Sea Glass Made with Second Chances

Serenity
Book 1

Stacey Wilk

Sea Glass Made with Second Chances by Stacey Wilk

Serenity, Book 1

This is a work of fiction. Names, characters, places, and incidents are either the product of the author's imagination or are used fictitiously, and any resemblance to actual persons living or dead, business establishments, events, or locales, is entirely coincidental.

Sea Glass Made with Second Chances

COPYRIGHT © 2025 by Stacey Wilk

Print ISBN: 979-8-9925372-1-5

Digital ISBN: 979-8-9925372-0-8

Cover Art by *Diana Carlisle*

Published in the United States of America

For Joanne
Thank you.

Chapter One

Everyone left Serenity by the Sea at some point. Many came back. Kassidy Russo fisted her hand around her morning find of green sea glass as a reminder that coming back hadn't been a sign of failure. Sea glass was once nothing more than a bottle or dish dumped in the garbage, but after time in the ocean, the broken pieces swept up to shore, smooth with the salt water's help, now speckled and beautiful. She wanted to be like the sea glass. Everyone should be allowed to recreate their lives at least once. Well, okay, maybe more than once.

She had picked up the old habit of collecting sea glass after her father took his final swim in the surf last month. She used to tease him about his constant pursuit of the ocean-worn glass that in some cases could be hundreds of years old. He loved wandering the beach at low tide, wearing his floppy sun hat and carrying a bucket in his hand. Her heart ached some. She missed her dad.

Kassidy brushed her long hair away from her face in a never-ending battle with the wind rolling off the ocean. She forgot a hair tie for her morning walk. She had been focused on other things instead. More important things. Matters that would change her life. Hopefully, for the better.

She walked past the dunes and onto the weathered boardwalk made gray by sun, sand, and spilled bottles of Coppertone. She had one stop to make before she returned home and cleaned up for the meeting with her sisters. Her flip-flops smacked the cement sidewalk as she navigated her way down Main Street past the small shops owned by locals. Most of the stores weren't open yet, except for Bella Notte bakery.

"Ciao, Kassidy." Giovanni DeFazio stopped sweeping the pavement outside the bakery and leaned on the broom. His arms were still corded with muscles even at his age. Muscles that lifted fifty-pound bags of flour since the 1970s and his arrival from Italy. His bright smile and blue eyes were as constant as the solar-powered streetlights up and down Main Street. She craved one of his giant chocolate chip cookies, the size of her head. Ever since she was a child, those cookies were a special treat when things went right or like today, when she was nervous.

"Good morning, Mr. D."

"Where are you headed so early?" His accent was faint, but still detectable. She liked the way the Italian language made any word sound soft and romantic. She could use a little romance in her life. Not a relationship.

That wasn't in her plan, but a bouquet of flowers or someone who could sing a love song might be nice for a night.

"Home. My sisters are coming today. I need one of your masterpieces this morning for courage." The extra sugar would take her jumbly nerves to the next level of hyper, but her brain associated calm with dessert and who was she to argue? Her sisters' arrival had her wrapped up like a rubber band ball. They didn't always see eye to eye, and for once she needed them to see things her way.

"Sometimes family requires a little bit of courage. Come inside. My chocolate chips are fresh from the oven. Your favorite." Mr. D leaned his broom against the wall and stood back to let her enter first. He was old-fashioned in his ideals, but his heart was in the right place, and she didn't mind. He was like the grandfather she never had.

The bakery smelled of just-baked bread and warm sugar. Her mouth watered as she approached the pastry case filled with goodies in pastels and primary colors. She wanted one of everything but would settle for the chocolate chip.

Mr. D wrapped the cookie in wax paper and handed it over the case. She gave him a five. "Keep the change."

"Ah." Mr. D waved a hand in the air. "Keep your money. You're a young woman, by herself. When are you going to get married?"

"I'm forty, Mr. D. At my age, I may never get married. And I will pay for the cookie, but thank you for the sweet offer." Her solitary existence could behave like a hanging scab, painful at the most unexpected times, even if these last months she didn't have time for a man. Not with her dad being sick.

Out of habit, she glanced at her phone. "I didn't realize the time. I need to go. I'm running late. Thanks again for the cookie." She pushed the five across the counter.

"Ah. Always running. You're like my granddaughter. Busy. Busy. Busy. Afretti. Don't be late." He waved her on.

She hurried the rest of the way home, wanting to wash off the salt water from her legs and put on clothes that said smart, confident, and capable, not sea glass searching bartender. Everything had to go as planned. She had too much to lose. She glanced at her lucky find of sea glass she had shoved in her pocket. Beauty or trash? Depended on who did the looking.

Turning onto her street, the toe of her flip-flop caught the uneven sidewalk. She tripped but righted herself before face-planting and crushing her cookie treasure.

"Whoa. You all right there, ma'am?" A tall man wearing a baseball cap and dark hair to his shoulders hurried toward her. He sported a neat and clean beard, not a ZZ Top type beard.

"I'm good. Thanks." She loved beards. A man with a little rugged edge made her insides hum as opposed to the clean-shaven type. Such a strange thought to have, but it was there, as clear as glass before it fell into the ocean.

"Your nose almost kissed the pavement." A Southern

drawl washed over his words. Not from New Jersey, that was for sure.

Working with her father in his tavern for the past decade made her an expert on locals versus tourists. She had wanted to change the fact The Blue Dot only saw the faces of the year-rounders, but she hadn't been able to accomplish her goal because of her dad. He could not handle a departure from the norm. And then when he became too sick to care about anything but stopping the pain, talking about menu changes seemed frivolous.

"That's what I get for hurrying."

The hot bearded guy squinted and ran his gaze up and down the street. He let out a long breath and muttered a curse, as if she hadn't spoken at all.

"Are you lost? You look lost. I don't have a lot of time, but I can direct you if you need some help." She resisted the urge to check her phone again. Her sisters would probably arrive soon and she wouldn't be ready if she helped this man, but something about him stopped her. He seemed almost familiar.

"I don't need any help, thank you. I'm where I'm supposed to be. I'm waiting for someone."

"Did you rent a tent for the summer?" The Topside Community was one of the most special qualities of Serenity by the Sea. The foldaway homes spoke of magic and wonder.

"My brother did. This was the address he gave me, anyway." The stranger checked his phone, much the way she wanted to check hers.

His hands were large. Strong hands that looked as if

they'd seen their share of hard work, but not so hard that his knuckles were snarled or scarred. Nice hands. Rugged hands. She shook the thoughts away. What was she doing, paying attention to the details of this stranger? But that was it. He was different and she wanted a change. She wanted to be like sea glass.

"Lucky you, then."

"Do you live in one of these tent things?" He hooked a thumb over his shoulder toward the small shed-style buildings.

"Me? No. I live in that tiny bungalow on the corner." She pointed to her house with its white chipped clapboards, more storm cloud-gray than white these days and the faded black shutters because no paint job could last more than a season with the salt air.

She would love to live in one of the charming summer houses, but the homes were hard to come by, often handed down generation to generation. Untouchable.

"Why do people rent these?"

"Because they're charming. They belong in a fairy tale." She glanced down the street with a sense of pride filling her lungs.

"If you say so." He arched a brow and pulled a face.

"I do say so. Give our little town a chance." She loved her town and its quaintness with local owned businesses, people who knew their neighbors, and the ocean as their very own backyard playground.

Serenity by the Sea was an old friend that could be counted on for its sturdiness in harsh times and its gentleness on wounded souls. Memories were made on the surf and in the sand that lasted.

"I won't be staying."

"If you say so." She echoed his words with a hint of sarcasm dashed on her own. She had overstayed her welcome.

An engine's rumble grew louder as a sleek black car came toward them. She hesitated. The man inside waved, then parallel parked across the narrow street. Her curiosity kept her frozen in place when she would be better suited inside, cleaning up. But it wasn't every day a handsome stranger came to town, even if he appeared a slight incorrigible.

The man hopped out, tall, like the man beside her, only lankier. Same coloring but dressed in pressed pants and a crisp button-down shirt with the sleeves rolled up to the elbows. A corporate guy. Not her type. Corporate guys hadn't been her type even when she thought they had been.

"Looks like you found the place," this new person said, walking toward them. A hint of a Southern accent coated his words too.

She switched her gaze between the two men. Must be the brother.

"Levi, did you actually rent this place?" her stranger said.

Well, he wasn't *her* stranger, but she did find him on the sidewalk right near her house like a shiny penny.

"You're going to love it." Levi sauntered across the street.

The two men faced each other, but neither one moved to shake or embrace. Instead, they stared each other down with a tilt of their chins and stiffness in their shoulders that looked ready to snap.

"I doubt I'll love another one of your crazy ideas," the muscular and unfairly handsome one said.

"Will you trust me?"

"No, thanks. No lame tents. Find me a hotel with some comforts."

She should mind her own business, but this town and all it had to offer were part of her fabric. She had to defend it.

"Usually, anyone who is lucky enough to procure a tent for the summer, or even a week, is excited and looking forward to everything Serenity by the Sea has to offer."

"Did you say procure? Who says that?" Her stranger, yes, her stranger, choked out a laugh.

"Someone who can read." She clamped her jaw shut on the rest of the words bubbling to spill out. If she kept talking like that, he wouldn't be anything but her enemy.

"Before you go insulting me, ma'am, maybe we should be properly introduced. My name is Grant. And this here is my little brother Levi, though he's anything but little anymore." Grant stuck out his strong hand. His smile was firmly in place. She hesitated for only a second, then slid hers into his grip and that wave of heat ran over her skin again.

Levi simply nodded.

"My apologies. I didn't mean to insult you. Now, if

you'll excuse me. I have to get inside." She eased her hand away, but the heat remained.

"Are you going to tell me your name?" A playfulness danced across Grant's smoky eyes and his lip twitched up in a devilish smile.

She could assume this man knew he was a charmer.

"I guess you'll have to wait to find out." She hurried inside her house without looking back to see if Grant and his rigid brother were still on the street.

She closed the door behind her and leaned against it. Had she just flirted with that guy? Grant might be nice to look at, but the last thing she needed was a man paying attention to her. She had no time for involvement. She had enough on her plate with her sisters coming to stay and the looming visit to the lawyer's office. A lot rode on this visit.

In fact, everything.

Chapter Two

With regret, Grant pulled his focus away from the outspoken woman leaving him in her dust. And for reasons he could not comprehend, he had just flirted with her, and he didn't even know her name. He hadn't meant to do that. Sometimes his mouth worked in overdrive, especially when he was tired and his back and legs ached. Not a real excuse, but the truth at least.

"I want to show you where we're staying. You're going to love it." Levi walked away without waiting for a response. Typical Levi. He always assumed Grant would do whatever he asked. And he usually did.

When Grant had passed through brick pillars at the entrance of town, he had driven down narrow roads filled with cars parked on both sides and small houses so close they almost touched. But each one was charming in its own way from white picket fences to colorful, pristine landscaping. This Serenity by the Sea was a very different landscape from the place he came from with its dirt for grass, space for the tumbleweeds, and double-wides.

On this street, tiny houses with white fabric roofs and striped awnings over small porches lined the road. Every house had some shrubbery and many boasted an American flag, waving in the wind.

Levi stepped onto the porch where a couple of rockers with yellow and blue floral pillows waited for someone to sit in them and drink sweet tea. The property sat on the corner, but on the other side of the street the houses went back to the small style he had seen on the drive into town. The first house belonged to his new neighbor.

"Well? It's great, right?" Levi spread his arms wide as if he had built the place himself.

"I have to admit that I'm curious."

"There's something I need to talk to you about," Levi said, sticking the key in the lock of the wood door.

"What's that?"

"I need you." Levi turned to him. The key dangled from his outstretched hand. The pleading look, one Grant was familiar with, crossed Levi's face.

"Oh no." He backed away. "I'm not writing a song for you. How many times do I have to say it? I'm done. Dried up. No good anymore." He should have known what this was all about. Levi had sent him a dozen texts asking for help. All of which he said no to.

"Here's the deal." Levi pushed the air with his hands. "You need to do this, or we will be sued for breach of contract. I know you don't pay attention to the date, but the two years the record label gave us is up. If you don't pull your act together and produce some songs for that final album, my career is over. And whether you want to hear this or not, it's time for you to find your voice again."

How had two years gone by so quickly? Grant wanted to help his brother. It was what he always did growing up. He stood in the way of their stepfather's fists when he had come for Levi. He would lay down his life for his brother, but he had failed Levi before. He couldn't bear to do it again.

"Can you put them off? Maybe next year. I still can't write." He hadn't been able to write another song since the bus accident. His muse left him that day, chased away by guilt and anger. He had walked away from his music career without a look back and hadn't regretted it. Most days.

"I tried. They won't listen to any more excuses. You need to do this. I can't afford to get sued and neither can you," Levi said.

"My writing is no good anymore. I don't have anything left to say." Every time he tried to write something new, his mind twisted around old memories of a rainstorm and a mangled bus. And his late wife's last words that he was a loser.

"It's just three songs. When the fans get wind you're back, the album will climb the charts. Your money problems will be over." Levi's face broke open in that devilish smile he had when he believed he was onto something.

He pushed past Levi, taking the key out of his hand.

He didn't want to talk about this anymore. But here he was, in some beach town on the New Jersey coast. He had suspected Levi was up to no good when his last text suggested a few weeks together at the beach. Like old times. He had been played.

The key slid into the lock like a knife through butter. The smell of a room closed off from the outside with its air tight and thick met him first. The space was small, but well maintained. There was a leather sofa on one wall with a surfboard hanging above it. The space also housed a table for two and a couple of cabinets. The tall bookcase was filled with fabric baskets.

"Not bad," Levi said behind him.

"Don't be so proud of yourself. We're here under false pretenses. Brother trip, my backside."

The tent was warm and welcoming despite the cold anger in his veins. At the back of the room was a doorway that led to the small kitchen, plus a bedroom and bathroom. The house had plenty of space. He had stayed in worse places than this and that was on tour, making money.

Money. His was running out because he hadn't written or toured in the past two years. His songs didn't rotate as much on the radio any longer, and the downloads weren't what they used to be. Grant Hawkins was disappearing faster than morning fog on the lake. The fans had moved on to newer singers popping up all the time. Younger and hipper musicians who were out in the spotlight and filling their social media feeds with funny photos and current hashtags. He didn't even have a Facebook account.

"I'm sorry I lied. But I was desperate. It's actually pretty nice in here." Levi flopped onto the sofa and stretched out his legs. "I picked this town in the middle of New Jersey because it may be a destination spot, but you have to dig pretty deep to find out about it. I mean, who even heard of Serenity by the Sea? It's not as if this place is famous like Asbury Park thanks to Springsteen."

"So you're saying I can stay hidden here. That no one will recognize me." He had taken to using a different last name in order to keep his identity under wraps when needed.

"That's exactly what I'm saying. It's perfect."

"It's still a beach town in the summer."

"Yeah, but no one will know who you are. You've done a good job of making sure that happened." Levi pushed off the couch and pulled his phone out of his pocket. His fingers flew over the screen. Without looking up, he said, "Sorry. I have to answer my clients who are willing to work."

"I don't want to face the fans," he said, ignoring Levi's jab about working clients.

"The beach will do you good. Inspire you even." Levi shoved his phone back in his pocket and patted him on the shoulder a little harder than necessary.

He was tired of moving around, not that he would tell Levi that truth. He hadn't told anyone he was ready to find a place to plant some roots. Just not a place that reminded him of his late wife Noel. Serenity by the Sea would have no connection to her. Maybe the summer here would do him some good.

Levi leaned against the counter that wasn't much more than the sink, a drawer, and a cabinet. "There's one more thing. The songs need to be written in three weeks. The label wants to slide you into an opening they have for releases."

"Three weeks? I can't write even one song in three weeks and you want... what... three?" He dropped the keys on the table and noticed the air conditioner. He turned it on to move the stale air around or to give himself something else to look at besides his brother's intense glare.

"We were contracted for twelve. The label has the nine you finished. So, yeah, big brother, that makes three on you."

"What if I can't produce something? I don't want to carry around the weight of your career on my shoulders. Find a way to get me out of this contract." He should have had this conversation ages ago, but as long as Levi wasn't asking for the songs, he hadn't brought anything up. It had been easier to pretend no one was looking for him than it was to remember that he had lost his edge.

"Can't do that. The clause is airtight. We're both going to be sued. End of story."

"Why did you ever allow that clause in the contract?" He had trusted Levi to negotiate on his behalf when the bigger label had offered a deal. He had just shown up and signed.

"Because when I left playing music to manage you, I was still a dumb kid from the south."

"You had more talent than I ever did." Levi was a better musician than he ever was. Levi was deliberate. He executed notes perfectly. All Grant ever did was slap some chords together.

"Thanks, but that's not true. Your talent was in your storytelling." He pressed his lips into a thin line. "Anything with your name on it will be a thousand times better than what I could ever write. You need this. Do you really want to spend the rest of your life moving from town to town and flipping burgers? You were meant to be onstage, making people happy."

Working as a cook gave him some cash, and he didn't mind the job. He met people along the way, but when he was done with a town, he moved on.

"Three songs?" He would also have to go to a studio and record them. He hadn't stepped inside a recording studio in years. There hadn't been any reason if he wasn't writing for the record label.

"Three." Levi held up as many fingers as if he couldn't count.

"Can I record them on my own?" He could get the equipment he needed and record right here in this tent. Hell, he could probably record them right on his phone. Then he wouldn't have to see the executives or the music engineers. He could produce a good quality song they could add to the rest. Musicians did it all the time.

"No way. Their studio. They're pissed enough at you. The studio time has already been booked anyway."

"I'll try."

Levi's smile spread wide across his face as if he had hooked him like an unsuspecting catfish. And he had. He would unearth his muse for Levi's sake. But he would only write those three songs, and then that was it. He didn't deserve to be onstage or writing music. Not when he was the reason his wife, his backup singer and best friend, had died.

Chapter Three

Kassidy dropped the sea glass into the mason jar on the kitchen counter. The green and white pebbles danced and clinked against the glass.

She threw open the windows in the kitchen and the living room to catch the cross breeze mixed with salt and took a much-needed slow breath. Her sisters would be here soon. Kassidy wasn't smart like Maren who had been destined for great things since she was four. And she hadn't been like Bailey who was the free spirit her father loved most, the wild child born to his second wife who had only become his wife on Bailey's second birthday.

With a few minutes left, she changed out of her shorts into a long skirt and tied back her bushy hair.

Her phone vibrated on the table. A text from Bailey.

I can't find a place to park.

Try in front of the church. It was Friday and those

spots were often open during the week because the church was just far enough away from the beach that the day visitors tried to avoid walking that far after a long day in the sun.

She took a quick peek out the front window. The new neighbor and his brother were gone, but the fancy car was still parked across the street. Sure, Grant's looks would make most women turn their heads, but that personality dulled his fine appearance. Well, that and those worn-out dirty clothes.

Bailey burst through the front door. She pulled a rolling suitcase covered in stickers over the threshold. It bumped against the doorjamb as if it were in a pinball game. Kassidy winced with each collision. The trim would need to be painted if Bailey kept that up. And she didn't need another thing to paint around here. The two oversized tote bags in bright colors, one on each shoulder, slid down her thin arms and tangled in the suitcase's handle.

Bailey shoved her sunglasses on top of her head while she stared open-mouthed. Her long spiral curls bounced against the shoulders of her white t-shirt tied in a knot at her waist. Bailey's striped wide-legged pants were typical Bailey style, free-flowing, casual, easy. Everything Kassidy had tried to be, but could never master with the same ease.

"Hey. I made it," Bailey said with huffed breaths. "You wouldn't believe the traffic even at this hour."

"It's Friday. The traffic started last night. Can I help

you with any of that?" She reached for a bag, but Bailey waved her away.

"Thanks. I'm good." Bailey dumped the bags on the floor and gripped her in a tight hug. "It's so great to see you." The smell of something minty flowing off Bailey like a cool breeze woke up her nose.

"Good to see you too." Her chest constricted against the vise hold. She patted Bailey's back and wedged herself out of the embrace. "I made up the middle bedroom for you. Do you want to get settled before we go over to the lawyer's office?"

"Ugh. The smallest, why me?" She stuck out her bottom lip. Also typical Bailey. As the youngest, and the one with the mother who didn't believe in rules, she was used to having her way.

"Maren is bringing Peyton. I gave them the bigger room in the front to share." Their older sister and her teenaged daughter were not happy about sharing a room during their stay, but the rent was free and Maren was tight for money while she fought with her soon-to-be ex-husband about their divorce.

"Well, okay. It's only for a few days." Bailey dragged her bags through the living room and into the smallest bedroom with the weird spiral staircase the last owner had installed for her teenage daughter to have extra space. The staircase led to an alcove in the attic just large enough to sit in. Shelves had been built into the wall for the girl to keep her books and treasures in. The staircase had charmed Kassidy when she purchased the home.

The idea that a mother had essentially created an indoor treehouse for her daughter gave flight to Kassidy's belief in the magical. Like her sea glass.

Her sisters believed they would only be staying a few days. The week at most, but she had other ideas. An idea they couldn't find out about. But if her plan worked, they would forgive her.

"Are you hungry? I could whip us up some breakfast before we go into town." She craned her neck to see Bailey toss the two totes on the bed. One flipped and fell on the floor.

"No, thanks. I had a banana in the car. How about coffee?"

"Coming up." She grabbed her ground coffee from the refrigerator. The best way to make coffee was a French press and not the single coffee makers, though she did have a mini one for those mornings or moments when she was too tired to go through all the trouble. Especially when she realized, at four o'clock in the morning on a breakfast day at The Blue Dot, that she hadn't grinded any beans.

"What time is Maren getting here?" Bailey hopped up on the counter.

"Really?" She pulled two mugs from the cabinet while the water in the French press heated up.

"What?"

"The counter. Why are you sitting on it? We put our food there." She shook her head. Nothing changed with Bailey. But Bailey would be the easier of her sisters to

21

convince to stay because Bailey was the one who hardly ever planned. How a health and wellness life coach could also be completely spontaneous was beyond her. But Bailey's clients loved the way she would drop off emails or calls at sporadic moments, checking in to make sure the client was doing okay. Sure, she scheduled client meetings like most people did, but with Bailey she could be conducting that meeting from a hut on the beach.

Bailey grunted and hopped off. "You need to relax. Let that beach view do you some good."

"I can't see the beach from here." But when she sat in the backyard, closed her eyes, and listened, the song of crashing waves against sand played on low in the background.

The front door swung open. "Hello? Anyone home?" Maren's voice bounced off the walls and filled the house.

"In the kitchen," Bailey said. "Kassidy is already being a drill sergeant. Come save me."

Her stomach clenched. Maren was the sister who would catch on to her game quicker than Bailey ever would. Bailey could barely remember where she put her toothbrush. Details weren't Bailey's thing, but Maren... Maren was a different story. She ran her home like a tight ship. Everything in its place and a place for everything. Maren never let her guard down for a second, always proving she was the best at whatever she did. She would sniff out the lie in a second if Kassidy wasn't careful.

"Were you swinging from the light fixture again?" Maren swept into the kitchen in her floral tank top and denim shorts. Her dark hair flowed past her toned shoulders in magazine perfect waves. Her lips were kissed with pink gloss and spread wide with a smile for Bailey.

Maren scooped Bailey into a hug and Bailey giggled as if she were still five and Maren had come home from school. She tried not to gag. The coffee was ready. She busied herself with pouring.

"I only did that one time," Bailey protested without much effort. "It was a dare from that cute boy. What was his name?"

"Marc Phillips," she and Maren said in unison.

"Right." Bailey snapped her fingers.

Maren gripped her in a hug too, yanking her away from the coffee preparation. "You smell good," she said.

"Thanks. It's called Dove unscented." Wasn't that the story of her life? Compared to her sisters, she was the understated one, looking to shine. Not that she was complaining. She wanted more now, that's all. She handed Maren a mug. "Where's Peyton?"

"She went for a walk on the boardwalk. She wasn't ready to come inside yet." Maren rolled her eyes. "We had a fight in the car. Teenagers will age you faster than the most damaging UV rays." She plopped into a kitchen chair and put her sneakered feet up on the opposite one.

"You know what we were like at that age," she said. Actually, she hadn't been all that daring. She had rarely broken her father's rules. Maren had tested the water more than she had. And Bailey, well, Bailey.

"I wasn't like that. I swear it. What time are we going

to the lawyer's?" Maren jumped up and grabbed almond milk out of the fridge. "No whole milk?"

"Whole milk isn't good for you," Bailey said.

"I stopped drinking it. I want to lose a few pounds." She patted her hips. The older she became the harder it was to get rid of the weight. As a kid, she could go up to the hamburger place across the street from the beach and chow down on cheese fries and not ever worry. Now, she couldn't smell cheese fries without gaining five pounds.

"As if you need to lose any weight. All that bartending and waiting tables keeps you thin." Bailey smacked her backside.

"Hey." She swatted Bailey away. Her job did keep her moving, and she loved that.

Once the lawyer confirmed that The Blue Dot was hers, she would take out a second mortgage on the business to fix it up and expand it. The way she had planned but couldn't convince her father to go along with while he was alive.

"Oh, come on, Kass, you have the cutest ass and legs. You don't need to lose a pound." Bailey twirled her hair. "Doesn't she, Maren?"

"I guess. Is Aunt Joanna coming?" Maren checked her watch.

"She sent a text, saying we had it all under control and if we needed her to shout. She'd come running." Kassidy had been relieved when her aunt mentioned she couldn't make it. Joanna had no idea how her brother had been living for years now and Kassidy didn't want her to find out for her father's sake.

"Well, if Aunt Joanna isn't coming, we should be going. I'll text Peyton and tell her to wait here while we're gone. I don't want her wandering around alone." Maren dug her phone out of her back pocket and tapped at the screen.

"This is Serenity by the Sea, not East LA," she said.

"Still," Maren said without looking up, as if Kassidy's words hadn't registered at all.

"How long are you staying?" Bailey said. "Kassidy gave you and Peyton the big room."

"Oh, that. I don't know. Maybe just overnight. I have to get back, and Peyton wants to spend time with her friends. Certainly not with me." Maren still barely glanced up at them while her thumbs flew across the phone screen.

"What are you in a rush to get back for?" She kept her back to Maren so she couldn't read the expression on her face. She had never been a good liar, but she had to act as if she didn't know the first thing about what was waiting for them at the lawyer's office.

She needed her sisters to trust her and spend the summer here. But if she had come right out and asked, they would both say no. Especially Maren who was in the middle of a divorce and felt as if she couldn't be away in case her soon-to-be ex changed his mind. Not that he would, and not that she should want him to. She didn't need him. She just didn't know it yet.

"Dave wants to bring a real estate agent to see our house. I think I should be there to hear what he has to say," Maren said.

"Can't they just phone you?" she said, stating the obvious.

Bailey nodded.

"You don't understand, Kass. If I'm not there, he's going to think I don't care. He won't know the right questions to ask, and he certainly won't remember all the renovations and changes we've made to the house. If I have to sell, I want to have a say in who the agent is."

"Honestly, does it matter? Why not just be glad to be through with him?" She bit her lip. The words were out before she could stop them.

"If you had ever been married and had built a life with someone to watch it tumble like a house of cards, maybe you would understand. Where is Peyton?" She went to the door without a glance back.

Maren's comment stung. So she hadn't been married before. It wasn't as if she didn't want to be. Marriage just hadn't worked out for her because her long-ago fiancé decided his career was more important than she was. Since then, she was too busy with the rest of her life to go looking for a husband. It wasn't as if she needed one. She was done needing men.

"Don't let her get to you," Bailey said.

"Whatever." She forced a smile on her face to prove she didn't care about what Maren had said. "We should go. We're going to be late."

"Do you think Dad kept a stash of money we didn't know about and that's why we've been summoned to the lawyer?"

"That would be nice, but I doubt it." She grabbed her purse and her keys.

"Then what do you think this is all about?" Bailey followed on her heels.

"I have no idea."

Lies. Every single word.

Chapter Four

Kassidy crossed and uncrossed her legs. The law offices of Benjamin West must believe lawyers had hotter body temperatures than most. She was pretty sure she could see her pulse-thumping breaths with each exhale.

"I'm sorry. Could you say that again?" Because she must not have heard Mr. West correctly. There could be no other explanation. Or the damn air-conditioning froze her ear canals.

"The Blue Dot is being left to the three of you equally along with the house." Mr. West folded his age-spotted hands on the large polished desk. Mr. West was a big man with a well-fed belly protruding over his belt and straining the buttons of his white dress shirt. His kind eyes held her gaze as if to say he understood her confusion and was sorry for it.

"But Dad said he was coming here to change the will." Her father and she had had many conversations about him changing the will before he became sick. She wanted The Dot. She had plans for The Dot. Her sisters barely stepped foot in it.

"I'm sorry, Kassidy. He never did." Mr. West had been her father's lawyer for his entire adult life. They had gone to high school together. They saw each other socially from time to time, and not once had her father thought to mention to his friend Ben that he needed or wanted to change his will.

"And what about that part where he wants us to clean out the house together. Is there a way around that? I mean, could we hire someone to do it for us?" Maren sat on the edge of her chair, leaning forward with a hand on the desk as if her imposing posture would change anything.

That house cleaning part could be changed. Because it wasn't real. She had asked Mr. West to say that. There was nothing in the will about her father's last wishes concerning the emptying of the house. Mr. West was doing her a favor because she was the daughter of his good friend. She didn't want to clean up that house alone and her sisters would leave her with the mess. They hadn't come to help her when their father was sick. Maren and Aunt Joanna had made a couple of trips—separately, of course—but each time her father had insisted they meet at Kassidy's little bungalow. He hadn't wanted Maren or his sister in his house, finding out his secret. Her father had been a proud man or maybe he had been simply embarrassed, but the only one who knew the whole truth about him was her. And for that alone, she should have been given the tavern.

She needed Maren and Bailey's help because what waited for them was insurmountable, and she couldn't think of a good way to keep them in Serenity except to lie.

"I'm afraid you all have to stick it out and clean up the house before it can be put on the market." Mr. West closed the folder and stood. This meeting was coming to a close, and she still couldn't get her head around her father's blunder about not changing the will.

She should have known. Or at the very least guessed he wouldn't do what he said, if the state of his home was any indication of his inability to handle difficult tasks. He had avoided confrontation the way a vegan avoids meat.

"There is no way on the earth that I'm spending one minute more than I have to in this town. I have a life somewhere else. A daughter to raise. I have no interest in cleaning out that house." Maren stood too and heaved her purse onto her shoulder.

"What about The Blue Dot?" Her mind finally snagged on a sensible thought. "I want the tavern."

"So buy us out," Bailey said, seemingly unaffected by all of this, and popped a piece of gum into her mouth.

"Can I do that?" she said to Mr. West.

"If you have the money." Mr. West dropped his gaze for a second before meeting her eye.

She didn't have to say anything further. He knew she didn't have that kind of money on her own. And still, her stubborn mind would not give up hope. "What about the sale of the house? We must be able to get around four hundred grand for it." Split three ways, she would have enough money to buy out her sisters.

"I'm afraid the house has a second mortgage for that amount on it. Your father needed that money for medical bills. The sale of the house will probably just pay off the debt. I'm sorry." Mr. West lumbered around the desk, tucking folders under his arm.

"The Dot must have some equity in it." Each idea was like reaching for a life preserver while she bobbed in the ocean.

Mr. West shook his head.

And then having that life preserver snatched away. "Wait a second." She put up a hand to stop Mr. West from walking straight out of the office. "Dad never mentioned anything about using the equity in The Dot. The building and the business should be worth something."

"He didn't want you to worry. He thought you'd have another good summer season and he'd be able to put things right."

"Does this mean we have to sell her too?" Her stomach coiled like a rope. The room that had been freezing was now too hot for her to breathe in.

"Why do you want to keep The Blue Dot, Kass? It's on life support as it is." Maren's brow creased between her eyes in a perfect line.

The Blue Dot had been in trouble almost from the beginning because her dad had picked a location two blocks from the beach instead of on the boardwalk. But they had persevered year in and year out, and the little tavern named after her father's favorite sea glass color, because blue sea glass could be seen against the sand, had managed to keep its head afloat.

"Because it's my life." Her voice shook and her eyes filled with tears ready to betray her. She had thought they would walk in here and the reading of the will would be simple. She would get the tavern and the three of them would get the house. And together they would clear it of the sadness that smelled of alcohol, musty cardboard, and death.

"I think maybe you ladies should take some time to discuss this." Mr. West hitched a beefy leg onto the corner of the desk.

"What's to discuss?" Bailey rummaged through her large tote—for what she had no idea. "I don't want The Blue Dot either. That tavern should be condemned."

"It's not that bad," she said. "How much time do I have before it has to go on the market?" She had to find a way out of this. She had already lost so much in her life. She couldn't lose this too. Tending bar and waiting tables was all she knew how to do. If she couldn't have the tavern, then she would have to start over working for someone else. Of course, there could be worse things, but owning something would prove she had made it. Made something of her life when she had nothing else to show for it.

"As long as you're making the payments, you can stay open. It's up to the three of you as to what you should do with the business. Kassidy, you own a home. You could take out a second mortgage on that to buy out your sisters."

She fought the unwanted tears harder. "It's mortgaged to the hilt." She had bought high when she had returned to Serenity by the Sea. She had had little money at the time and taken a loan with a hefty interest rate. By the time she could refinance, a hurricane had blown in and dropped a tree on her roof. Her basement had flooded and living near the beach meant insurance companies didn't want to pay for floods.

Mr. West let out a long breath. "I know you weren't expecting this. Your dad had money troubles, and then he went ahead and asked you to take care of the mess he left in the house. But you three will come to an agreement. I'm sure of it."

"I cannot spend the summer here. I have a child to raise and a divorce to get through." Maren huffed.

"A summer at the shore with her aunts won't kill her." Bailey pulled out her flowered sunglasses and plopped them on her head.

"Are you saying you'll stay for the summer and help me clean out the house?" She still had to figure out what to do about The Blue Dot, but at least she wouldn't be alone all summer sorting through her father's things.

"As soon as Maren turned on her *my life is more important than your life* argument that she so conveniently uses, I decided. I want to go through Dad's things. There may be something worth keeping."

"I don't do what you just said I did." Maren crossed

her arms over her chest and tapped her foot to some impatient beat only she could hear.

Bailey spit out a laugh. "Yeah, okay. You always do that and especially to Kassidy. I'll rearrange my plans. I was going to visit Marty in Oregon, but that can wait. And I can meet with my clients using a video chat. I do that all the time. If Dad wanted us to take the summer and clean out his house, then I'll do it. It's the least we could do for him. You should stick around, Maren. You owe it to Dad."

Maren clutched at the collar of her shirt and pressed her lips into a thin line. She didn't say anything but held Bailey's gaze. Bailey must have hit a nerve, and she was grateful for the help. Their father was far from perfect, but he had done his best for them. He had loved each one of them fiercely. Bailey was right. Cleaning out Dad's house was a simple ask. She hoped.

"Let me think about staying," Maren said.

That answer would have to do and Kassidy wouldn't push now.

"But we sell The Dot, if Kassidy can't buy it out from us." Maren pointed her glare at both of them. A moose couldn't move that determined look in her eye when she got like this.

"What if I can't find a way to buy The Dot?" There was a time she had thought what she needed was a college degree and a fancy job that required her to wear a suit. She had believed climbing the corporate ladder would bring her happiness, but life had taught her that priorities had a way of changing.

"Then we sell it. Like I mentioned," Maren said. "We can't carry the burden of that debt indefinitely. It will strangle us. If Dad hadn't prepared better, he's left us no choice. We sell." Maren turned on her heel and marched out.

"I know keeping The Dot is important to you," Bailey said. "But you'll have to consider selling if you don't have the money. Maren isn't going to budge. She's too wrapped up in her own problems right now to consider holding on to the place."

"My life is in that tavern." Over the years she had allowed every inch of that place to weave its way into the fabric of her being. Her friends were there. Her community was there. She had no backup plan, which made her stomach queasy as if she stood on a rocking boat in the deep sea.

"You look like you need a second alone. I'll meet you outside. Thanks for everything, Mr. West." Bailey stuck out her hand.

Mr. West slipped his meaty paw into Bailey's. "My pleasure."

Bailey exited through the doorway, her tote bouncing against her hip.

Mr. West turned to her. "How long do you think you can keep the truth from them?"

Her father had kept a truth from her; maybe she could go the entire summer without revealing anything to them. She wanted her sisters back in her life, and that was worth the risk.

But she wanted The Dot too, and that was a problem she hadn't anticipated facing while she lied to her sisters.

"They never need to find out I'm the one who wants them to help clean out that house. They are going to be shocked enough when they see what kind of state it's in. Without this fake stipulation, they'll both run. You see how determined Maren is to get away, and I can't do it alone. I won't be able to. I loved my father, but he had issues."

"You can't build a future on lies."

"I know." But she could try.

Chapter Five

Grant pushed out of bed. The mattress sagged in the center and turned his back into a baker's hard pretzel. He stretched, arms reaching for the sky, and his vertebrae responded with a symphony of pops and clacks. He hadn't been able to sleep much, not that he ever did. Since the bus accident, he and sleep avoided each other like lovers in a divorce.

He padded over the thin, rough carpet to the kitchen. The sun wasn't up yet. The tiny house, or maybe he should say tent, was muted with dark grays, but his eyes had adjusted enough to make his way around. He guessed the time had to be around four in the morning. His usual waking time.

The cabinets and the fridge were sparse except for the dishes and silverware provided by Phil, the landlord. Phil had called Levi to see if they had settled in okay. He was spending the summer in North Carolina, so if Grant or Levi needed anything, he could call his nice neighbor Kassidy Russo. According to Phil, Kassidy came to his rescue all the time. In fact, Kassidy was quite the helper Phil had told them.

Grant had swirled her name around his mouth and enjoyed the feel of it against his tongue.

He didn't doubt Phil after Kassidy's curator style explanation of the Topside Community. She wasn't the only one who could use big words. He had a few stored up too for pulling out when he needed them. He just saved his words for his songs. Songs he didn't write anymore, so he wasn't sure what he was saving up for. He hadn't wanted to talk much either. Not his style.

The cabinets might be missing food, but they had the pots and pans for cooking. He should have found a grocery store yesterday. He'd put that on his list for today. The list was short. Buy food. Write a song. He needed a different list. He was also going to need a job.

He slipped past Levi snoring on the couch and went out onto the porch. The damp sea air stuck to his skin like a wet blanket, giving him goose flesh. He shivered, but the cold went right to his bones. The smell of salt and something he didn't quite know, something tangy or bitter, coated the air too. He had been to a beach town before, but none that smelled like Serenity.

Kassidy Russo was probably still asleep in that house of hers like most normal people were at that hour. He had noticed her return late in the day yesterday with two other women. But did she have a man sleeping in her bed? He shook his head. Not only did he need a job, but he needed something else to think about besides his neighbor. What was he going to do in Serenity for the next three weeks? Even if he could write three songs, which he doubted he'd be able to, he wouldn't spend twenty-four hours a day on it. That might make him go insane.

He should never have allowed Levi to rent a place like this one. He should be in a city where things went on all the time. He could use a coffee shop that opened early or a theater that played old movies well into the night. When his mind was occupied, he couldn't get stuck on what he'd done to Noel, to Levi, or to the other members of the Grant Hawkins band. Or what happened to his youngest brother Emmet.

He went back inside and threw on a sweatshirt and a pair of sneakers. Sleep wouldn't come back, and he couldn't sit in the small space, waiting for Levi to wake. A walk might do him good.

He went east toward the boardwalk. The horizon line pulsed with rays of orange. The sun would climb into the sky soon. Wind swelled off the ocean, and he was grateful for the extra layer he wore. Ocean Avenue was quiet without anyone walking or driving, and he crossed the street to the boardwalk. Benches faced the water all along the worn-out boards, waiting for someone to come sit on them and keep them company. Streetlights did little more than spill a small cone of yellow, but the bathhouse burned bright with bulbs all around it. Serenity by the Sea wore the early morning hours like a debutante.

He hung a right onto Main Street where all the shops

were. He stole a quick glance at the sleeping music store named Beach Rhythm. He loved the small independent stores where albums could still be bought and instruments could be tried. Though he didn't go in them much anymore. They were also the places where someone would know his name.

The bakery had a light on inside. He hesitated outside the door of Bella Notte. A short man with balding hair caught him staring and waved to him. He opened the door and hesitated right inside.

"*Buon giorno.* Good morning. Welcome to my bakery. I am Giovanni." The man's smile invited him in the rest of the way.

"Good morning, sir. Are you open?" The bakery was warm and took the chill out of his bones. A black-and-white marbled floor sparkled in the fluorescent lighting. Old photos with scalloped edges and neutral tones showing happy people laughing and eating hung behind the cases of cookies and pastries. Dean Martin crooned softly in the background.

"Ah, not so much, but I never turn someone away who's standing outside my door. What can I get for you?"

"How about two coffees?" He'd bring one back for Levi, and if his brother wasn't up when he returned, then he'd get him up and ply him with caffeine. If he couldn't sleep, neither could Levi.

"And a pastry? Or better yet, the bread is warm." Giovanni pushed through the swinging doors and came back with a long loaf of bread. Without waiting for his reply, Giovanni put the bread in a white bag. He poured coffee into to-go cups with lids.

"Where are you from, young man? Your face, it's familiar, but you not from around here, no? That will be *cinque* dollars." Giovanni laughed. "Five dollars, please."

He dug out his wallet, doubting Giovanni would know him or his music. And he was fine with that. "I'm from down south. My brother and I are renting one of the tents for a few weeks."

"I love seeing new faces. This is a beautiful seashore town. You and your brother will have a wonderful vacation. Did you bring your wives?"

Even after two years, the question of a wife made him stop and take a breath. "I'm not married." He handed over a five without explaining the real reason he was alone.

"It's that long hair. You should cut it." His words were direct, but the humor in his gaze indicated Giovanni was not malicious.

"But I like my hair. I think some of the ladies do too." He enjoyed the bantering.

"Ah, well, then don't listen to an old man."

"You wouldn't happen to be hiring right now, would you?" He could learn to bake bread and make pizza dough. The pastries might take more effort and skill than he had, but he wasn't afraid to learn.

"No, no. It's me and my three boys. Why work while you're on vacation? Enjoy the sunrise."

"It's not exactly a vacation. But yes, I wouldn't mind

41

working." He needed to work just to keep his mind occupied and a few dollars in his pocket. Levi was right about his money running out.

"Keep your eyes open. You never know what this town will bring you."

He thanked Giovanni for the coffee, tucked the bread under his arm, and pushed back out into the early morning. Main Street remained languid. Next to the music store was a bookstore. He would be sure to stop in there and find something to read that had big enough words to impress his neighbor. Funny how thoughts of Kassidy continued to slide into his mind. He didn't expect a chance encounter to stick with him that way.

The quiet street and the cool ocean breeze pushed the stress from his shoulders. Maybe he didn't need the lights and noise of a big city, at least for a little while. He slowed his pace, enjoying the time to himself before his return to the tent and Levi standing over him while he attempted to write.

A pair of headlights turned down the street and headed his way. Some other person eluded by sleep. He half wished it was Kassidy. Maybe because he didn't know anyone else in this town, or maybe because her smart-ass personality gave his mind something to chew on. A woman like that would have an opinion about everything. He needed distractions, but he wasn't sure she would be a smart one.

With thoughts of Kassidy occupying his mind, the pavement reached up and snagged the toe of his shoe. His foot stopped, but the rest of him kept going. He threw out his hands to break his fall, sending the cups and bread end over end into the air. The lids popped off and the coffee met its death on the cement. He smacked the heels of his hands on the ground. His chin came within an inch of kissing the sidewalk cracks.

"Well, hell." He picked himself up and then the cups, tossing them in the metal garbage can. His hands stung right along with his pride. The bread was still in the bag and seemed okay. If thinking about Kassidy was going to land him on his ass, he'd really have to find something else to think about. Like how to put one foot in front of the other.

He found his way back to the tent. Inside the lights blazed as if the house was in full party mode. Most of the other tents were still dark. At least Levi wasn't blasting music, but the front door was unlocked.

"Where have you been?" Levi opened his mouth wide and let out a loud yawn. Heavy bags hung under his eyes.

"Trying to get some breakfast." He held up the bread but longed for the coffee. He should have turned around and went back to the bakery, but admitting he was clumsy because thoughts about a pretty lady tangled his feet together was too much to admit. "Looks like you had a rough night. Are you sure you want to spend the next few weeks sleeping on that couch?"

He wanted Levi to return home and allow Grant to wallow in his lack of inspiration alone. He would get far more accomplished that way. He also wasn't giving up the bed no matter how uncomfortable the couch was on Levi's back.

"I just need some coffee. There's no food in this place. Why did you get a loaf of bread and no coffee?" Levi opened and banged shut the cabinets.

"You're giving me a headache." He cut a piece of the bread and handed it to Levi. He would not mention his trip and fall. Levi would never let him hear the end of it.

"No, thanks. I think I'd rather have eggs. I've been thinking." Levi crossed his arms and leaned against the table.

"This can't be good."

"Just hear me out. I want the two of us to go onstage and sing one of the new songs. I can get us a spot at the outdoor Hats and Ropes Music Festival."

"Oh, no. Never." He tossed the knife in the sink. He wasn't hungry anymore. That music festival was the biggest in the south. Thousands of people came to see ten to twenty bands play each year.

"Come on. We'll do it together. You and me, like old times."

"Old times when it was you, me, and Emmet and we played some dive bar where the crowd consisted of a couple of drunks. Leave the past where it belongs, Levi." He was tired of explaining that performing and writing were a foreign language to him now. He didn't recognize himself when he stepped onstage. He shut down, his voice failed, the lyrics and notes left him, because he didn't deserve to be there. He hadn't been able to save

Emmet from himself or save Noel and Sean from the bus accident.

"When are you going to get back on the stage?" Levi would not back down. He pushed and pushed until the anger boiled inside Grant, wanting to push back.

"I said I'd write the songs, but I will not perform. I'm through with the stage and touring. That's not my life anymore, and you will not ask me to make it so. The label can sue me all they want. They can take every penny from the album because I will not stand in front of a microphone and sing for a crowd." He stormed past his brother. Levi grabbed his arm with a viselike grip.

"I know how much you lost when Noel died two months after Emmet, but I'm still standing here. I want my brother back, and whether you like it or not, the fans want you back too. Every time I make a call about another client, someone asks about your return."

"I'll write the songs. That's it." He pulled away and went into the bedroom because there wasn't anywhere else to go. His back hurt and his leg hurt from his stupid fall earlier, but the worst hurt was deep inside him. He had been somebody once, and he had blown it.

"Let's get some breakfast. I'll buy." Levi leaned against the doorjamb.

"No more talk about performing or I swear I'll beat you like you were ten all over again."

Levi barked out a laugh. "Yeah, okay. I'd like to see you try that now. But no more talk about performing for the time being. Just keep in mind, if you don't take to the stage after the album is complete, you won't make the same kind of money."

"You mean *we* won't make the same kind of money." Levi made a commission on everything he made. Downloads paid pennies. The real money was in touring.

"Can you blame me for wanting to keep my cash flow?" Levi's eyebrows climbed into his hairline.

"I'm serious. No live shows."

"Okay. Okay. No live shows." Levi held his hands up in surrender.

"Thanks." Relief washed over him, but a twinge of disappointment hit him too. He had drawn the line in the sand about performing, and for the first time Levi sounded like he might be listening. But for a brief second, so brief he almost missed it, his heart turned toward the idea of standing before the crowd at the music festival. He wasn't expecting to feel any of that. He had made a promise to himself when he woke up in that hospital room, that if Noel couldn't be onstage anymore, then he wouldn't be either.

He grabbed his keys again, and they headed out. "Isn't New Jersey supposed to be famous for their diners? We should find one." He hitched a leg into the truck. Something must be open by now.

Levi slid in beside him. "Have you ever heard of a car wash? Your truck is filthy."

"Knock it off, will you? I live in my truck."

"I see that." Levi held up a crumpled bag from Dunkin.

"Where to?" He ignored Levi's scrunched-up face

and his shift to sit closer to the door, as if that would keep him away from the wrappers and empty water bottles, and instead eased out of the parking space and onto the narrow road.

"I saw a place when I drove in. The Blue Dog or The Blue Fish or maybe The Blue Moon. I don't remember. But the sign did say they served breakfast Fridays through Sundays."

"Any idea what street it was on since the name stuck with you so well?" A man as successful as his brother, negotiating contracts and organizing concert tours, stalled out trying to find which way north pointed.

"I don't remember the street name. Just drive around. We'll find it. The town isn't that big." Levi huddled farther into the door.

"Why do I listen to you?" He turned away from the beach and snaked the roads that might lead back to the highway. He could plug in a couple of words to the map app and probably find the place, but he also loved to track. Growing up, he'd hike into the woods with nothing more than his sense of direction.

"You listen to me because you're my big brother." Levi propped his boots on the dashboard.

"Shouldn't that be the other way around? The little brother listening to the wisdom of the big brother. And get your feet off my dash." He turned right at the end of the road.

"Now you care about your truck?" Levi dropped his feet. "You know, I've been listening to you my whole life, following you around like a baby goat. When you set me

47

loose after the accident, I could barely think for myself. What you did—not driving the bus, I don't give a damn about that—but you telling the world to go to hell, including me, that cut me in half. You weren't the only one who lost a brother."

He gripped the steering wheel with both hands. When he had realized the length of the damage he had caused, all he could think to do was run. He ran as far and as fast as he could away from the music scene and everyone left behind who gave a damn about him. He wanted to run straight off the edge of the continent into the ocean, if he could, just to get away from the pain inside him, eating him up.

"I don't want to talk about this. Plug that restaurant into Google Maps. I don't want to drive up and down every street either." His voice echoed in the truck, but he couldn't keep the growl out of it.

"We are going to talk about it. That's why I'm here. More than the songs. You're going to hear about how I feel." Levi tapped at his phone screen.

He didn't have the words to explain his disappearance. If he had, he would've written a thousand songs about it. He didn't know how to pull himself free from the chains he locked around his own heart.

The female voice on the phone directed a left-hand turn, and like magic The Blue Dot tavern appeared. Two cars sat in the pockmarked parking lot that made the truck bounce on its shocks. The cedar shakes on the building's side were worn and tired. The roof looked original, and the windows were small. It wasn't much, but the open sign flashed red and blue.

He parked and turned to Levi. "No discussions about the past or the accident. I'm sorry I left you. I had my reasons." One of the biggest reasons was he couldn't take care of his brother any longer. That job had consumed his entire life. At first, he figured he needed a little time, but days turned into months and he found himself unable to do the job of protector. He had failed Levi, Emmet, and Noel.

Levi shoved the door open and stepped out. "I know what your reasons are. I don't blame you."

"Fine, then. Let's drop it." He started for the door. Levi wasn't onstage anymore because of that accident. He wouldn't perform without Grant, which was foolish, but Levi wouldn't hear of it any other way.

"I don't want to be a manager anymore. That wasn't my dream. It was supposed to be a detour until you felt better." Levi's words stopped him in his tracks. "After you finish those songs, I'm quitting. If you won't play, neither will I. It's not fun without you, and I'm tired of waiting for you to stop feeling sorry for yourself."

"Enough." He pounded the top of the truck with his fist. No one had told Levi to quit playing. He didn't want to be responsible for Levi turning full-time manager.

"Fine. Big, tough guy is done talking." Levi marched past him, kicking up gravel in his wake. He went into the building without looking back.

Grant ran a hand over his face. He should drive away and never come back. The hell with the songs. He unlocked the truck door and shoved himself inside. The roar of the engine as it kicked over was like splashing cold water on his face. He couldn't leave town. Levi needed him to write those songs. His bank account needed it too.

But once those songs were done, he would take off—alone. He wasn't good for anyone, not for Levi, and not for another woman who could have the power to come along and break his heart again.

Chapter Six

"What do you mean you're quitting?" Kassidy stared at Charlie Reynolds as if he had two heads. Charlie was as much a staple in The Blue Dot as her father was. They were best friends for twenty-five years. "Wait a second. You're joking, right?"

This had to be a bad joke because she needed Charlie to help her run The Dot. He had been the one in charge of the kitchen her entire life. She wouldn't be able to pull off the breakfast service. Without offering breakfast, she was sunk. Not that she wasn't already sunk because her sisters wanted to sell her second home, and she had no way—yet—to buy it away from them.

"I'm sorry, Kass. This is no joke." Charlie folded his stained apron with his long fingers and put it on the counter.

She stared at him, waiting for the punchline. Instead, she noticed the loose skin around Charlie's jawline that she hadn't paid attention to. And the deep lines around his mouth that in his youth wouldn't have been there but had formed from years of smiling. His shoulders, once razor-sharp straight, curved with the weight of age. His transformation had happened right under her unobservant nose while she was busy living her own life. Shame on her.

"But why? And why right now? And you can't just walk out on a Saturday morning without any notice." She tried to reel her voice in, but it took off and shook the ceiling. Okay, maybe he was older and maybe he was tired, but she needed time to find a replacement.

Charlie pressed his lips together. "I've been trying to tell you for two weeks that today was my last day. But you never listen to me." He clasped his weathered hands in front of his thin waist.

"You mean all that balking about quitting was real?" She had thought he was kidding. Charlie was a practical joker. He was known for gluing shoes to the floor or putting too much spice in your food. Never a customer's food, but an employee? Definitely.

"But it's Saturday." As if that should explain everything.

"I'm sorry about that. I wanted to move on a Monday, but my daughter couldn't get the extra days off. I sold my house, Kass. I can't afford to stay in Jersey anymore, and with your dad gone and all, I just don't see the point in dragging out my stay."

"What am I going to do without you?" She couldn't process what was playing out in front of her. Charlie was her best cook, and the only one who worked the breakfast shift. The most important shift at The Dot. They made as much during three days of breakfast as she did all week at dinner.

"It's time to sell." He patted her shoulder.

"I'm not selling. This is my home. You're my family." Her heart ached and the tears threatened to betray her again. Charlie was like an uncle to her. He had been at every holiday and major event she could think of. Not that she had had many events lately, but he had come out to Chicago for her college graduation years ago. She had taken six years to finish college at night, and Charlie had been as proud of her as her father had. "How can you leave when I need you?"

"I will always be your family. If you ever need me for anything besides being your line cook, I'll come right back. I promise. But if I were you, after the summer ends, I'd consider selling."

"But you'll work today's shift, right?" She needed to get through the breakfast shift, then she could digest everything he said. Yes, they were like family, and if she needed a kidney, Charlie would stand in line to be tested. But what she needed more at the moment was someone to make breakfast.

"No, honey. My daughter is in the parking lot with my U-Haul. Take care, Kassidy." He headed for the swinging doors but stopped and turned to her. "Oh, by the way, Annie won't be in today either."

"What did you say?" Her hands went up as if to block the blow of his words. "Hold on... Annie too?"

Annie, her best server, was leaving too? On the same damn day? She forced her mind to recall the past two weeks of memories like scenes from a bad movie. Annie had written her a note and left it on the top of her computer in the office. She had shoved it in a pocket, intending to read it, but never did. There hadn't been time.

"She wanted to say goodbye to you yesterday, but you were at the lawyer's office. I'll call you when I get to North Carolina." He placed a soft kiss on her cheek. He smelled like Old Spice, which made her think of her father. Her heart hurt more.

Charlie went through the swinging doors and out of her life. She should have been paying better attention, but her father had been sick, and she had The Dot to run. She never believed Charlie was serious. Now what was she going to do? She couldn't get a cook to come in this morning. She might seriously have to close today and couldn't afford to lose the money.

Kassidy stared at the griddle. She hoped if she stared long enough, the thing would decide to make breakfast.

"I think you have to turn it on with your hands to make it work. You can't mind meld with it." Bailey barreled into the kitchen, her hair bouncing along. She did a sidestep and landed next to her.

"Do you know how to cook?" She glanced at Bailey, then back at the grill.

"Me?" Bailey hooted with laughter. "I can barely boil water."

"But you teach people how to eat for a living."

"I can toss a salad. I'm great at cutting up fruit or baking a potato in the microwave. But if I want grilled chicken, I buy it that way. Wait a second. You can't cook either?"

She held Bailey's gaze and shook her head. Even though Bailey was her younger sister, they hadn't lived together for many years. And even though she helped her father run The Dot, she hadn't bothered to learn to cook. She mixed drinks and served. "I never got the hang of it. Dad and Charlie did all the cooking."

"Where's Charlie?" Bailey turned in circles as if he would appear from the walk-in. She almost wanted to check in there just in case this was a bad dream.

"He quit this morning and took our morning waitress Annie with him." That wasn't fair of her to think. He wasn't taking Annie, per se. Annie had been taking nursing classes. She had tired of bringing people their food, listening to their complaints. Food service was a tough business and could wear out the very best. And Annie needed better health benefits.

"This morning? Why?"

"He said he had enough of New Jersey. He can't afford the property taxes on his house anymore. Since Dad died, he decided to move in with his daughter and son-in-law in North Carolina." It seemed more and more people were racing out of Jersey for a less expensive life in another state. Every year another local sold their home and drove out of sight. She was beginning to think that might be a good idea. But she stopped herself. No, she wasn't ready to wave the white flag.

"They didn't give you any notice?" Bailey hopped up on the prep table.

"Charlie said he had tried, but I wasn't listening. I think I would've heard *I quit.*" But she hadn't. "We can't tell Maren. I'll figure something out. How hard can it be to cook eggs, right?" She pulled her hair back in a ponytail.

"Why don't you want to tell Maren?"

"Can you put up the coffee? If Maren finds out we don't have a cook or a server, and I can't cook, she'll double down on her argument to sell."

"Just hire another cook. You can wait the tables." Bailey jumped down and rummaged through her tote, pulling out a bag of carrots and gnawing on one. Not exactly making coffee.

"I can't do that either. Hire another cook, that is. The coffee is in the pantry. Can you work that machine?" Since she couldn't hire another cook, she would have to pull on her big girl panties and get to work. If she could mix drinks, she would be able to pull off a breakfast shift or two.

"I'm afraid to ask why you can't hire another cook. Are we serving cat or something?" Bailey put her carrots down and fiddled with the coffee machine.

"Gross. And don't go spreading that kind of rumor." She pointed at Bailey. "Charlie hadn't taken a raise in ten years. Dad paid him in trade to make up the difference. He would paint Charlie's house or build a garden for him, things like that." She grabbed the eggs and butter from the fridge. Maybe they could go without the menu for the day. Everyone would get sunny-side up eggs. She'd make it a special. See? Easy.

Bailey held a hand to her head. "No wonder Charlie can't afford his bills. Okay, no new cook for now. What about lunch and dinner?"

"Dad stopped offering lunch, which is a shame. People coming off the beach are looking for something to eat. We lose out to Max's on the boardwalk and the pizzeria on the corner a block in." She wasn't sure he even tried to build a lunch crowd. The Dot was two blocks in from the beach and off Main Street. In the summer, everyone wanted to be on the sand. During the offseason, the year-rounders didn't offer enough business for lunch.

"Without a cook, we won't be able to offer it either, and we'll need that. We need to expand the menu. Why don't we offer some healthy organic options that include locally grown?" Bailey asked.

"I like that idea, and when I find the money to buy you and Maren out, you can sit down with me and help me come up with a new menu." *A menu someone else will cook.* "I wouldn't mind expanding to lunch when I can afford it." Her business plan had included adding breakfast on more days and booking more bands for the weekends. They hadn't been offering entertainment much these days. Her father always fought her on bringing in bands. But with live bands, they could stay open later than ten which would attract a younger crowd. Her father hadn't cared about expanding to a younger crowd. He liked his crowd best.

"Kass, why didn't you ask me to help you with the menu before?" Bailey stood with the ground coffee in her hand, hovering over the coffee maker. "I would have."

"I know." But did she really? "I didn't want to bother you when Dad always fought me on changes. I figured if I could convince him first, then I could ask you for your input."

"Maybe if you had asked me first, it would have helped your case."

Ouch.

"Anyone here?" A male voice punctuated the air from the dining area and nearly made her drop an egg.

Bailey raised her eyebrows. "It looks like we have customers. See, ask and the Universe will provide. I'll go take their order."

"We're only offering eggs." She didn't believe in things she couldn't see. She believed in spreadsheets, balance sheets, and butts in the chairs. She didn't even trust the meteorologists who guessed at the weather half the time.

On a long breath, she slapped a slab of butter on the griddle and crossed her fingers for things to go her way. They only served breakfast until ten thirty and the morning promised to bring some fog and drizzle which meant the beach crowd would be light. If luck could land on her side, the breakfast crowd would also be light today. Then she'd spend the rest of the day trying to figure out how to get someone to cook. Maren was a great cook, but she doubted her sister would jump in and help. She had refused her offer to come in today even to see the place.

"I know it's a dump," Maren had said.

She had left Maren sitting at the kitchen table, scrolling through her phone with an oversized mug of coffee in one hand. At least she had promised to stick around for more than a day or two. It was a start because they still had to go over to Dad's house and shuffle through his mess. And when Maren saw that, losing Charlie would seem like a walk in the park.

Bailey pushed through the swinging doors. "We have two hotties at table four."

"You know the table arrangement?" She had no interest in the heat barometer of her customers. She only cared about the color of their money.

"I have no idea. I picked a number out of the air. Anyway, I took their order. I could swear one of the guys looks familiar." Bailey ripped the order off the order pad.

"Why would someone in Serenity by the Sea look familiar to you? You're hardly ever here." She cracked eggs onto the griddle.

"I don't know. He looks like someone I've seen before. He must have that kind of face. And a family of five walked in. They would like breakfast too. But they're hoping for Joe's pancakes. They come to Serenity every summer and never miss out on his pancakes. At least that's what they claim they do."

"What did you tell them?" Her heart beat like a wild racehorse. Her father's pancakes were the best, but he used some secret ingredient to make them fluffy. A secret that he had taken to his grave and Charlie took to North Carolina. She yanked her phone out of her pocket and sent Charlie a text for that ingredient. She'd need it when she found a cook.

"I told them the cook would be happy to make pancakes." Bailey flashed a bright smile and swung her hips.

"Bailey, are you nuts? I don't know how to make those. I don't even know the ingredients or if we have them. Oh, I could strangle Charlie, leaving me like this." She turned in circles. She was in over her head. Why didn't she ever learn to cook? Stubborn and stupid. That was what she was. Charlie hadn't responded to her text.

"Let's not panic. We can do this. You Google how to make pancakes. It can't be that hard. I'll bring out the drinks and how about some fruit? Do we have fruit?"

"We can't afford to give away fruit. Bring the drinks. I'll figure it out." She grabbed her phone and searched. A million "easy" recipes popped up. Her father had never believed in writing down his recipes. He used to tap his head and say it was up there in his fireproof filing cabinet.

"I could use a peek into that cabinet now, Dad." She decided on the second recipe after she'd read a dozen on the search page. Something burned. She crinkled her nose.

Smoke swirled off the griddle. The eggs. The edges had browned and the yolks were almost solid. She had the griddle up too high. She lunged for the knobs and slipped. Her hand landed on the hot metal of the griddle and seared her palm. She screamed and jumped back, swinging her arm. She knocked the carton holding the rest of the eggs. They splattered to the floor in a gooey mess of clear and yellow liquid.

She bit back the foul language bubbling to the surface and ran her hand under cold water. That was the last of the eggs because she hadn't been to the store to get more. Charlie was supposed to do that, but he hadn't gone to the grocery store either.

Maybe she could run to Mr. D's bakery and buy muffins and loaves of bread to serve. Or she could just send everyone home and agree to sell the business.

"How are the pancakes coming? Uh-oh." Bailey stared at the floor, then back at her. "What happened?"

"I happened, that's what. I can't fix this." She threw her hands in the air. The burned one throbbed. She had dreams of making the tavern better, and here she was acting like she had no experience. She was still reeling from the meeting in the lawyer's office and Charlie quitting. She needed a do-over today. That was all. Everyone was entitled to a bad day or two—or twenty.

"Two more tables of people showed up. And the ones who have been waiting are getting grouchy." Bailey handed her a dishtowel.

"Okay. Okay. I'll handle it. Make more coffee. And toast. Make toast." She pushed past Bailey and swept through the swinging doors.

The seating area was dim even for the early hour of the day. The dark paneling and dirty windows were the cause of that. The place needed a facelift. Something light and airy and remnant of the beach. Restoration had been her plan once she had taken over The Dot. Looked as if that plan was on permanent hold.

The restaurant was full. They didn't offer a ton of seating, and she had plans to add seating outside, but for now, the ten tables all had occupants. She should've locked the doors before the place filled up. She couldn't throw them all out now.

Rick, the local dog trainer, waved to her. He had lived in Serenity all his life and had recently taken in his father. They had a small house on the edge of town by the highway. Rick was amazing with the dogs. People, not always the case.

"Hey, Rick. Do you want coffee?"

"Can I help myself to a soda from the fountain behind the bar?" He unfolded his thin frame from the chair. He had a habit of turning his body slightly away from whoever he spoke to, as if to protect himself from whatever they might say.

"Sure. I'm a little short-staffed today. Sorry about the wait." She often allowed her regulars to use the soda machine when they ate with her. The money she had probably lost from doing that might add up to a lot if she took the time to figure it out. But she liked the year-rounders to feel like they were more than customers.

"I saw Charlie's daughter in the parking lot. I guess he finally pulled the plug. You're probably not far behind him." He pushed a laugh through his teeth.

"I'm not going anywhere." She controlled the desire to huff and puff all over the place. Why was everyone ready to see her close the doors? "Excuse me for a minute," she said and moved along the tables.

The door opened and another group of people gathered by the hostess station. Not that there was a hostess. Or better yet, it was her. If she had to be the cook and the bartender, she would try and recruit her beautiful niece to help out. Peyton needed a job.

The family of five seated near the small stage was the group who wanted the pancakes. As she zigzagged through the seats, someone else waved to her. Her new neighbor and his brother were at table four. Bailey was right. They were both attractive, but Grant drew her attention like the heat of the sun.

His smile was quick and small. He was probably pissed off about waiting for his food, but it couldn't be helped. She made a detour and stopped at his table. The family of five was busy making a game out of straws. They didn't seem to have a clue pancakes weren't coming today. She needed it to stay that way for as long as possible.

"Hello again. How can I help you?" She shoved her injured hand behind her back.

"When will our order be ready?" Levi said.

"Your eggs will be right up. Can I get you anything else while you wait?"

"We didn't order eggs. And I don't want eggs. I ordered avocado on toast. Did your waitress get the order wrong?" Levi's upper lip curled in a snarl.

"Levi, relax." Grant turned to her. "My brother doesn't know when to keep his mouth shut. I'm sorry."

"No need to be."

"I know your secret." Grant stood.

Her heart stuck in her throat and she had to swallow to breathe again. How could he know about Charlie quitting? "What secret is that?"

She hoped her voice came out natural and not strained.

"Your name is Kassidy." He straightened his shoulders as if proud of his revelation.

"How did you know?" Because she had left him with the distinct advantage of knowing his name while hers remained in question.

"The man we rented the tent from said you were the best neighbor on the block. It's nice to meet you, officially." He extended his hand.

She hesitated, but for only a second, wanting to know what his hand felt like against hers. His grip was warm and solid, sending heat up her arm.

He knew her name. She shouldn't like that so much. "Phil is very kind."

"What about the avocado toast?" Levi interrupted them.

With effort, she turned to face him. "We're a little short-staffed this morning." She sounded like a broken record. "It's eggs for everyone today. I apologize for any inconvenience."

She also would have liked to say the order was on her, but she needed each and every sale, especially after what Mr. West had said about the extra mortgage.

"What kind of a place is this?" Levi pushed out of his chair.

"Levi, take it easy." Grant clenched his jaw, then motioned for her to move closer.

She leaned in and was rewarded with his wintergreen smell. She bent a little more to get a better whiff and lost her balance. Without thinking, she gripped the back of the chair to keep from falling into his chest. A sharp pain ran across her burned skin. She gasped and clutched her hand to her chest.

"Are you okay?" Grant took her wrist, turning her hand over. Her bright-red angry palm gave her away.

"I'm fine." She forced her gaze to hold his intense dark one while the heat from her hand turned into the heat of embarrassment running up her neck.

"You don't look fine. This might blister. Did you put anything on it?" He continued to hold her wrist.

"I'm good. Really. Just a clumsy accident in the kitchen." She eased out of his hold with some regret. She appreciated his concern, and it had been ages since a handsome man touched her even if it was only to offer medicinal advice.

A table of two snapped to get her attention. She gave them the one-minute sign. The father at the table of five who wanted pancakes checked his watch and strained to look around the dining area. She needed to appease these people before they all walked out and left bad reviews online. "If you'll excuse me, I have to see to my other customers."

Grant leaned in again. She forbade her nose to sniff

him. "This might be none of my business, but you have a full house and no waitstaff taking orders. You look like you've got a third degree burn on your hand, and the only thing on the menu today is eggs. I'd say you are anything but fine."

"It's the Saturday special. We do it once a month for fun. The regulars love it." Oh, the lies she told. If she kept this up, she'd be a pro by noon.

Grant scrunched up his nose like he smelled... well... rotten eggs. "Really?"

Levi pointed to the door. "I watched three sets of people walk away since you've been chatting it up with Grant because no one greeted them. And there goes another group." The customers who had walked in walked right out.

"Like I said, my staff didn't come to work this morning. By dinner we'll be right as rain." *Right as rain?* Sweet Lord, who was she becoming?

"Do you need some help?" Grant said.

"No, why would you think that?" She forced a laugh and swatted the air to prove that was the most ridiculous thing she had heard all week. Her hand throbbed more.

"Kassidy, could you come in here a minute?" Bailey poked her head out of the kitchen doors.

"If you'll excuse me a second. Can I get you more coffee while I'm in the kitchen?"

"I'd like my eggs. Not that I ordered eggs, but I'm so hungry I'll eat anything," Levi said.

"Levi," Grant warned.

"What? She's making me wait for my food." Levi held his hands up.

"Excuse me." She hurried back to the kitchen. "What is it now?" She gripped Bailey's arm.

"I broke the coffee machine." Tears filled her hazel eyes.

"The whole machine?" This couldn't be happening. If she had eaten breakfast today, it would be on its way back up her throat. No morning had ever gone as badly as this one.

"I don't know. It started gurgling, then it stopped making coffee. Do you have one of those old-fashioned metal carafes that make like thirty cups of coffee?" Bailey wiped at her forehead with the back of her hand.

"We don't have one of those. Oatmeal. I could make oatmeal." She would have to figure out how to fix the coffee machine or she'd have to run to Dunkin and buy their coffee in boxes. Or, dare she think it again, she'd have to close this morning. Not an option.

"Nobody ordered oatmeal." Bailey's words brought her back to center and gave her an idea.

She grabbed her purse and shoved her wallet at Bailey. "Go to the market and buy up all the eggs. I'll serve fruit while you're gone and juice even though I should make them pay for the fruit, but beggars can't be choosers. We have enough bread for toast and we have bacon and sausage. I'll get all that going. Now, hurry."

Bailey spun around and slipped in the egg goo still on the floor. Her feet flew out from under her, and she landed on her back in the eggs with a plop.

"Oh, gross." Bailey held up her hand and the egg dripped from her fingers.

Kassidy couldn't help but laugh. She didn't mean to, but the fizz of uncontrollable cackling burst over her lips like a spewing bottle of shaken soda and bent her in half. "Are you okay?" She managed between chuckles. She was a terrible sister for cracking up, but if she didn't hoot with laughter, she might cry.

"Excuse me?" That Southern male voice again. Deep and sultry with the hint of bad boy charm. She leaned into that sound as if it were a gift just for her. She could listen to that man talk all day. Grant waited just inside the doors. He ducked his head and scratched at the back of his neck.

"Yes?" She forced thoughts of Bailey falling and Grant's sexy voice to the back of her mind. She needed to focus on eggs and breakfast. The opposite of sexy, but necessary.

"I hope you don't mind me saying, but I've worked in enough kitchens to know you're having a problem back here."

"Help me up, Kassidy." Bailey waved her hand from her spot on the floor.

"By the looks of her and your weird egg menu, I think I'm right. Is there something I can do to help?" Grant peered around her to Bailey slipping on the floor.

"I don't understand why helping me is so important to you." She grabbed Bailey's hand and righted her on her feet. "Who are you? Some kind of food critic in town to write an article on bad restaurants?"

He dipped his chin again. "No, nothing like that. My momma raised me to lend a hand whenever a hand needed lending. It's the right thing to do, and you have a boatload of ornery customers out there. I suppose you don't want to lose any more than you already have. And since you're my new neighbor and all, I thought I could pitch in."

"He's a prince and spot-on. You can help us, whoever you are. I'm Bailey, Kassidy's younger sister. Thank you for the help." Bailey washed her hands.

"Bailey, this is a family matter," she said through gritted teeth, hoping Bailey would get the hint she didn't want the help of a stranger. She had no idea who Grant was except for some hot guy who seemed put off yesterday at the tent and her appearance at it. Was she supposed to take his word for it that he could cook? What if he were actually a serial killer?

"Kass, without Charlie and Annie to help us, we're kind of in a bind here. You want to make this place work; we need some help." Bailey glared back at her.

"All right. Help. But I don't know what you can do that I can't." She hoped her face hadn't turned bright red to confirm the humiliation sloshing around inside her like kitchen grease. At least Maren hadn't come in today to witness this whole meltdown firsthand.

"Can you cook?" Bailey said.

"Yes, ma'am."

"There you go." Bailey waved a hand in the air. "And please don't call me ma'am. She's the old one."

"Hey." She smoothed her hair back with her injured

hand and winced. Her appearance shouldn't be something to worry about at the moment, but she must look a mess. She hadn't bothered with makeup this morning and her curly hair had probably frizzed. Not to mention, Grant was the picture of handsome rugged man.

"Okay. Older sister. I have to go home to change." Bailey pulled her wet pants away from her legs.

"You can't do that. You need to go to the store."

"Covered in eggs? No way. I'm going home first. Look at me." Bailey was beautiful with her dark hair and bright-hazel eyes. Her olive skin shone with a vibrancy that made others turn their heads.

"How about if I get my brother to run to the store for y'all? Your sister can change into something dry, and you tell me what we need to do." Grant's long legs carried him through the kitchen to the sink where Bailey had just been.

She explained the lack of food and cook situation, and how they no longer had a server for the morning shift. She gave him a list of items they needed. He went out to the sitting area with it and came back in no time.

"Levi is finding the store now. I've been a line cook for a few years. I'll take over the kitchen. You wait the tables." He grabbed an apron on the nearby hook and moved around the kitchen as if he were born to do it.

Bailey scooted out the back and returned a half hour later to help them. They worked in unison for the next few hours, not saying much but who needed what food and what table was ready. It was the best breakfast service she'd seen in a long time. Grant put Charlie to shame in the cook department. She hated to admit that because Charlie and her father had been friends for so long, but Grant knew how to handle the food prep with ease.

He was also a lot better to look at in his white t-shirt sticking to his muscular torso with the sweat of hard work than Charlie in his baggy pants, stained shirts, and eyebrows bushy enough they dusted where his hairline used to be.

When the last customer left for the morning, she locked the door with an exhausted sigh of relief. Her legs and shoulders ached from hard but satisfying work. The three of them had done it. Her heart swelled with excitement for the future possibilities of The Blue Dot. She returned to the kitchen and found Grant cleaning the griddle and Bailey loading the dishwasher.

"Thank you, Grant. I don't know what I would've done without you today." He had been quite the surprise this morning. Yesterday, she had almost considered telling him off. Good thing she had had the sense to walk away.

He smiled and shrugged and continued to clean the griddle.

Bailey raised her brows in question and pointed to Grant. She had no idea what Bailey was getting at, but she did have a burning question on her lips.

"Grant, is there any chance you're in need of a job?" She crossed her fingers behind her back. Not that she wished unemployment on anyone. She knew firsthand how difficult it could be to make ends meet, but if Bailey was right about her Universe theory, she really hoped Grant had been delivered to her doorstep both literally and figuratively.

"No, ma'am. I have a job." He kept his gaze on the grill.

She stifled a groan. "Any chance you'd be interested in another part-time opportunity? At least temporarily until I can hire someone?"

"Come on, Grant. You have to admit it was fun working this morning with my sister and me. She's very good at what she does. You could do the breakfast service. It's only three days a week. We'll find someone else for the dinner rush until we get the lunch menu going." Bailey dried her hands on a towel and offered Grant the smile that usually got her what she wanted.

Kassidy tamped down the ugly feeling churning in her stomach. She had no reason to be jealous of Bailey with all her beauty and charm. Bailey was her sister and deserved all the love and happiness in the world. And if she flashed Grant that stunning smile, she must want his attention besides in this kitchen.

Grant's gaze moved between her and Bailey. He scratched the back of his neck. "If I only work the breakfast shift, what will you do for dinner tonight?"

"I'll handle it." She straightened her shoulders and held his gaze. She appreciated what he had done for them this morning, and she planned on paying him what Charlie would've received, but she didn't need him. She would never need a man again.

Bailey tossed the towel at her. "She's so stubborn.

This is a temporary arrangement, Grant. If you could swing the dinner shift tonight, our other sister will take over dinner tomorrow. I've already spoken to her."

"You have?" That was news to her. She wasn't sure if she wanted to wait tables while Maren barked orders around the kitchen.

"Yup. Maren will start tomorrow."

"I'll help y'all out in the mornings until you find a replacement, and I'll handle your dinner tonight."

"Thank you." Relief pushed her lungs wide open. "Let me get you some money for today." She wanted him to know how much she appreciated what he was doing for her. He was helping her make her dreams come true, and he didn't even know it.

"No, ma'am. Keep your money. I don't need it." His gaze hovered somewhere near her mouth. He either couldn't meet her eye or he had a thing for lips. Or worse, she had something in her teeth.

"But you can't work for free." She would not owe him. She paid her way.

"You let me eat here when I'm working and that will be enough. I'm sure you'll find a new cook in no time at all."

"You have to take payment for your services. I'm not a charity case." Her shoulders snapped to attention again. She had no problem with a man being chivalrous, but she needed to maintain some of her dignity.

"Don't argue with her, Grant. You have no idea how relentless she can be when her mind is made up," Bailey said.

She wasn't relentless. She had caved plenty of times in her life. She had given up her life in Serenity because Bear Foster, her former fiancé, wanted to move to Chicago for work and she went too. When Bear didn't want to get married because she was hurting his corporate image with her waitressing job and lack of education, she didn't beg him to take her back. She didn't even fight him all that hard. She had asked only why he had waited so long to tell her. If she had known sooner that she had embarrassed him to that degree, she would've stayed in New Jersey.

Bear hadn't given her a good answer about why he had waited to mention his dissatisfaction with her. He had only thrown his clothes into a suitcase and wished her luck. He was moving on and moving up. Without her. Since him, and it had been several years since that night, she had focused on herself and trying to get her career off the ground. She had stumbled a couple of times. She had had relationships too, but when a man started to talk about a permanent future together, she bailed.

She was determined to make The Blue Dot work this summer and prove to herself and her sisters that she had what it took to be a successful businessperson. Though her fiasco this morning proved otherwise, but once Grant stepped in, things turned around.

She was also determined not to allow a man to break her heart again. Especially not a man who wandered from place to place and that was who Grant had to be. She didn't know how she even knew that, intuition she guessed, or the sad look in his dark eyes that hung around like storm clouds.

She didn't wait for Grant to agree to the money. She marched past him into the tiny office filled by the metal desk covered in paper. She grabbed the petty cash box and pulled out enough to cover the breakfast and dinner shifts.

"Here," she said when she returned with the money. Bailey was gone. Only Grant was left, leaning against the counter of the prep table.

Grant stared at the cash. He raised his gaze to hers. "Thank you." He slipped the money from her fingers and grazed her skin with his. An electric current shot up her arm and made her chest tingle. She wanted to curse physical attraction. Grant didn't want her and would probably be no good for her anyway. He would just be a distraction.

He cleared his throat. *Was she staring in some kind of weird stalker way?* "Your sister left. She said to tell you she'd see you at the house. She had stuff to do."

"Oh. Okay. Well, thanks again for this morning and for tonight. I'm really trying to get this place in better shape." If he had noticed that the stove was from thirty years ago or that the pans had been used for so long that the copper on the bottom would never shine again, he hadn't said.

"I understand. This is a family business, I guess."

"My dad owned it for decades. He passed away recently. I want to keep it going. My sister Maren wants to sell. I think after today Bailey might be ready to keep it. Do you want something to drink? I could use a Diet Coke." She went into the walk-in refrigerator and pulled out two Diet Cokes.

"No, thank you. I'm good. I'm sorry about your dad. I lost my mom some years back. I know how hard that can be." He remained in his spot by the grill, but a soft smile tugged at his lips.

"Thanks. We're doing okay. I think. Sorry about your mom too." She poured the soda into a tall glass and let the foam from the bubbles tickle her nose.

His smile receded a little like a wave on the sand, and he shrugged. "Life happens. She got sick and didn't tell anyone until it was too late."

"That seems sad." Her mom had left one day without saying anything to her or Maren. When she had come home from school, her mother had left a note with a few pieces of sea glass next to it as if that would soften the blow of her mother walking out and leaving her behind. But she and Maren had had their dad, and even Bailey's mom for a short while, because Dad was never good with relationships. Before she knew it, Bailey and her mom were gone too.

"Sadder for her. Her life ended too soon."

"What kind of work do you do?" She wanted to know more about him, if he was going to work with her temporarily. She also wanted a reason to keep him talking for a little while longer.

He hesitated as if he didn't know how to explain his employment. She hoped he wasn't into organized crime or something. "I have a family business too. I work for my brother, Levi."

"Do you find it hard to work with a sibling?" Because if she had her way, both of her sisters would remain in Serenity by the Sea and together they would run The Blue Dot. But even though they were sisters, they weren't exactly friends. They didn't meet once a week for drinks or anything like that. Time and life had drifted them apart like the broken pieces of wood washed up to shore.

"Hardest thing I've ever done was work with family." He dropped his gaze.

"I was hoping you'd say it was great." She sipped at the Coke and relaxed against the counter opposite him.

"It was once, when things were good, but it hasn't been great in years." A wistful look crossed his face.

He probably had snagged a memory of when things were better than they were now. Memories tangled up like that for her all the time. She had learned to try and cut them loose and wash them away. Sometimes successful. Sometimes not.

"Then why do you stay?" For her, the reality would be if she and her sisters couldn't make this business work, no one would stay. They would sell everything and move on. She would have to cave and agree to sell The Blue Dot even though she didn't want to with all her heart.

"Family sticks together no matter what."

"It's that lend a helping hand thing you mentioned earlier?" When her sisters found out about the shape of their dad's house and how hard it would be to clean it up, would they worry about letting her down if they left? She hoped so because she could not take on the task of clearing it out by herself. They needed to get over there and soon. The house wouldn't clean itself.

"Something like that." He tapped the counter with his knuckles. "Well, I best be getting on. I have some things to do before tonight's shift."

She finished her soda while he pushed through the swinging doors and out of sight. He was easy to talk to. Too easy, in fact. She hadn't seen a ring on his finger, but that didn't mean there wasn't a woman in his life. And she was pretty sure Bailey had piqued his interest some. She had that power with men. Men always picked Bailey.

She grabbed her purse and headed out. She still wanted to collect sea glass today. After that, she and her sisters would go to their father's house. She dreaded what they would say, but it couldn't be avoided any longer.

She couldn't put her finger on it, but something rang familiar about Grant. Maybe she had heard his voice somewhere before, like in a movie. A laugh escaped her lips. Right. A famous movie star had walked into The Blue Dot and generously offered to cook her customers breakfast.

Things like that only happened in make-believe. Not in real life. And never for a girl like her.

Chapter Seven

Grant's boots scraped against the pavement as he walked away from The Blue Dot. Levi had left with the truck, stranding him. He could have called Levi to come back, but a walk would do him some good. Clear his mind. Maybe inspire him to write something. Three weeks wasn't much time to create three songs. Three songs in three weeks. Why had he ever agreed to that? Even if he had three months, he doubted he'd be able to pull it off.

He should have kept his backside in the chair of that restaurant this morning, but no. He had to help the pretty lady. He had watched as several customers left without being attended to and heard more than a few complain about the service. When the kitchen door had swung open and Bailey had come through, he had caught a glimpse of Kassidy and the panicked look on her face. No other activity was happening in a kitchen that served breakfast, and that was bad. He knew that from experience.

If Kassidy hadn't caught his attention the day before at the tent with her untamed hair, bright smile, and that determined tilt of her chin, he might have been able to control the impulse to help. He should blame his momma for that impulse. But she had been right and the smartest woman he had known. "Help the underdog, Grant," she had said from the time he could walk himself and his brothers to school alone. "They just need someone to hold the ladder for them. They'll climb it just fine once you do."

His heart had folded in on itself the night he missed Emmet's phone call—his last. Grant had been onstage when the call landed in his voicemail, and he often wondered if Emmet had picked that exact time, knowing Grant wouldn't hear the message for hours.

Grant could still hear Emmet's voice swollen with tears, asking Grant not to be mad at him. Emmet had always been the underdog, and Grant hadn't helped save his brother. He had been so wrapped up in his music career he hadn't seen how much Emmet hurt. His mother would be disappointed in him.

He could use her advice now. Maybe even her song-writing skills. He and Levi had learned to love music because of her. She would sing in the kitchen with the radio on the windowsill turned up as loud as it would go while she made dinner or washed dishes.

The end of the street came to a T with the top of the T running along the boardwalk. He crossed in between cars moving too fast for a road crowded with people walking and on bicycles and leaned against the metal railing. The sun was out in full force. Tourists covered the sand with blankets and umbrellas, barely leaving enough room to get around. Lifeguards in their red bathing suits with thick white sunscreen on their noses sat up high in their white wooden chairs. Surfers challenged the waves. He'd seen bigger on the west coast, but that didn't discourage a group of five from riding waves in and paddling back out. This beach was a popular one. He'd give it that.

Too bad more of these people hadn't had breakfast in Kassidy's place. She and he had settled in right nicely while working together. She seemed to know what he needed before he did, a spatula, another flap of butter. Her laugh was full, as if she had so much emotion it had nowhere else to go but over her lips and into her eyes.

He had taken a big risk wandering around town in the early afternoon at a crowded beach. Someone might notice him even if the fans had dwindled more and more over the past two years. He was amazed how quickly he could be forgotten. Part of him wanted to yell that Grant Hawkins was on the beach just to see what the others would do and to prove to himself they still cared, but then he could end up with a lot of questions to answer, and he wasn't ready for that—not by a long shot.

He pulled down his cap and walked north along the boards. He had seen the comments on social media when he bothered to look, which wasn't often. The fans wanted to know where he was and what he was doing. Some were understanding, mostly the women, but some were not. They didn't care about his personal life. They wanted his music and his performances as if he owed it to them. And maybe he did, once. He also owed them the best he could be, and he wasn't that now.

He stopped short, as if his legs could see what was on the beach before his brain could catch up. Kassidy's full head of dark hair fought against the ocean breeze. She brushed it out of her face, but the wind gripped the untamed strands and swatted her again with them. A small laugh tilted over his lips at what had to be her frustration. She was cute when she was mad.

She bent down where the water pulled away from the edge of the beach and ran her fingers in the sand. She scooped something up, gave a little fist pump, and skipped on to the next spot.

She hadn't been that animated all morning except for when some old guy hassled Bailey and refused to pay his bill. He had been ready to march out to the dining room and set the guy straight, but Kassidy took care of him. The guy had paid and apologized.

He moved along before someone, especially Kassidy, noticed him. He didn't need to get caught staring at his new boss. And he needed to get back to the tent and mess around with his guitar for a while before he returned to The Blue Dot tonight.

The walk back eased some of the tension in his shoulders. The town was scenic with a mix of Victorian homes near the beach and smaller houses with postage stamp size lawns farther inland.

He turned onto his street. The line of tents stopped him for a second. Each one had an awning in some bright solid color or striped in the same hues. Every home was taken care of with pride. Several sported the American flag. Tent really wasn't the right word for these dwellings. Fabric house maybe. He could live in his tent year-round, really. The cold never bothered him much. He didn't need a lot of space. He was tired of moving, anyway. The south held nothing for him anymore. He would never go back to singing and touring. That world was over. Not that he had any plans for making a life in a place called Serenity by the Sea, but he could see why someone would want to. Someone like Kassidy who had a passion for this community.

He unlocked the door and found Levi sprawled out on the couch in sweatpants and a t-shirt, watching something on his phone.

"What are you doing?" He tossed his keys on the table.

Levi pushed up to a seated position and tossed his phone to the side. "I've been waiting for you to come back so we could work on the song."

"I'm working on the song. Alone. Go do something. Or better yet, go home. Your presence is stopping my creativity." He didn't need or want the pressure of Levi looking over his shoulder.

"I'm not leaving without those songs." Levi stood inches from him. That wasn't hard in the little space, but Levi wanted to make his point. He didn't always appreciate being the little brother who got told what to do by him.

"I can send it to you. Technology, you know." He held up his own phone but stepped back to give Levi some room.

"Listen, I appreciate what you're doing and how hard it is. If I were the songwriter you are or half the musician, I wouldn't be the manager. You've been in a dark place for far too long. I'm not leaving and taking the chance you can't pull those songs together in time. You might be done with music, but I'm not. I can't afford to piss off the record label. The music business is how I make a living. I'm not interested in slinging hash for a few bucks."

"Point taken. I won't let you down. Not this time." After the bus accident, Levi had been in the hospital for two weeks, then four months of physical therapy before he was better. He had let Levi down in a big way that night. He would find a way to pull these songs out of his backside. But what scared the hell out of him was trying to put his heart into those songs. The fans would know if he didn't. They always did. And he wasn't sure he could.

He needed some air and went into the kitchen. The fridge was stocked and so were the cabinets. His little brother had done the grocery shopping while he was at work. Maybe he would let Levi stick around for a short time.

"Hey, you didn't let me down the last time either." Levi stood behind him. So much for getting space. "And you didn't let down Emmet. You can stop carrying the weight of the world on your shoulders."

He ducked behind the fridge door, pretending to look for something inside. He had let everyone down on that bus. He shouldn't have been driving. Plain and simple. "Thanks for going to the store." He pulled out an apple and wiped it on his shirt.

"So, that's it. You still won't talk about it." Levi blocked his way out of the kitchen. The only place to go was the bedroom or bathroom. He could write sitting on the toilet. It wouldn't be the first time.

"Nothing to talk about. I messed up. I know that. I made my amends with the families." He had shown up at the doorsteps of everyone who had been on the bus. The hardest people to look in the eye were Noel's parents. Her mother had broken down, turning her face into her husband's shoulder, and sobbed with gut-wrenching wails. Noel's father had only shaken his head and slammed the door shut.

"How about with yourself? You could let yourself off the hook too."

"Get out of my way. I have work to do before I go back to The Blue Dot." He pushed past Levi and settled at the table.

"What do you mean go back?" Levi followed fast on his heels.

"I'm helping out there temporarily." He flipped open his laptop and booted up the songwriting program. He preferred to write with pen and paper, but he didn't have any at the moment and messing with the computer gave his hands something to do. He tossed the apple in the garbage. He didn't really want it.

"You can't work at that bar. This morning was one thing, and I knew I'd never be able to talk you out of it. You had that look in your eye you get when you're about to take on the world. You're just like Mom that way. She had that same look. I always knew it was going to mean I'd have to pack a thousand boxes with food for the food pantry or play my trumpet at the nursing home. You have to write three songs in three weeks. All your energy should be put to that. Not slinging grease."

"Don't tell me how to use my time. The ladies needed help. Their cook quit this morning." He kept his gaze on the screen. There was no point in explaining about the difficulties writing would cause him. He needed the distraction from facing a blank page.

"Are you sure this doesn't have something to do with the fact that Kassidy is pretty?" Levi crossed his arms over his chest.

"I hadn't noticed."

Levi gave a half laugh. "Yeah, okay. A blind man would notice those two women. I caught Kassidy stealing a look at you when I came back with the food you wanted. She looked like she was ready to lick you clean from the plate."

"You should shut up, really." On a long breath, he closed the software program. He needed to open his mind a little more first. Or get Levi to stop yapping. He was like their mom that way. She had talked nonstop when she wasn't singing to them. She and Levi could sit at the kitchen table for hours gossiping like two middle school girls.

Someone knocked on the door.

He and Levi exchanged a glance.

"What are you up to now, little brother?" He pushed out of the chair. It would be just like Levi to surprise him with something disagreeable like a songwriting coach. Levi had tried that before. It didn't go well.

"I swear I haven't done a thing." Levi backed away with his hands in the air.

He wondered how true that statement actually was. "I guess there's only one way to find out."

He went for the door. A petite woman with red hair —even he could tell that red came from a bottle—and creased skin the color of tanned leather held a foil-wrapped plate and a bright-white smile. Her yellow blouse with orange flowers was thick in the middle where it met her green shorts. Definitely not someone on Levi's usual list.

"Can I help you?" He held the door open.

"I'm your new neighbor, Kate. I live two doors down with my husband Howie. We're here every summer." She pointed off to her right. "I wanted to welcome you to the Topside Community."

"That's mighty nice, ma'am, but my brother and I are only here for a short vacation." Visitors at the door with food was like his hometown. He hadn't expected people in New Jersey to be so neighborly.

Her gaze searched behind him. When she landed on something, that smile grew three more sizes. He glanced over his shoulder. Levi stood there waving like a fool.

"Oh, I know you're here for a few weeks. Your landlord and I are old friends. I like to make all his renters feel welcome." She held out the plate. "That's my specialty—crumb cake. I make it from scratch. Goes great with a cup of coffee in the morning. At least that's how Howie and I like it. Go on, take it. It doesn't bite." She laughed and pushed the cake closer to him.

He took the dish for fear she'd grip his hands and wrap them around the plate. "Thank you." His new neighbor reminded him a little of his mother. Not in appearance. His mother was tall and thin with blond hair that fell to the middle of her back, but she loved to meet new people. She was always baking something to bring to a new neighbor or for someone new at her church. She had fit right in back home in that small town of theirs.

"I know everyone in Serenity by the Sea. My tent has been in my family since the nineteen twenties. My grandfather won it in a poker game." She leaned in and whispered as if *poker game* were bad words. "Anyhoo, if you boys need anything at all, just holler. Howie and I are grilling tonight. Why don't you both come for dinner?"

"That would be nice," Levi said.

"I can't. I'm sorry. I'm working." He shot a look at Levi as if to say, *you want to eat dinner with someone old enough to be your grandmother?*

"Working while you're on vacation?" Kate's dark eyebrows furrowed together. He suspected she dyed them too.

"It's a working vacation." He handed the plate to Levi. "Would you like to come in?"

88

"Oh, no. I don't want to bother you. I just wanted to say hello and invite you to dinner. I hope you'll join us after work. Well, where are you working, actually? I could give you the skinny on the business."

"The Blue Dot."

"Oh, the Russos' place." She tsked and shook her head. "Such a shame about Joe. He died so quickly, leaving that place for his daughters to deal with. I shouldn't gossip, but I heard Joe was in debt up to the ceiling." She marked the spot above her head with a flat palm. "The best thing for those girls would be to sell it. Have you met Kassidy? She's lovely. I don't know the other two. They never came to visit their father. At least that's the gossip. But you know the saying. Believe half of what you hear and all that."

"Is the place for sale?" Levi crowded him at the door.

"I heard it was. Their business has been slow the past few years. I don't know how Joe kept the doors open. A lot of the locals would go there for dinner, just to help him out. Howie and I had done that a few times when word spread Joe was in financial trouble. Anyhoo." She waved her hand in the air. "I have to run. Dinner is at six, if you boys change your mind."

"Can I come without him?" Levi leaned past him.

"Of course you can, dear. See you then." Kate waved again and hurried down the sidewalk.

"Why do you want to have dinner with them?" He closed the door.

"You're going to be working. And I have to eat." Levi

lifted a shoulder. "Do you think your new boss would like an offer on her place?"

"Why do you want to buy a tavern in New Jersey? You're not actually taking to this place, are you?"

"I don't know. I like being near the beach. I've thought about opening a bar a few times. Maybe you're not the only one who needs a new line of work."

"Knock it off. You love music. I don't see you bringing people their food."

"I don't want to wait tables. But an investment property might be nice. I could start my own line of tequila or something and sell it right from my own bar. Like Sammy Hagar did."

"Now I've heard it all." He pulled back the foil from Kate's cake. Notes of cinnamon and vanilla floated up to him and sang under his nose. He grabbed a knife and cut a thick slice.

"You aren't going to cut me any?" Levi actually had the nerve to look hurt.

He dropped the knife on the table. "You want to be a restaurant owner. Cut it yourself."

"Nah. You're right. Buying a tavern is a dumb idea." Levi handed him the knife with assuredness all over his face.

And like he always did, he took care of his brother—and cut the cake.

Chapter Eight

Kassidy held her breath and unlocked the front door to her father's cottage. Bailey, Maren, and Peyton were behind her, scattered down the porch steps and onto the front walk. This house, located on the south side of town, would sell and pay off the mortgage, if they could get it cleaned up—and that was a big if. Her hands shook as she turned the knob. Her sisters would probably go running when they saw the inside.

She had wanted to tell her sisters and her aunt what was going on, but her father had begged her not to. He didn't want them to see him this way. Of course, he had allowed her to have a front-row seat to his problems. He had said she was stronger than her sisters and that she could handle it better than either of them would. As for his sister, he only said Joanna wouldn't understand. She hadn't known what to say to either of those declarations.

Her father had spent years visiting Maren at her house, saying he liked taking long drives. Maren had never argued, busy raising a child. Maren had appreciated Dad coming out to her. As for Bailey, Dad enjoyed hopping a plane and following her anywhere she went. Her home base was Hoboken. When she was in town, Dad went to her too, using the same excuse. After the funeral, everyone came back to The Dot. Neither Maren, Bailey, nor Aunt Joanna had noticed they never stopped at Dad's house. She had made sure of it. For his sake.

"Here we are." She hip-checked the door which stuck in the humidity and let them into the living area.

"For the love of all things holy, what is happening here?" Maren put a hand over her nose and mouth.

"Yeah, about the smell..." She followed the path made by piles of junk on either side of it, covering the sofa and the chair and most of the available floor space, to the back door and opened it to let in a breeze. Most of the windows were too hard to get at anymore because of the accumulated clutter and who knew what else was in the way. The kitchen window, above the sink, was accessible, but it had been painted shut for some reason. Other than letting light in, it offered no other useful purpose.

"You can barely walk in here," Bailey said.

The house was small with a galley kitchen behind the living room and two small bedrooms and a bath to the right. They had all lived in this house once. Strange to think of that time when not almost every space was filled with stuff, useless stuff like unopened mail that had sat for years or receipts for every purchase Dad had made since the nineties. Boxes of files from all the years he owned The Dot and the house had accumulated like static buildup. He had piles of magazines all over the kitchen counters. Used pizza boxes and empty soda bottles that might come in handy because he was afraid of facing the future.

"When did he become a hoarder?" Maren said.

"About six years ago, right after a pretty bad hurricane. He started leaving the old receipts and magazines around. He was afraid he wouldn't have what he needed if another one came along." She suspected he always fought the urge to keep things. Even when they were young, he would shove receipts into the cabinet until the cabinet was so full all the paper would fall out. She had cleaned up after him several times both here and at The Dot. But after the hurricane, and after he had fallen off a ladder and banged his head, he couldn't seem to control the urge to keep things. Wait until they saw the basement and the attic.

"The hurricane could've wiped him out even with all this stuff," Maren said. "And this explains why he never wanted me to come over. I thought he was doing me the favor."

"It's not logical." It was a mental illness. She had read up on it after she found him keeping piles of mail and coupons that had expired. When she had tried to throw them out like she had thrown out his other stuff, he had become furious and irrational and threw her out of the house instead.

"But The Blue Dot doesn't look like this," Peyton said.

"It could have. He had started making piles in the office. One day I told him the employees and the customers would find out if he didn't let me clean. Honestly, the mess in here could be worse. Some hoarders fill the place with garbage bags because they won't even throw out their garbage. He didn't want the neighbors catching on, so he made sure to put his cans out each week."

"Thank God for small favors," Maren said, still covering her nose. "Why didn't you tell us?"

"He asked me not to." She had threatened to call Maren once, so he would allow her to throw stuff out. He had given in that time, and she had cleared off the kitchen counters, but he went right back and did it again. When she threatened again, he broke down. She hadn't the heart to call anyone after that. Watching her father cry was more than she could take. Maybe she was the coward, not him.

"What about the bedrooms?" Bailey peeked down the hall.

"His room was fine. After he passed, I threw out the mattress, everything in there that reminded me of him being sick. I even managed to slap a coat of white paint on the walls. I couldn't sleep for the first couple of nights." Every time she had closed her eyes, the weight of cleaning this house sat on her chest, making it hard to breathe.

She had paced her own house, worrying about what

to do. That was how she had come up with the idea of telling her sisters that their father had requested they clean together. They wouldn't be able to deny his last wish, and she would not drown under the anxiety of hauling each and every piece of trash out of this house alone. Even now, the problems in front of her, losing The Dot, and this house, had the power to reach inside her throat and choke the air from her lungs with a strong fist.

"I'm not touching anything in this place." Maren threw up her hands.

"It needs to be cleaned out so we can sell it," she said.

"Then we hire a service," Maren said.

"Are you paying for that? Because I don't have the money." And she wanted the help. She wanted to sift through some of this stuff in case anything valuable was tucked in. Even something from their childhood could be in the attic or the basement.

"We'll have to rent a dumpster, but I think we should go through everything. He might've tucked money in one of these shoeboxes." Bailey pointed to the stack of shoeboxes that went up the wall between the living room and the kitchen.

"I'm not staying all summer to do this, and it will take all summer if it's just the four of us. I have a life to return to," Maren said.

"Mom, I want to stay and help. This is the saddest thing I've ever seen and Grandpa asked that we do this together. Don't you think we should honor his last wishes?" Peyton stared, wide-eyed.

She wanted to hug Peyton, but she didn't because her

father had said no such thing. In fact, he had said the opposite. He hadn't wanted Maren, Bailey, Joanna, and especially not Peyton to see how he lived. Charlie was the only other person who was aware of his condition. She couldn't give him that last request. By herself, cleaning this house would take years and a toll on her she wasn't ready to handle.

She missed her sisters and wanted a chance to spend time with them. That had been the real motivation. They had grown apart. After her father died, she realized she was alone. She had no one and nothing except The Blue Dot. Now, she might not even have that. A few weeks with her sisters would help her heal. She wasn't asking for a lot, just a chance to have a family.

"Let's see the attic and the basement." Bailey pulled the string on the door in the hallway ceiling. The door creaked open, inviting them into the attic's secrets that could no longer be held. Like an octogenarian unfolding from a chair, the ladder steps uncurled at their feet.

"I'm staying down here. For all we know, the ceiling will collapse." Maren lifted a stack of magazines off the kitchen counter and dropped them back down as if they were hot. Dust burst into the air and snagged in the sun's rays like a shower of tiny stars.

She and Bailey climbed into the attic, leaving Maren wiping her hands on her legs and Peyton staring at her mother.

"Whoa." Bailey stopped short before she finished climbing, only her head and shoulders poked out of the opening in the floor.

"Yup." No other words formed on her lips. No other words were necessary.

Bailey climbed the rest of the way in. The attic ran the length of the cottage with a high ceiling that allowed them to stand. Even though it was early afternoon, the space with its walls of pink insulation already cooked.

"On one hand it's actually pretty up here. On the other, what do we do with it all?" Bailey said.

Buckets and baskets of sea glass in all colors and sizes perched all around the perimeter of the attic and in between boxes of who knew what. She had counted the last time she was here and there were a hundred containers filled with sea glass. The sun streamed in through the one window and reflected off the colors. Bursts of blues, greens, browns, and whites shot around the room like a kaleidoscope. If the whole thing weren't so sad, she'd take a few pictures for her social media sites.

"I don't know what to do with the sea glass. Sell it, maybe? We could sift through it to see if he came across any of the rarer colors." Red and orange were the hardest to find and worth the most money, but sitting like that in those buckets the stones commanded about a hundred dollars. Put into jewelry the piece would be worth more, but nowhere near enough to solve the money problems she had.

"Kass, why do you search for sea glass at the beach when this is all here?" Bailey grabbed a fistful of sea glass and dropped it through her fingers and back into the bucket like a rainbow waterfall.

"It's relaxing. I can clear my head. It was something I

used to do with Dad. I didn't know he had so much, though. Charlie said Dad used to take trips to beaches all over the world, looking for sea glass." She had known about the vacations, but never gave his time away much thought. Her father was entitled to time off, but he had probably used money he borrowed against The Dot for the trips. His search for sea glass seemed as much of an illness as keeping everything he had ever crossed paths with.

If she had known he had such a large collection, she might not have searched for her own stash. She didn't want to be like her father in this way, hoarding, searching for something he couldn't find.

"I wish I had known about this so I could've asked him," Bailey said. "I didn't think anything of all those holidays at Maren's. She has the space and the big yard. It made sense."

"If you asked him what he was doing, he either would've changed the subject with a vengeance, or he would've told you not to worry. Or he would've become angry and told you to mind your own business. He would never have let you remove any of it."

If his habits had become much worse, she would have had to find a way to convince him that these trifling items had to go, but the cancer had come back, and then all the hoarding didn't seem to matter. If keeping useless objects had given him some peace during his last days, that was the least she could gift him.

"I feel like I didn't know him at all." Bailey grabbed a

tennis racket and twirled it in her hands. Dad never played tennis that she knew of.

"The hoarding wasn't all of him. Just a part that got confused or crossed or something. He's still the dad you remember." That's how she had to see it or she might lose her mind in all this mess. He was still the man whose face lit up when any of his daughters walked into a room. And the same man who came to their school events and sat in the front row, clapping the loudest. He wasn't the best with money or women, but he loved her, Bailey, and Maren, even when he wasn't always showing it.

"My brain can't figure out what to think. How is it I didn't know this part of him existed?" Bailey tossed the tennis racket back in the box.

"Give it time. This is a lot to take in at once. The first time I realized how far the hoarding extended, I needed a week just to look Dad in the eye. Come here, I want to show you something." She turned sideways in order to follow the narrow path to the back of the attic. The dust kicked up around her and tickled her nose.

Her father had tucked away an old record player and a couple hundred vinyl records in the corner. She pulled out an old Dolly Parton album.

"Do you remember when we were kids, we'd put on records and sing like we were in a band?" She would grab a hairbrush and sing at the top of her lungs. Bailey would pretend to play guitar on a cane their father had, and Maren usually wanted to be the band manager. She laughed at the old memory of all of them, spending time together like a family. She hadn't had an intact family in so long she wondered if she even remembered it right.

"Yeah. Dad used to pretend to play piano on the back of the couch." Bailey gave her a wistful smile.

"I hate to get rid of these records." Some of them had to be warped and unplayable now, but keeping them anchored her somehow. She put Dolly back in the crate and wiped her hands.

"We should try to sell them. Any extra money we can come up with will help you keep The Dot." Bailey flipped through some of the records, stopping at a Sammy Davis, Jr.

"I doubt a few old albums will change anything."

"Wow. Look at all of this." Peyton charged into the attic and practically dove for the buckets of sea glass. "These are so pretty. Why didn't Grandpa tell us he had them? I could make like a thousand crafts with them." Peyton stuck her hands in the bucket and giggled as the sea glass tumbled over her skin. A few pieces fell to the floor and rocked against the wood planks.

"Take what you want," she said. Less they'd have to throw away. But she couldn't toss all that sea glass into the garbage. At the very least, she would sell it online to someone who could make use out of it. Again, not giving her enough money to save The Dot, but maybe enough to take Peyton to dinner.

"Really? Thank you, Aunt Kassidy. Mom, come up and look at this," Peyton yelled down the steps.

"We could make mosaics and frames and sell it all online. You know, on those small business sites. I could make an Instagram account for the pieces too." Peyton plopped down in front of another bucket and pulled bits out, grouping them by colors.

"You know, there's a beach festival in a few weeks. Vendors set up tables on the boardwalk. The Blue Dot has one. If you want to make some things to sell, you could put them at the end of the table." She had selfish motivations for suggesting the crafts. If Peyton wanted to stick around, Maren was less likely to say no. But she also wanted to make Peyton happy because her parents' divorce was eating her up. Peyton hadn't smiled like she was now with her hands in the sea glass since she arrived.

"I would love that. I need a job and haven't found one. I already have some ideas for all this. I'll have to go to the craft store and get supplies. Can I take a couple of buckets back with me today?"

"Please. Less things we have to worry about," she said.

"It's almost as bad up here." Maren's head popped up through the opening in the floor.

"Mom, look at all the sea glass. Did you know Grandpa had all this?" Peyton's eyes were wide with wonder.

Kassidy wished something as simple as sea glass could bring her so much joy. She loved searching for it because it was the thrill of the search. She even believed in its beauty, but she had grown too old to believe magic was waiting around the corner in the form of sea glass or any other form for that matter.

"If I had known that he was keeping enough sea glass

to sink a boat, I would've taken it all back to the ocean and dumped it back where it belongs." Maren climbed the rest of the way into the attic.

"You're so grumpy. Look at the beauty that's here." Bailey waved her arm.

"All I see is an attic full of garbage that needs to be thrown out," Maren said, wrinkling her nose. "And now it's our job, which I don't appreciate because the last thing I need is another job to do."

Peyton flinched. If Kassidy could climb over Bailey and the boxes, she would grip Peyton in a hug. Maren didn't realize the bite of her words. The divorce had frayed every one of her sister's nerves, and understandably so, but Maren continuously flicked her unhappiness all over everyone else.

"Well, I'm going to make mosaics and frames and sell them at Aunt Kassidy's table during the beach festival." Peyton tucked her hair behind her ear, and her jaw was set.

"Are you, now?" Maren arched a brow.

"No point in letting all of this go to waste." She pretended not to notice Maren's intense look or that it might mean a war between mother and teenage daughter was about to begin, and she didn't want to end up a casualty.

"What about your friends back home? Don't you want to see them?" Maren said.

"I can see them later this summer. I want to be in the festival." Peyton took her bucket and went down the ladder.

"You told her about the festival to keep me here, didn't you?" Maren turned on her now. Looked like she might end up a casualty after all.

"I told her about the festival because she was so excited about making stuff out of the sea glass. Besides, Dad asked us all to work together to clean out this house. You have to stay."

"I don't have to do any such thing. I also can't believe I considered cooking at The Dot while I'm here either. You know, I could use a vacation. My life fell apart. Did you ever think I just wanted to come to the beach and relax?"

"It wasn't me who put a dying request in my will." She turned away from her sisters so they couldn't see the lie all over her face.

"You can have plenty of time to relax," Bailey said. "Go to the beach in the mornings. We can spend a couple of hours each day here. The Dot is closed on Mondays. You're not even going to be working that hard."

"I don't want to work at all. I want to go home. Back to my real life." She fisted her hands on her hips, but the steam had seeped out of Maren's words.

"Your old life is over. Time to make some changes. Take a bucket." Bailey handed Maren a plastic beach pail filled with more sea glass.

Maren growled and went down the ladder with the bucket—at least.

"She'll come around," Bailey said. "But we need a plan. How are we ever going to get rid of all this stuff?"

"I'll rent the dumpster. We'll make piles. We should start in the basement and work our way up."

"There's more in the basement?" Bailey's eyebrows shot into her hairline.

"Unfortunately."

"This is going to take forever."

That was the plan.

Chapter Nine

Kassidy rubbed her aching feet. The dinner shift had gone better than she expected. Grant showed up on time, for which she had been grateful. No one else had quit. Bailey helped her wait tables, and Peyton had played hostess much to Maren's dislike. Which was probably why Peyton had agreed to do it. Peyton was quickly becoming entrenched in Serenity by the Sea, intrigued by its charm and a mountain of sea glass. She only wished Maren would feel the same way.

Grant had said less during dinner than he had earlier in the day. The ease in which they had worked together to make breakfast for a handful of customers had disappeared during the dinner rush. She had blamed it on the number of customers, but even after the shift was over around ten and they were all calling it a night, he seemed a million miles away. She hadn't wanted to push for information. It wasn't her place.

The sun had set about an hour before they closed The Blue Dot and taken some of the humidity with it over the horizon. The breeze had picked up off the ocean, and though the houses often blocked the wind, tonight it had blown around the bungalow and cooled her heated skin.

She stretched her legs out on the chaise in the backyard. It wasn't much, but she liked it all the same with her patio and fire pit. Across the street to her right, was an old Victorian that towered over the road and gave the second floor a perfect view onto her property. She was pretty sure her neighbor Josephine, the older widow whose children had left town and barely ever returned, sometimes watched her sit here at night with the fire pit going while she made her way through two glasses of wine. Josephine was a lonely busybody that Kassidy tried not to judge. She understood too well people and their eccentricities thanks to her father and his hoarding.

Sitting out by the fire had become her nightly getaway since nursing her father during his last days. The flicker of the flames and the distant hum of the ocean lulled her into believing she could make a real life for herself here again, a life with a family. The fire pit and the chaise lounge had become her sanctuary. She relished the peace and solitude it offered her.

"I brought stuff to make s'mores." Bailey appeared with a tray full of graham crackers, marshmallows, and chocolate bars. Tucked under her arm were three sticks for roasting. Her oversized t-shirt nearly covered her very short shorts, and the smile that danced across Bailey's face as she offered the goodies prevented Kassidy from expressing her desire to be alone.

It wasn't as though she didn't want to be with Bailey. The whole reason she had concocted this crazy scheme to lie to her sisters about their father's wishes was because she wanted her family back together. A house filled with the noise of living people was far better than the sounds of machines ticking away the last seconds of life.

But she hadn't been ready to share her outdoor space just yet. Another night, certainly, but tonight, after the day she had had, she wanted nothing more than the song of the cicadas. Spending any time in her father's home drained her like water from a bathtub. And after all the tension with Grant during dinner, alone time was the only way she knew how to unwind the knots in her shoulders.

"I can't eat those. I'll get fat." She pushed herself into a seated position and eyed the chocolate with longing. Chocolate could unwind a few knots but would certainly add a few too many pounds to her middle.

"Oh, please. You have the best figure. I thought it would be fun for the three of us to, you know, make dessert, celebrate a good day, and hang out. Like sisters." Bailey plopped herself down on the neighboring chaise.

"We hang out." But not enough. Not nearly enough. If she were being honest, that was her fault too. She had run to Chicago, following Bear like a Labrador puppy. She had gladly dumped her family for the prospect of a fancy life. And when she had returned, scraped up from all her failures, she had avoided her sisters, too ashamed to admit her mistakes out loud.

At the time of her less than triumphant return to Serenity, Maren was happily married with five-year-old Peyton skipping off to kindergarten with her pigtails and princess sneakers. She and Maren hadn't had anything in common, and Maren was always too busy to make time to get together. There was always a school thing, a church thing, a David thing she had to attend.

"Us spend time together? You must have us mixed up with the Marsh sisters. Here." Bailey handed her a big fat marshmallow on a stick.

When Bailey was in middle school, she would come to stay with them for the summers. They piled onto Maren's bed, and she would read *Little Women* to them, acting out every scene and giving each sister her own voice. It was the only time Maren lightened up, and *Little Women* was Bailey's favorite book. Maren loved the way Bailey would stare up at her in wonder, as if Maren herself had pulled the words out of the sky with nothing more than a twitch of her nose.

"Where's Maren?" Kassidy glanced over her shoulder toward the house. She hadn't seen Maren for a good hour.

"She's on the phone with he who shall not be named." Bailey followed her gaze as if Maren might appear behind her and find out they were talking about her.

"Really? Why? What does he want now?" She didn't

envy what Maren was going through. Even though she and Bear had only been engaged when he left her for his career, her world had been torn apart. Everything she thought she knew about herself had changed. Maren must be thinking similar things.

"Apparently, he's sending her the divorce papers here. Great way to ruin a sister trip." Bailey rotated her marshmallow over the fire.

"How do you know that?" She hadn't thought about this time together as a sister trip, but she did like the sound of it. She had friends who went away every year with their sisters or closest friends, but the three Russo girls had never even spoken of such an idea.

Kassidy had believed they were like every other family with their weirdness, but as soon as each of them had been able, they took off for other opportunities. She had only come home because she couldn't make it in Chicago. She returned to working at The Blue Dot and somehow a decade had passed.

"She had him on speaker and since the house is about the size of a cutlery drawer, I couldn't help but overhear." Bailey shrugged and smooshed her marshmallow between chocolate and graham crackers.

"Were you eavesdropping?" If Maren found that out, she'd pitch a fit. And the whole neighborhood would hear that, giving her neighbor Josephine plenty to chew on.

"No." Bailey winked.

"Bailey, you were listening to me, and is there any more wine?" Maren barreled outside. The wooden screen door slapped against the frame like an exclamation point on a sentence. She grabbed the bottle from the small glass table.

"You shouldn't use a speaker if you don't want to be heard," Bailey said.

Maren brought the bottle to her lips and took a giant swig. Kassidy bit her lip against the retort of how gross that was and that Maren should get herself a glass. She had wanted her sisters back home. Here they were in all their natural glory.

"I guess I'm done drinking from that bottle," Bailey said.

"That was the last bottle in the house." Okay, she couldn't keep her mouth completely shut.

"I'm sorry. I should've asked first. I'll buy more tomorrow." Maren took another swig.

"What did the jerk say?" Bailey bit into her s'more and groaned with pleasure. "Better than sex sometimes," she said around the food.

"The usual stuff he always complains about. He doesn't want to wait to get on with his life. He wants to sell the house and thinks things will move faster if we're already divorced. He believes if on paper we're still married, then I'll put up a fight to keep the house." Maren took another swig from the bottle and flopped down on the remaining chair.

"Damn it, how dare he assume I don't want to live in that house just because he doesn't. I love that house. I decorated every square inch of it. By myself, I might add. Peyton's little handprint is inside her closet in pink paint.

Do you remember when I had her do that?" Maren drank more.

"No," Bailey said.

"Yes," she said at the same time. She had been there when Maren had taken Peyton's three-year-old hand and dipped it into the bubblegum-pink paint. Peyton had squealed with delight, and Maren tried not to flinch at the paint dripping on the floor.

Bailey had been in college or traveling or something. Honestly, she couldn't remember. Bailey had a wandering soul as if the idea of staying put for too long in one place would hollow her out.

"You could take a picture of her handprint," Bailey said. "Then you'll have it forever."

"Where will I live if we sell? The houses cost too much in our town for me to afford one by myself. And I have to get a real job now. Be glad neither of you are married."

The offhand comment stole her breath. Maren must not realize what she had said, or that such a thing would even bother her. She had downplayed the disappointment when she finally told her family her engagement had ended, but she had been devastated by the breakup. She had to redefine herself and come to terms with the fact she would never be the corporate exec she had wanted to be. She had grieved for the loss of that version of Kassidy. She wasn't ready to grieve again by losing The Dot and the identity she had attached to it. She was still grieving her father.

"You could live here." Her mouth betrayed her. She

wanted to push the words back in, but it was too late. Overwhelming Maren with ideas of moving across the state and back to Serenity would be too much at the moment. Maren was the ultimate planner. She made lists for her lists. She still needed Maren on board not to sell The Dot. She couldn't distract Maren with crazy ideas of living together. Maren would never want to do that.

"Yeah, right. Live here. In this house? And what about Peyton? She's in high school. She has friends and activities. I can't take her away from all that."

"Of course. I don't know what I was thinking." She wasn't thinking; she had been feeling for a brief second, even believing a night like this one—surrounded by her sisters and getting along—could repeat itself.

"Make a s'more. You'll feel better." Bailey handed Maren a stick with a marshmallow.

"I have never had one of these," Maren said, taking the stick.

"How is that possible? We used to do this with Dad all the time." She kept her gaze on her marshmallow. She wasn't ready to make eye contact with Maren just yet. The sting of her inevitable rejection still pulsed.

"Not me. You and Dad could bond over anything. When it was the three of us, I usually felt like the third wheel. I did better with Dad when it was just him and me, and we'd do things like read together. You know, nerd stuff. Then Bailey came along, and for a while, I didn't like you."

"Gee, thanks." Bailey licked her fingers.

"I know that sounds terrible, but to me, you were the

reason my mother left. I know that's not true, but I was so mad at Dad because he and your mom had an affair. I know now I shouldn't have been mad at you, but I was. And in my defense, I was a teenager mad at the world. You and Dad would make s'mores too. Kassidy, the ever-present people pleaser, was right there beside the two of you. I never wanted to join in."

"So, what's different now?" Bailey mushed a second marshmallow between the chocolate and graham crackers. Chocolate oozed out the sides and landed on her leg. She wiped it with her finger and shoved her finger in her mouth.

"Besides the fact I'm not a child anymore? Dad's not here. We are." Maren bit into the marshmallow and chased it with the wine. She hadn't even held it over the flame. "I should have come to visit Dad more than I did. I had no idea he was hoarding. I feel terrible about that."

"He didn't want you to know," she said. The hiding was part of the illness. She had read up on it, trying to understand their father a little.

"I still should have come. He had made it so easy for me to stay away." Maren reached for the wine bottle then turned it in her hand.

"I'm glad the three of us can hang out like this now. I always wanted to spend more time with the two of you, but when you were together, you usually pushed me out," Bailey said with a swift change of subject which she was grateful for. She didn't want to go into the whys and why nots of her father's problem tonight.

"I just had different interests. I was happy sitting by

the window reading or on the beach reading. I didn't like board games or cards like you two did. I felt like no one wanted to do the things I wanted to do." Maren turned to her. "You never rode your bike with me to the library like you would ride up and down the boardwalk with Bailey."

"I would have if you had asked." She wanted to defend herself, which seemed childish at this point. She had always believed Maren preferred to ride off to the library or the arcade alone or with a friend instead of her.

"I wanted you to do all kinds of things with us, but other than acting out scenes from *Little Women*, you never wanted to do the same things we did." She had followed Maren around for years, wanting to be just like her and wanting her older sister to notice her in some way.

"You pushed me away when Bailey came to live with us." Maren turned away from the fire, practically putting her back to them.

"I never pushed you away." The fire was in her belly now, shoving her out of the chair. Was that how Maren remembered their childhood?

"Do you think it was easy being the third sister and the only one with a different mother?" Bailey stood too.

She had never considered how difficult it must have been for Bailey coming into a family of two sisters who had shared every secret of their lives. They hadn't been introduced to Bailey from her birth. She was more like meeting a cousin than a sister.

Kassidy had always seen Bailey as the lucky one. She was the one who had both parents who loved her. Her and Maren's mother had left, and barely returned. "We were all trying to figure things out," she said.

"You and Maren are still trying to figure things out where we're concerned. For better or worse, we're family. But you two always want to do things your own way and without the others. Maren, you won't even consider keeping The Blue Dot and why not? It's not as if you have a whole lot to go back to in that country bumpkin town you live in. And you"—Bailey pointed at her—"when are you going to realize you have two sisters who love you? Two." Bailey stormed off, slamming the door on her exit.

"Did I miss something? Why is she so upset tonight?" Maren tilted the wine bottle upside down and looked inside.

"I think she's still mad because we didn't let her play Barbies with us." She shoved another marshmallow into the flame.

"She was four and always tried to tear their heads off." Maren threw her head back and laughed, teetering on the edge of the chaise. She windmilled her arms and fell into the grass, howling on the way down.

Kassidy bent over and laughed too. Her insides hurt and tears filled her eyes. The marshmallow stuck to her hair, and they laughed harder.

"I want to sell the tavern. I'm hoping we can make a profit of some kind. Any extra will help me. I need the money. I know it's your livelihood, but I can't keep it and you can't afford to buy it from us. Please try and understand," Maren said. "It's not personal, Kass. I'm desperate."

She wanted to understand, but she didn't. The Dot was personal to her. She had nothing left but The Blue Dot. Maren had Peyton and her life filled with PTA friends. And Bailey had her life coaching business complete with a set of friends they didn't know and a world of adventures she didn't include them in. Would she have gone if Bailey had ever asked? She wondered.

She was alone now. And if she wasn't careful, she would end up like her neighbor Josephine, looking out the window onto the street, hoping to be included in something—anything, even if it wasn't hers to be included in.

"Maren, please spend the summer here with me. I can show you how important The Dot is. Not just to me, but to some of our regular customers whose butt prints are on the seats. Please let me have more time to find a way to buy you out." She should tell Maren that she wanted her to stay because there was a hole in her chest that she couldn't fill, but she stopped right at the entrance to those words. Maren would scoff at her sentimentality. Their relationship wasn't built on that.

Maren pushed off the ground and wiped her hands on the back of her shorts. "I'm leaving at the end of next week. Dave is sending the divorce papers to Serenity via FedEx. They should be here by Tuesday if he actually goes to FedEx on time to send them. I won't leave before they come. I know Peyton wants to stay for this beach festival, but that can't happen. I'm sorry, Kass. My plan will never be to stick around."

Maren retraced Bailey's steps. The overused screen door only clapped closed this time. What remained of the fire flickered in the soft breeze but was ready to quit. Just like her. Her plan to keep her family close and intact wasn't going well.

She walked around to the front of the house, giving a quick glance in the direction of Grant's tent, but the front yard was empty. She followed the side street and crossed Ocean Avenue. The wood and cement bench faced the ocean, and she plopped down on it. A cool wind sent shivers over her skin. Even in the heart of summer, the beach could provide a chilly night. She had always loved to sleep with her windows open to catch the breeze and the smell of salt air. She wondered if Grant had figured that out about the tent. She would have to remember to tell him tomorrow.

She would need longer than a week to convince Maren to stay. If she wouldn't even come to The Dot, she would never be able to see its possibilities. Maren had an eye for the creative. But even if Maren did, and she was willing to sell her portion, where would Kassidy come up with the money? All her planning and telling that white lie did not factor in her money issues. She hadn't known her father was in hock. But she should have. She'd been flying blind. Again.

Bailey's outburst tonight had surprised her, though it shouldn't. Their childhoods had not been filled with picnics and kite flying. She had resented Bailey for many years, the intruder who had sent her mother away. Her father had had an affair with Bailey's mother. Kassidy's mother had discovered it and left. Not long after that, their father had told them about Bailey. And like Maren, Kassidy had placed the blame of her broken home on a baby. Because she had been a child too. A child desperate for the love of her mother.

But she didn't believe that any longer. She wanted her sisters with her. She wanted a family to share her life with. That was the only reason she had come up with the crazy idea to tell them Dad wanted them to work together to clean out his house.

She should have thought the idea through better than she had. Maren proved difficult to convince to stay. But clearly, stating the truth and asking her to stay hadn't worked either. She still had a chance with the lie.

She was being selfish. She didn't want to comb through all the clutter and mess at her father's house. She didn't know what she would find, and it scared her. She didn't like thinking of her father as a man with a mental illness. He had held his life together with tape as if it were a broken box and the tape had dried up now. Was he hiding something in the center of that chaos? And even if he weren't, because she doubted very much there was anything like a dead body in there, sifting through the debris would change the way she saw him. She needed him to remain the strong man she believed he was. Having her sisters hold her hand while they dug out his clutter would help her, but not them. This wasn't their problem. She would send them all home tomorrow. It was what was best.

She walked back to the house and gathered the tray and their garbage. She looked at her little bungalow. She had been a fool to believe a family could be created out of a lie. She'd just have to go on the way she always had been.

Alone.

Chapter Ten

Grant pulled into the parking lot at The Blue Dot and turned off the truck. The sun tipped its hat over the horizon, turning the morning sky from gray to orange. He could use a hot cup of coffee and a few more hours of sleep, but he had promised Kassidy he would work her breakfast shift until she found someone else.

He had been up half the night reading post after post about him. Hats and Ropes, the live music festival, scheduled this summer wanted him to perform. Fans and haters alike had left their opinions like dirty shoe marks on a welcome mat. Some thought he should show his appreciation for the love and well wishes fans had sent to him after the accident and because he hadn't in the way they wanted, he was ungrateful. One guy thought he should never step onstage again. He was washed up. No good. Ungrateful. Selfish.

Each word was a punch to the gut. Maybe he was all

those things. He wasn't pretending to be dead. He had only wanted to step away from the music scene. He had wanted to grieve in private and leave the stage to give the spot to someone more deserving. Someone who hadn't been at the hand of two people's deaths.

And others—many in fact—understood how hard it was to lose a spouse and a brother and told him to take his time. They would wait.

He couldn't face any of them. He had been appreciative, still was, for the prayers, cards, and notes from fans. But he needed to stay out of the limelight because he had lost the desire to play music. If his heart wasn't in it, he wouldn't do it. He had never begun playing for the money. He played because music brought him peace of mind.

He didn't understand why the festival claimed he would perform. Except that Levi had implied that he would to someone who leaked it all over the place like a busted ballpoint pen. He would talk to Levi later when the anger slowed down to a simmer. Hopefully, work would help with that. He pushed out of the truck and stretched his back. He took a deep inhale of the salt air.

He needed to focus on writing the songs. As much as he could use the extra cash, Levi was right. Working in Serenity by the Sea was more of a distraction than a help. Especially because of Kassidy and her wild hair and smart mouth. She had him thinking things better left alone. He headed inside to give his notice. Hopefully, she didn't throw something at him when she found out.

The kitchen was dark and smelled like burnt food.

The whole place could do with a fresh coat of paint and a new floor. Maybe some bigger windows out by the seats too. Kassidy ran through the kitchen from the basement with a bucket and toppled his thoughts.

"Good morning," she said on the tailwind she created as she flew by. The muscles on her bare legs flexed with each step. She had nice legs.

"What's going on?" He followed her through the swinging doors into the dining area, but she didn't stop there.

She made a sharp left and headed down the hall where the bathrooms were. A puddle of water ankle deep ran out of the ladies' room and into the hall. *Well, hell.*

"Did you turn off the water?" He leaned through the doorway. She mopped at the water with an old braided mop that had seen better days.

"Of course, I turned off the water. But from the main line because the knob on the toilet is stuck or rusted or something which is why I have a river down the hall. By the time I got downstairs in the basement, there was enough water to paddle through." She swatted her wild curly hair away from her face. "I swear this is the last time I forget a hair tie."

"What can I do to help?" His resignation would have to wait until after the breakfast shift. He had some sense not to make her morning worse than it already was. Customers would arrive in less than an hour. Without water to the kitchen, she'd be sunk. He couldn't leave her hanging.

"Can you unclog a toilet?"

"Maybe." As long as it was something simple. Plumber was not on his list of skills.

"There's a plunger in the basement where we keep all the cleaning supplies. And if you see anything that resembles a towel, please bring it up. I need to mop up this water."

He did what she asked, but the plunger wouldn't do the job. "You're going to need it snaked. You'll have to call a plumber."

"I can't. I don't have any extra money this month. And my sister Maren finally agreed to come see the place today. Would you believe she hasn't stepped foot in her father's tavern in, oh, I don't know, maybe ten or fifteen years." She threw her hands in the air. The mop toppled over and splashed in the water. "I don't know why I'm bothering with any of this. She is determined to sell this place. And she's probably right."

"Now, hang on. There must be a local plumber in town. Take it out in trade. He snakes your toilet and you give him a week's worth of dinners or something like that." His stepfather used to do that plenty when money was tight.

"I can't ask for help."

"Why not?"

"Because I don't want anyone to know how much debt this place is in. Don't you see? My father was suffocating under his medical bills and didn't even tell us how bad it was. The lawyer says we have to sell this place to pay off the debt, but I don't want to sell. My sisters do and why wouldn't they? It's not their livelihood or life about to be washed away."

He didn't have the heart to tell her about Kate and her coffee cake. If Kate knew about the debt, chances were everyone in this small town knew too. Small towns were the same no matter what part of the country they were in. Everyone was knee-deep in everyone else's business.

She arched her eyebrows. "Well, say something."

"You want me to comment on what you just said?" Noel had taught him not to speak when she was... what had she called it? Venting. When she was venting. Kassidy's red face and rush of words sure reminded him of Noel. But the similarities stopped there.

"Isn't that how a conversation works?" She pushed past him with the wad of wet towels. He followed her back into the basement where she dumped the towels in the slop sink.

"Let me get this straight. You want to keep the tavern and your sisters want to sell it?" He hadn't been expecting her to want to hear his opinion on her situation. He did want to help her and erase that crease between her brows, but he figured keeping quiet would do it.

"Something like that." She marched back upstairs with a glare in her eye as she glanced at him over her shoulder.

"And you don't want to call a plumber because you think you're giving your father's secrets away."

"He's as smart as he looks, ladies and gentlemen."

She swept her arm through the air. He couldn't help but laugh. She was feisty. He'd give her that.

"If you leave that bathroom broken because your pride won't let you call a plumber, you're going to prove you have no business running this place."

She stared at him with wide eyes. Her small mouth hung open. He may have said too much. At least he didn't tell her about Kate.

"I could learn how to fix it." She tilted her chin.

He didn't doubt that she could learn. She was smart and assertive. She was just a little frazzled by this morning's unexpected situation.

"Not by the breakfast rush. And not by the dinner one either. Your problem surpasses your plunging skills. And if you don't have the money, I'll lend it to you." Not that he had extra money to spare, but he wouldn't let this woman go without water to her bathroom. She needed a helping hand. He would give her one.

"Oh no, you won't." She pushed past him again. He caught a whiff of her coconut scent. She smelled sweet and tangy all in one. "I don't need your charity." She pumped her arms like a speed walker, racing to the kitchen.

"Are you always this stubborn?" He hurried after her. "You want me to tell you how to handle this, but deep down you really don't."

"Taking care of things by myself is how I've gotten by in this life."

"Then why do you need your sisters to give you the high sign to keep this place? Just buy them out."

Her whirlwind came to a halt in the middle of the kitchen. The steam left her, and she deflated against the counter.

"I can't buy them out. I don't have the money. My house is mortgaged, and that's my only asset. No bank will give me a loan on what I make here. And even after we sell my dad's house, if there's any money left over, we have to put it toward the debt here."

"I'm sorry." He knew better than anyone how life's plans could change in a second. He had been going along thinking he had everything he ever wanted or dreamed of, but life's unexpected and unwanted intrusions changed all that.

"It's not your fault. I need a miracle. Once the summer season ends, without said miracle, it won't make sense to stay open. I'll have to sell." A darkness passed across her eyes, and her shoulders drooped with the weight of her problems. She swiped her hair out of her face and let out a long breath.

"Let's just worry about this morning for now. Call the plumber. You need to turn the water back on or we can't cook. Put a sign up on the bathroom door, and tell the ladies they're sharing the men's room. I'll get the food prepped."

"Thanks, Grant. I don't know what I would've done without you this morning." She gifted him a small smile and placed a hand on his arm. Her fingers were thin, but her touch scorched his bare skin.

He forced his hands to remain at his sides because he would like nothing more than to take her hand in his and offer her more comfort. She had lost a lot recently and was about to lose more. If he could shield her from some of the pain, he would because he wanted her to know she didn't have to face the world alone. Instead, he would cook for her and not wonder if her lips tasted the way she smelled.

"I didn't do anything except grab you a plunger and some towels. You did all the hard work." He busied himself with pulling ingredients from the fridge.

"This is going to sound crazy, but it's something about your voice. It's soothing and kind of familiar. I don't know why that is." She dipped her chin, and her face bloomed a deep red, but not with the frustration from before.

He stiffened but returned her gaze, hoping his expression didn't give him away. "You're not used to my Southern drawl. Y'all from New Jersey drag words out too long or something." He added a forced laugh to throw her off. The next time he took up space in a small town, he would ask who listened to rock music first.

"I guess that's it. Anyway, thanks for listening to me. I'll call the plumber so we can get the water back on. In case I forgot to say it, thank you for taking the cook's job too. It's a weight off my shoulders for now." She pushed through the swinging doors.

His announcement that he couldn't work here would have to wait. He wouldn't quit on her while she was trying to work through her issues with her sisters and the plumbing. She might want to take care of things all by herself, but he knew that rarely worked out in the end.

He'd been trying to grieve alone for two years, and he wasn't any closer to being done.

She returned with a smile on her face that lit up her eyes. That smile could lead a broken heart to its fixing station. His breath stuck in his throat. That line wasn't great. But he could work with it.

"I spoke with Bob. He'll be here in twenty minutes. I caught him at the right time, he said."

"Well, look at that. Your luck is a changin', Miss Kassidy Russo." He tipped the edge of his cap.

Her smile went high-voltage, and his insides sang for more. A man could get used to being looked at that way.

He continued to gather the things he would want nearby when the orders started rolling in, and he hoped for her sake the morning was busy. He stole a glance at her. She picked at her fingernails. "Something else on your mind?"

"Why are you in Serenity by the Sea? It isn't for vacation, is it?"

He debated for a moment, telling her the whole truth. He could come clean about who he really was. But she would probably ask all the questions people wanted to know. *Why were you driving the bus? How do you live with the deaths caused by that accident? How do you feel about missing your brother's call?* Or worse. *Would you play here to bring in a crowd?* He couldn't summon the words even as he tried.

"I'm a wanderer. Never stay put in one place for too long."

"Is that a fear of commitment thing?"

"Haven't found anything worth committing to, that's all." He turned his back so she couldn't see the lie in his eyes. He didn't want to be found out, and he didn't want to see the disappointment on her face. She might be sizing him up like a man who was selfish and didn't care about anyone but himself. Kassidy was a woman who believed in commitment if her determination to keep this tavern was any indication.

She didn't say anything. He risked a glance over his shoulder. The doors to the sitting area swung back and forth. She was gone.

Kassidy had another problem she didn't know how to handle. She needed to stop looking at Grant's butt every time she passed him in the kitchen. Sweet Lord, he was bound to catch her and what was she going to say? But those jeans made her want to fan herself. Or it was the heat from the stovetops. She needed to reel those emotions in. He wasn't going to stick around in Serenity. He had said so himself. No point in being interested in a man who weaved and dodged his way through life. The next time she got involved, she wanted a man who could commit to her exactly the way she was.

Maren was due any minute. She had told her to come around ten fifteen when things would slow down for the kitchen, but the place would still be packed. Her hands leaked sweat like that toilet that spilled water this morning. She was bound to drop a plate on someone's lap if this kept up. She had no reason to be nervous. Maren was her sister, not some high-end investor.

She bumped into Bailey who was refilling coffee mugs. "What is with you this morning?"

"Nothing. Why?"

"Oh, please. She doesn't bite anymore." Bailey snickered. "She outgrew that by the time she got to high school. You don't have to be nervous."

"She's going to leave by the end of the week. I have to convince her to want this place long enough for me to find a way to buy you both out."

"I know this is important to you, but she's too caught up in her problems right now. She doesn't want something else to have to dig out of. Literally and figuratively. I can't believe Dad's house." Bailey shook her head. "Don't push her too hard. She'll come around to giving you more time."

She couldn't let Maren go home. Back at home, all the beauty and charm of Serenity would be forgotten. She needed another plan to make Maren see not only the possibilities of The Blue Dot, but the charm of Serenity by the Sea. She stuck her hand in her pocket and wrapped her fingers around the piece of sea glass she found on her first day back. It was blue and oval. An unusual find. She wanted it to be a sign that good things would come her way for once.

The entrance door swung open, and Maren stood inside. Her lips were pressed in a thin line as she surveyed the dining area. She had secured her hair back and gold tubular earrings dangled from her ears. Her wide-legged linen pants brushed the floor as she walked around the tables.

"I'm here. What do you want to show me that I haven't seen before? Same paneling on the walls. Same small dirty windows not letting in enough light. The tables are full, but we don't have that many because of the stage and the counter."

"You're being loud. Even Tom from the post office can hear you and he forgot his hearing aids today." Bailey leaned in and spoke by Maren's ear. "Give her a chance."

She glanced over at Tom sitting with Ralph in his hardware store smock. Tom waved. She stifled a groan.

"Come in the back for a minute," she said and turned to Bailey. "Do you have everything handled out here?"

"All good." She held up the coffee pot.

Maren followed her into the kitchen. "Grant, this is my older sister Maren. Maren, Grant is the nice man helping us out that I told you about. He's the one living next door in the tent."

Grant wiped his hand on his apron and held it out to Maren. "Nice to meet you. This is a mighty nice place you and your sisters own." His smile ignited the sparkle in his eyes. She appreciated the effort he made to impress Maren.

"Have we met before?" Maren slid her hand into Grant's and they shook. Maren's gaze searched his face, as if she too was trying to place where they could have met. Strange. But stranger would be that they knew him somehow.

"No, ma'am. This is my first time at the Jersey Shore." He adjusted his cap and went back to cooking.

Maren turned to her and whispered, "He's Southern."

"I noticed." She had noticed other things better left unnoticed. Like the line of his shoulders and the taper of his waist into his jeans. Or that his legs bowed a little at the knees, and his walk was slow and purposeful, as if he had all the time in the world to get there. Unlike most people in Jersey who raced to their next place, always in a hurry or in fear they might miss out on something.

"My accent stands out here amongst y'all, that's all," he said over his shoulder. The hint of a laugh followed. Heat burned her neck. He had heard them.

"I don't have an accent," Maren said. "Do I?"

"Not to me. Come on. I want to show you something in the office." She nodded to Grant and slipped inside the office that was more the size of the broom closet. Her father had kept a few piles here too, but nothing like at home. His desk had always been messy. He swore he knew where everything was, and she didn't argue with him. He must have been working hard to control his need to hoard here. After he passed, she cleaned up the office so it didn't feel so claustrophobic.

Maren shut the door. "The new cook is good-looking."

"I hadn't noticed." She pulled a file out of her tote bag, avoiding Maren's knowing gaze.

"Oh, come on. Are you kidding? Those eyes twinkle when he smiles. And his jawline all dusted with a scruffy beard. He's in great shape. Unlike Dave who let himself go. I should've known when he decided to go back to the gym another woman was in the picture. I think I read somewhere it's the number one sign of infidelity."

She gripped Maren's hand. "Dave doesn't deserve you. He has no idea how good he had it, and he will miss you if he doesn't already."

Maren pulled away and tapped at the corner of her eye. "Thanks for saying that. I don't want him back. I really don't. So, I don't understand why this divorce hurts so much."

"Because it does." She didn't know if she would ever fall in love again. She never wanted to feel so broken and ugly as she did when Bear left her. Love might be great at times, but love could hurt like scraping your leg on a piece of coral.

On a long breath, Maren said, "Okay. Enough about me and my problems. What's in that folder?"

Her hands shook as she pulled out the photos she'd taken off Pinterest. "I've been putting together a business plan to improve The Dot. She needs a little facelift, a new menu, and entertainment. I want to pull in a younger crowd who will stay later at night and drink. The money is in the booze. And I'm good at bartending." She'd rather be making drinks and talking to the customers than waiting tables or pretending to cook as she had been. At least she hadn't burned any more eggs.

"Let me see what you have." Maren held out her hand.

She hesitated. She had been gathering ideas for

months—years. She had sat down night after night constructing a way to improve this place and really make it something even after all the times her father fought her on changes. It was his business, he had said. He wasn't changing anything. She had never expected to lose the opportunity to turn The Dot around before she even got started.

Maren waved her fingers with a huff. She handed over the folder as if she might be handing over her child.

Maren flipped through the photos. "You want to redecorate?"

"Not just redecorate. I want to increase the prices on the menu too. We could also expand our seating to outside. We have that side piece of property doing nothing. We probably have to get permits and whatnot, but imagine if we could also offer outdoor dining at night? We could have a band play out there and in here."

"Or you could open up that wall where the band plays now and bring the outside in."

She hadn't thought of that. "Great idea."

"If you offered more seating, you would probably need more staff. We can't afford more staff. And we can't afford to renovate. I looked at the books, Kass. This place sucks up money like a vacuum. Why do you want to keep it so badly?"

"Because I believe I can make it better. I know I can take this run-down place that people still come to because of the friendships and make it profitable. I want to make it the place tourists drive miles for." She also wanted her family intact. Was that too much to hope for?

"Did you talk to Dad about this before he died?"

"I tried talking to Dad about this a hundred times, but he wouldn't budge. Is it any surprise considering his other problems? Once he got sick again, I stopped talking about it." She had spent years studying what the managers and owners from other bars and taverns did. She had made so many plans to improve The Blue Dot inspired by the sea and how it helped her heal.

"What about the costs? We have to do something with the debt."

"I'm thinking about that. I don't have it figured out yet. I can't get a loan. But I'll come up with something before the summer ends. In the meantime, we can do some of the labor ourselves. You can handle all the redecorating. You've always been great on a shoestring budget."

"Flattery will get you everywhere." Maren picked up the photos again. "We could capitalize on the beach theme. Not that it hasn't been done a thousand times before. Maybe something charming like farmhouse and beach resort rolled into one? Lots of whites and ecrus. Light blues." She stood and smoothed her pants.

"So, you'll do it?" She had been ready for the argument and had rehearsed all the ways she could handle Maren's objections.

"I need to think about it. Peyton is ready to stay thanks to you and those buckets of sea glass. That's not a fight I feel like taking on at the moment. And staying is a small thing I can do for her since Dave and I disrupted her life too." Maren handed back the folder. "And after the other night in the backyard, I have to admit, I was being a bitch to you. I'm sorry."

"It's okay. The summer in Serenity would do you good too. You always looked good with a tan. And it's high time Dave handled some of the things around the house. Let him deal with the real estate agent if he wants to sell the house." She hated using the thing Maren was most vulnerable about, but Maren deserved to find herself again.

"I could use something to focus on besides the divorce." Maren tugged at her oversized earrings.

She bit her lip to keep from squealing. Her sister was ready to cave. She hadn't thought it possible under all that armor Maren kept wrapped around her.

Maren pointed a finger at her. "Don't get too excited. Let me look over your business plan too. If you can come up with a way to buy us out, and you want to deal with the debt hanging over this place, I might be willing to wait until the end of the summer to see this place go."

"If I make these changes, I'll make money. I know it." She tapped the folder. In her heart, she believed she could do this. She had to find a way to buy her sisters out —that was all. As if finding money was a small thing. Well, it wasn't, but she would find a way.

"Life doesn't come with guarantees, Kass. We don't always get what we want."

"I know that." Her stomach twisted around the uncertainty that had become her existence. Maren didn't have to remind her that life was unpredictable. All of her plans had washed away like the tide more than once.

"I never loved living here," Maren said.

"I used to think that too." She had believed a shore town had nothing to offer, that only a city with its museums and traffic and businesses had everything she could want. But that wasn't true, at least not for her.

"But you're different. The beach is in your blood. Not me. I didn't even like getting sand in my shoes. I've been asked countless times by the people in my town why would I move away from the beach. But they don't understand that living here isn't special. The beach didn't keep me safe from life's problems. I'm still the person whose mother left her. I'm the person whose father didn't know the first thing about picking a good wife and making us suffer because of it, and apparently, his problems went deeper, but he hid them. The beach doesn't stop bad things from happening."

"Bad things happen everywhere to everyone. The beach offers peace and a chance to get away from those problems. We were lucky growing up with the ocean in our backyard. Some people never even see the ocean."

"I wanted to be someone else. I still do." Maren crossed her arms over her middle and stared at her shoes.

"Oh, Maren. Don't say that. You're incredible. You're smart and beautiful." She gripped Maren's shoulders, wanting to shake some sense into her.

"Really? If I were those things, why did Dave look somewhere else for them?" Her bottom lip trembled. "And if I'm so incredible, why would Dad keep his problems from me? Didn't he think I could help him?"

She gathered Maren in her arms. She stiffened at first

but gave in and hugged her back. Poor Maren. She only wanted to be needed, by her husband and her father. She needed to do a better job of showing Maren that she loved her and wanted her around.

"Dave is a poopyhead." She hugged Maren harder.

Maren barked out a laugh and eased away from her embrace. "Did you just say poopyhead?"

"I was trying to be nice."

"What if I wanted to stay? Would you find a place for me here at The Dot?"

"Of course I would. If we can stay open." Which she wished for with all her heart.

"Give me some time. I want to talk to Peyton and see what she thinks. I have a lot of decisions to make, and I'm overwhelmed. And there's one other thing," Maren said as she headed to the door.

"What's that?"

"You need to ask the hot cook out on a date." She winked.

"Maren, that's ridiculous. Why would I do that?"

"I mean it. I've never seen you blush so many times in one minute. And when was the last time you went out on a date? The nineteen nineties?"

"I'm not interested in a date. And he would never be interested in someone like me." She couldn't take the time to get involved with a man who had no intention of staying in Serenity. It was hard enough trying to convince her sisters to stay. And even if her whole plan fell apart, she wasn't leaving again. She wanted to finish out her life at the beach, searching for sea glass and running her own business.

"He'd be a fool not to want a date with you. Don't be like me. Don't play it safe when it comes to love. Take a chance." Maren opened the door and went through the kitchen. She shouted a goodbye to Grant and Bailey before the swinging doors swallowed her up.

She didn't have time for a romance. She could be on the verge of getting this place and proving to everyone else she had what it took to make something of herself. Family mattered, but her career mattered too. Plus, her sisters wouldn't break her heart the way a man could. Grant might be easy on the eyes, but on the heart, he would be nothing but dangerous.

The breakfast rush was over. Grant and Bailey had the cleanup under control. The pile of paperwork on her desk could wait. Maren almost acquiescing felt like a victory. She should celebrate and knew the best way to do that. She checked her high tide app. The tide would be going out soon, making now a good time to search for sea glass. She grabbed her tote and shouted goodbye to Grant.

By the end of the summer she could have this place in top shape, a formidable career as a tavern owner, and her sisters and her niece in her fold.

What else did she need?

Chapter Eleven

Grant hesitated outside Beach Rhythm. Walking in there could be a big mistake. Someone well versed in all music genres could spot him and start asking questions. He'd been picked out other times during his two-year hiatus, but he managed to get away without taking a photo or having to explain a whole lot. Those couple of fans had respected his wishes to be kept off social media. They had offered their condolences and left him in peace. But not all fans were like that. And none of the media outlets. They had wanted a piece of him, and he had nothing left to give.

He could have just ordered the sheet music online. But he missed the smell of an old-time store with instruments hanging on the walls and aisles of vinyl wrapped in plastic. He had spent his teen years sucking up every piece of knowledge and information from the local music stores within a twenty- or thirty-mile radius of his home as if his very existence relied on such measures. Music had given him an escape from growing up in a house where his stepfather thought his stepsons were more of a nuisance than a blessing.

He stole a glance through the window where the candy apple red drum kit was displayed. He hoped if he spent a little time in a genuine music store, his muse would wake up some. He needed her. He hadn't been able to write a thing yet, and Levi was breathing down his neck.

He gripped the warm metal door handle and forced himself into the store. The bell above his head gave him away instantly. He almost ducked out but planted his fleeing feet. Levi was right. Grant needed to start making his way back into the music world. He had no plans to tell Levi he was right, though. That would encourage him to continue to stand over Grant's shoulder while he tried to write.

"Hey. Welcome to Beach Rhythm." A guy with white hair pulled back low on his neck and matching white mustache sitting behind the glass counter gave a wave. The man closed his tablet and arched his back in a slow stretch.

He knew how the guy felt. His back always ached ever since the bus accident. "Howdy." He tipped his cap. The rest of the store was empty of patrons, only the typical instruments hanging from the wall, an assortment of basic keyboards off to the side, and another drum kit decorated the space. Behind the cash register, above the man's head was a quote from Dick Clark. "Music is the soundtrack of your life." Mr. Clark had that one right. But for now, Grant's radio was off.

"Where are you from, son?"

"Is my accent that obvious?" At least the first words the man said weren't, *"Well, shit. Grant Hawkins is in the store. Let me get my camera."*

"To someone like me, born and bred at the beach. Been in Jersey my whole life. Plus, I know just about everyone in Serenity by the Sea. You're not from town. Are you on vacation?"

"Something like that." He wandered over to the vinyl section and out of habit he went to the *H*'s. One Grant Hawkins Band was tucked in toward the back. It was his second album. Hadn't done that well in sales, but the fans had shown up for the tour. He had still been getting his feet wet in the business and foolish enough to believe that high would last forever.

"Can I help you find anything? I'm Kenny, by the way."

"It's right nice to meet you. Name's Grant. I'll be needing some sheet music, if you have it." His fingers continued to dance over the albums.

"I've got some in the back." Kenny slid from behind the counter and sauntered to the back of the store, returning with a wirebound notebook of the paper he wanted. "Country singer, right?"

"Country music suits my twang, but my first love's rock." He forced a laugh, but Kenny stared at him, stone-faced.

"I'm sorry for your loss, son." Kenny stuck out his hand.

"I don't know what you mean." A fire churned in his belly, and heat spread through him like he was a wood-stove. He was as cornered as a raccoon in a trap and went back to glancing at the albums in hopes that Kenny would believe him.

"It's an honor to have you in my store, Mr. Hawkins."

He could try and deny it, say he wasn't Grant Hawkins, but there was no point in insulting this man. He looked around to make sure the place was still empty, that no one had come in from the back. Maybe if the person behind the counter was a teenager, he would have been fine. But not a man who probably had the years of experience under his belt like this Kenny guy.

"You're safe here. I know you left the music business and you don't want anyone to know where you are. The media would only hound you with questions that are none of their damn business. You've got my word. I won't tell a soul."

"Pardon me, but how can I believe you?" He took a step toward the door.

"I'm not interested in taking one of those selfie things the kids like to do. I also don't believe a man's personal life should be all over the internet. You have my word, and my word is gold." The earnestness in Kenny's eyes convinced him.

"Thank you."

"I protect my town and the people in it. I'm not the sheriff or anything, but I love Serenity by the Sea. She's been good to me. And music has been good to me. And I will always respect the people in the business who have shown respect. And you have. I followed what you did for that charity and those children."

The heat in his veins burned hotter, but not from anger or worry. He had only helped those children because they needed help. He had insisted there be no cameras when he arrived. He didn't want the entertainment channels finding out about his visit and using it for their benefit. But someone had leaked the information about his appearance. And it went viral.

"It was nothing. Anyone would've done what I did." Once he had started making a name for himself, he wanted to help kids who needed a break—like he, Levi, and Emmet had needed.

"It was more than nothing, and no, you're wrong about most people. Most people would not spend their own money to build a school where underprivileged children could go after the regular school day to take free music lessons. Instruments and teachers cost a lot of money."

"Music saved me. I wanted to help. That's all." He had spent every penny he had back then. Noel had been furious with him, but he couldn't stop himself. He had learned about the music program getting pulled from too many schools. Music healed. Those kids needed some healing.

"The notebook is on me."

"No, sir. But thank you." He dug his wallet out of his front jeans pocket. He didn't want to owe Kenny. Kenny probably needed the money from every sale. Small music stores like this one rarely made it anymore when online shopping was faster and cheaper.

Kenny put a hand to stop him. "I'm paying you back for taking care of those kids. It doesn't come close to what you did, but I'm not looking for anything in return."

"That's mighty nice of you." He shoved the wallet back in his pocket, not wanting to hurt the man's pride by still refusing. Grant understood a thing or two about pride and how it bruised.

"How long are you in town?" Kenny slid back onto his stool.

"Three weeks. I'm staying in one of those tents with my brother." He wished Levi would go home. His presence in the tent shrunk it by a mile.

"Levi?"

"Yes, sir."

"Looks like you might be ready to come out of retirement." Kenny handed over the notebook.

He took it. "Not quite yet, I'm just messing around with some ideas, but I'll let you know if I decide while I'm in town."

"I'd appreciate that. If you ever need anything, you let me know. I'm always here even when the store is closed. I prefer music over people most days."

"I understand that. Music doesn't judge." Grant held up the notebook. "Thanks again." He pushed outside and walked toward the Topside Community.

He hadn't expected to find someone as kind as Kenny inside that store. Serenity by the Sea was full of surprises.

And maybe not such a bad place to be. He could get used to having the beach a block away and seeing a pretty dark-haired woman every day. What would she say when she found out he had lied to her about who he was? She didn't seem like a woman who appreciated being kept in the dark about anything.

He stopped back at the tent, ready to give his new notebook a try, but Levi was strumming on the guitar with earphones plugged in. His brother looked up and waved, but thankfully went back to his playing. Grant wasn't ready to sit down in this small space and write, while Levi plucked strings without effort. The tent walls closed in on him. He signaled to Levi he was going back out.

He had no idea where to go, but his boots took him toward the ocean. The sun warmed the back of his neck. He might have to buy himself some shorts and a shirt from the clothing store next to the bakery and across the street from the music store.

People packed every inch of the beach with their towels. Maybe Kassidy wouldn't care that he left out his real identity. Levi hadn't hidden who he was, and she hadn't recognized him. But she wouldn't if she didn't follow the music. Levi had been in the band but had never taken center stage.

Levi had toyed with the idea of a solo career, but he couldn't get any traction. His skills had been in managing the band. He had gathered a few other clients and hung out a shingle. He was proud of his little brother taking a bad event and turning it into something good. Grant hadn't been able to do that. He was stuck like a tractor in the mud. Maybe he should enlist Levi to write the songs with him. He certainly hadn't picked up the guitar recently.

He leaned into the metal railing and soaked in the enjoyment of those running in and out of the ocean. His body spotted her before his mind could register the image of her squatting on her haunches where the sand was wet. She held her shoes in one hand while she ran her fingers in the sand with the other. Just like last time. He had no idea what she was doing, but he wanted to know. The more time he spent with her while she hustled to make customers happy, bringing them their food and drinks, the more he wanted to know about her. He took the wooden steps that led down to the beach. More wooden planks made a walkway about a quarter of the way down the sand.

The sun cooked his arms and neck. Jeans and boots were a mistake for the beach. The sweat ran down his back as fast as the seagulls flew away with bread in their mouths. He sank with each step, having to lift his legs higher to keep moving and not fall over. His leg complained from all the extra effort it had to put in to get him to Kassidy.

She dipped her hand into the water, then moved farther down the beach closer to the pier and away from him. He could try to yell, but the crashing and banging of the waves, along with the wind howling across the clear blue sky, and the yelling from the people on the beach would drown him out. He'd only manage to cause a scene and get himself noticed.

She turned back in his direction and held her hand over her eyes. She stopped as if she noticed something and waved. He looked behind him to see if someone else was waving too, but no one was any the wiser. When he glanced back at her, she had thrown her head back in laughter.

Something tugged low in his belly as she came closer. This woman was making his body wake up and take notice of things he'd forgotten about like the way a woman's hips swayed when she walked across the sand to him. Or the way Kassidy's lip curled up on one side when she smiled. And she smiled big and wide like she loved smiling. Smiling was hard for him. He almost forgot how.

"Excuse me, are you Grant Hawkins?" A woman probably around his age with a large sun hat in black and white stripes and a black one-piece bathing suit to match intersected him.

"No. Wrong guy." He wrangled his accent in as best he could. But the woman searched his face as if trying to decide if she believed him.

"You look a lot like him." She pressed her lips into a thin line and tapped her cheek with a finger.

"So I've been told. Would you excuse me?" He tried to step around this perceptive person, but she moved into his path again.

"I don't mean to be a pain, but I never forget a face. I saw you in concert three years ago when you came to the PNC Bank Arts Center. I had fourth-row seats with my sister. She is a huge fan of yours. I wish she were here to see you." Her gaze trailed his body. "Plus, you're wearing jeans and work boots on the beach. Your baseball cap is on backward. You're screaming Grant Hawkins."

He had played that outdoor venue. He and the band had opened up for Jason Aldean. The stage was small, the seating capacity was limited, but everyone was close to the stage because of it. He had ridden the wave of the audience's energy all night long. He didn't doubt this woman was in the fourth row with a good view of his face on the stage and on the giant monitors. And she was spot-on about his poor choice of clothing.

"I'm sorry. That isn't me. Please excuse me, I'm meeting a friend." He waved to Kassidy in hopes the lady would get the hint.

"Okay, then. Sorry to bother you. But you sure do look like him. Too bad." The woman returned to her beach chair. She leaned over to talk to her friend. He imagined she spoke about him and what she thought she saw and how she wished she had taken a photo to prove her point on social media.

"Did you run into an old friend?" Kassidy said as she saddled up near him. She held out a fisted hand. Something green or brown poked out between her fingers.

"That woman? No. She thought I was someone she knew." He tried to shrug it off, but he wasn't sure if Kassidy would buy into his indifference.

"That happens a lot to you. What are you doing out here?" she said.

He took her quick change of subject as acceptance to

his story. He did want to know what she would say if he told her the truth. Would she be mad at him or would she understand his reason for wanting to fade into the background?

"I saw you and thought I'd come down."

"Boots aren't exactly the best shoes for the sand. You might've wanted to wait until I came back up." Her laugh was sweet and simple. It danced over him and settled in his chest.

"I'm seeing that now. Maybe I should head back to the boardwalk."

"I'll go with you. I have to get back to the house. But let's hurry because the sand is getting too hot to walk on." She slid in step beside him, handling the sand like a professional while he wobbled with each step.

"What do you do down here by the water? It looks like you're digging for something." The wood planks were a relief to his legs and his ego. They climbed the stairs to the boardwalk and he was back on solid ground.

She opened her palm to reveal small smoky colored stones in green and brown. "Sea glass. Isn't it pretty?"

"You search for sea glass?" So, that was what she had been doing by the water. He had never searched for sea glass. He had seen plenty of pictures of it, even some jewelry made from it, but never in person. He'd only been to the beach a handful of times in his life.

"Sure. It's relaxing. I can clear my head out here near the ocean. My dad and I used to do it when I was a kid."

"You've been through a lot losing your father." The loss of his mother had knocked him as hard as a wild horse kicking him in the chest. He could guess what she was going through right about now.

"Some moments are harder than others. I'm managing. I guess."

His back complained about the walk. He shoved his fists into the small of his back to release some of the pressure.

"Are you okay?"

"Sore back. Gets to me sometimes, but I'm fine. Having your sisters around must be helpful." He wouldn't have gotten through losing his mother if he hadn't had Levi and Emmet. His brothers had given him something to focus on. But Levi wasn't able to offer any support after Noel died. He was suffering too. Levi hadn't wanted to talk, couldn't find the words to say what was eating him up inside. The guilt and the anger had stolen every breath and every desire he had had too.

"Having my sisters around is great—when we're getting along. They aren't thrilled about cleaning out my dad's house."

"Families fight especially when times are hard. I'm sure they'll do the right thing and help you pack up his belongings." What little he knew of Bailey told him she would jump in and help. That woman had been at The Blue Dot every day to help Kassidy after her morning staff quit. Her other sister was a harder read.

She worked her lip under her teeth. "My dad... well, he liked to collect things. They weren't bargaining for the amount of work. Never mind my problems. Do you want to sit? For your back?"

His back still complained. He could use something hot against his aching muscles or the touch of a good woman.

"It's better to walk. I could walk you home, if that's where you're headed." He wanted to kick himself. He must sound like a boy with a crush wanting to carry her books. She was a grown woman who didn't need him to escort her. Though he really wanted to.

"I would like the company." She dropped her gaze. The sun drew streaks of golden brown in her curly hair. He made a fist to keep from trying to find out if the strands bouncing by her neck were as soft as he imagined.

"Did you always live in Serenity by the Sea?" He offered her his elbow, and she slipped her hand into the crook of his arm. Heat bloomed in the center of his chest as they strolled down the boardwalk.

"I moved away for a while. I went to Chicago thinking I'd have a big career and take over the world. Silly, huh?"

"Not at all. I've heard crazier dreams than that one." Like his own idea to be a famous singer. He'd been nothing more than a poor kid from the south with a step-father who didn't like him much. He'd just been at the right place at the right time when the world opened up to him.

"When things didn't work out in Chicago, I moved back. That was about ten years ago. Now I want to make The Blue Dot the summer destination. You probably think I'm out of my mind now that you've worked there a few days."

"Not if that's what you want." He could tell someone else to run toward their dreams, but he didn't know how to take a step back in the direction of his.

"I do." She gifted him that smile again. His chest burned hotter.

The walk unwound the knots in his shoulders and even eased some of the pain in his back. No one else noticed him, and Kassidy fit on his arm. The day was shaping up even if he couldn't write a song.

"Is your mother still alive?" He hadn't seen or heard even a mention of her father having a wife. Only the three sisters seemed to be tangled up in the estate issues.

"She is. She lives in Pennsylvania Maren and I don't see her very often. Motherhood wasn't exactly her thing."

"I'm sorry to hear that. She misses out on three daughters."

"Bailey has a different mother."

"Oh. My mistake. I assumed." He tried to pull the boot out of his mouth, but still tasted the leather. If a sibling showed up some day and said he or she was related to him, he wouldn't be the least surprised. Their biological father had a sinner's streak a mile long, and he was as untamed as they came. He had taken off for parts unknown without a glance backward, leaving his three boys behind.

"Don't worry about it." She gave his arm a squeeze. "Easy mistake to make. We have a bit of a modern family. We try to make it work. It doesn't always. I'm hoping this summer will bring us closer together."

They arrived at her front walk. The house wasn't

much bigger than the tent he was staying in. The white clapboards could use a fresh coat of paint, and the black shutters had faded from all the sun and salt air. The boxwoods in front of the cement porch could use a going over. She had a lot on her plate and probably didn't have the time to worry about the upkeep any house needed.

He could offer to help here too, but he'd done enough by cooking for her restaurant. He loved cooking. He had started doing it when his stepfather didn't make dinner and Levi and Emmet needed to eat. Then he did it when they were on tour because it helped him relax. He kept doing it after Noel died to find a way to make a living. He'd lied to past employers about his cooking experience, but Kassidy had been in too much of a bind to question his ability.

He shrugged off the desire to assist this woman. She might be an underdog with the odds stacked against her, but he wasn't sticking around after the end of the summer. And she didn't want his help.

His phone pinged in his pocket. "I'm sorry. I need to check that." He wanted to make sure it wasn't Levi watching out the window and telling him to come inside and work.

"Sure. No problem." She pulled out her own phone and tapped at the screen.

Sure enough, his pain in the backside brother wanted to know where he was. Well, Levi could just wait it out.

"Sorry about that." He shoved his phone back in his pocket.

"No problem. I have a bunch of things to do before the dinner shift. Will you be back to work on Friday?"

She didn't serve breakfast during the week, but she should. Her breakfast crowd was more consistent than the dinner one. He had stopped in to see last night. The place was busy in the earlier hours, but by seven thirty, the crowd had thinned out. She was catering to families and retirees who liked to eat early. The late-night crowd wanted the bars on the boardwalk with the entertainment. He'd been in and around big cities most of his life. The bars with the music rocked till they closed. She had a stage. Now she needed a band or several to draw a crowd. She could tend bar, but she wasn't fast enough. Unless she asked, those opinions were his alone. And he wasn't about to suggest live music.

He'd have to wait five days to see her again. He needed that time to write, but he wasn't sure he wanted to go that long without that smile.

"When will you be searching for sea glass again?" He said the first thing to pop into his mind. He shouldn't have said it based on the rise and arch of her brows.

"I prefer to come down to the beach when no one is here. You know, early mornings even before the lifeguards get to work, but the best time to find it is when the tide goes out. Sea glass likes to hide in the wet sand."

"What do you do with it after you find it?"

"You're full of questions. Have you never searched for sea glass as a kid? I thought everyone did that."

He should shove his boot right back into his mouth. He had no business with this woman. 'Just curious. We didn't go to the beach. I've been to a couple of islands for vacation, but I didn't search for anything."

"I put them in jars around the house. I have more jars than I need. Another weird thing about me."

"It's not weird if it makes you happy."

"I do love the idea of something unwanted turning into something beautiful with a new purpose." She shook her head. "I'm sorry. I must sound like a children's movie." A blush rose up her neck.

His fingers itched to touch her skin.

"Nothing to be sorry about. You looked... peaceful right then. More beautiful." He was asking for trouble now.

She drew back, her eyes growing wide. "That was kind of you to say." She pulled the pieces from her pocket and handed him a green one.

"I can't take this from you. It's your treasure."

"I want you to have it. Besides, I have plenty. Too much, probably. And it's not as if it's worth money. I'm just sentimental and looking for a purpose in my life. I'm saying way too much to you today."

He took the sea glass and their fingers touched. The heat that ran up his arm made the summer sun seem like frosted glass. He was headed into long-forgotten territory and risking it all.

"Something to remember you by when the summer is over." He curled his fists around the stone.

"Right. Yes, when the summer is over, you'll be on to wherever it is you go. I hate to cut this short, but I need to get inside. Thanks for walking me home." She smiled, but it didn't reach her eyes.

She must see him as nothing more than her employee. She was being nice to him, and he had misread her signals. He'd been out of practice for a while. He had forgotten how to engage with a woman.

"Would you like to grab dinner on Monday?" He couldn't stop the words from coming out if he had lassoed them with a new rope. And he definitely didn't want to wait all week to see her again.

"Monday? Um, yes, okay. I'd like that." She smoothed her hands on her shorts.

"I'll pick you up at six. And thanks again for this." He held up the sea glass.

"See you then."

He waited. She turned at the door with a quick glance back and a small wave. He was in too deep. Deeper than the ocean. A tingle ran down his spine. Words he could use in a song.

Maybe.

Chapter Twelve

"Where are you going all dressed up?" Maren passed by Kassidy's bedroom door but did an about-face and came back. Maren leaned against the doorframe with clothes in her arms. Her hair was pulled back in a bushy ponytail, and her face was wiped clean of makeup.

"Out." She hadn't mentioned to either of her sisters that she was going to dinner with Grant on her only day off. Maren and Peyton had spent the day making crafts. Bailey had gone to the beach and was now at Dad's trying to make sense of the piles. She had wanted to go along too, but Bailey said to stay. That she needed some time alone at Dad's place. The little white lie wasn't so bad. She had brought her sisters home, and they were sticking around longer than they had originally planned. She loved having them all in her house. All the noises they made filled in the spaces that echoed with loneliness.

"Out? In that red tank top and those jeans that look

painted on. You're going somewhere with a guy. Who would waste that top on a trip to the grocery store? Spill." Maren dumped the clothes on the floor and plopped onto her bed.

The red tank top had been a splurge purchase last summer and never worn. It showed off her shoulders, and she loved her shoulders. The jeans were her darkest pair and seemed to be suited for nights out. Since she didn't go out much at night, the jeans still looked fresh from the store.

She had chosen her clothes with some care. She didn't want to wear anything that made her seem too desperate because she hadn't been on a date in a very long time. If tonight even was a date. He hadn't said officially. But she had shaved her legs just in case. Not that she planned on sleeping with him or anything—at least not yet. Clean-shaven legs made her feel sexier.

"There's nothing to spill." Heat climbed up her neck and burned her cheeks. "I made plans with a friend. That's all."

"Well, if that's all, then can I come along?" Maren's eyes twinkled in the golden glow from the lamp beside her bed.

"You'd be bored." She dabbed on a little lip gloss and smacked her lips together.

"I don't know. I might find it interesting to watch you and the hot cook all cozied up together." Maren flopped back on the bed and laughed.

"What are you talking about?" She didn't know how Maren knew she was going out with Grant.

"Bailey told me how you two look at each other at work. And if I looked that good in that top, I'd only wear it out on a date too." Maren fluffed the throw pillows.

"It's not a date. It's just dinner." She wasn't going to call it a date. If the night ended in a kiss, then maybe, but for now, she was having dinner with a friend. A very handsome and sexy friend, but still a friend.

"So, you are going out with him." Maren clapped her hands and bounced on the bed like a middle school girl.

"Okay, maybe I am." She jumped on the bed beside Maren and grabbed her hands. She hadn't had a girls' talk in ages. She didn't have a lot of friends in town because she was just too busy with The Blue Dot. She should change that. Maria from Intentions Clothing was hilarious and a great talker. Maren would love her.

"I'm so nervous." If the sweat under her boobs was any indication.

"Why?"

"Because I haven't been on a date in forever, and the last few times I did, they were disasters." During dinner on one date, the guy told her he was in finance and under investigation for fraud. She had left that second without offering to leave any money for the food, worrying that he would pocket the cash and take off.

"Just relax. Be yourself, but not too much yourself."

"What does that mean?" She yanked her hands away.

"Oh, come on, Kass. I don't mean it in a bad way. Just go easy on the guy if he says something you disagree with. Ease him into the full spectrum of your charm."

The heat in the room stifled her breathing. She got

up. "For once, I thought maybe we could talk like sisters do."

"We are talking like sisters." Maren climbed off the bed, putting distance between them.

"You're always judging. Don't you ever see the good in anything?"

"I was just offering some advice. I don't want you to blow it again."

"Maybe it's you who should soften that bite of yours. Did you ever think Dave got sick of his head being handed to him?"

She grabbed her purse and stormed out, not wanting to see Maren's reaction. She suspected Maren's face fell in disbelief. It wasn't like her to snap that way at either of her sisters. Or her father for that matter. She allowed everyone to go on doing their thing at whatever cost it was to her. Wasn't that exactly why she and Bear broke up? She hadn't once asked him—no, demanded—he treat her the way she deserved. Instead, she was happy with his scraps because she foolishly believed he loved her for her.

She paused on the porch. Her stomach twisted into an oily knot and made her nauseous. She hadn't meant to say what she had said to Maren, but Maren was a pro at pointing out everyone's flaws and it stung like a jellyfish bite. With a glance at the door, she debated on going back inside and apologizing.

Instead, she pushed the thoughts and the sick stomach feeling away and focused on the night ahead. She deserved some fun and a night off, didn't she?

Grant waited on the sidewalk in front of his tent. Her breath caught, and her feet slowed at the sight of him. His solid frame was almost a silhouette in the last of the sun's evening rays. He turned as if he could feel her gaze on him and smiled. Her worries dissipated into the warm night air.

His hair was wet and slicked back. His t-shirt was a vivid blue and wrinkle-free. His jeans still hung on him in all the right places. But the best part was, he had trimmed his beard to a soft smatter of dark hair coating his jaw. She let out a long breath.

"You look great," he said.

Her voice stuck in her throat. She swallowed and tried again. "So do you. Were you waiting long?

"Just came outside. I thought we could walk to dinner. I've been inside all day. Do you mind?"

"It's a beautiful night. Why not? Where are we headed?" The humidity had taken a vacation and was replaced with the cool air and soft breeze that caressed her skin. She wouldn't regret wearing her jeans if they walked.

"It's a surprise." He offered his arm, and she slid her hand around his bicep. His muscles flexed under her touch. She liked that Grant wanted to stroll as if they were a couple from a bygone era, and not modern people always in a hurry. Bear had never been one for public displays of affection of any kind. He didn't even like holding her hand in front of others. Grant was a gentleman. She could get used to that. Which she should not.

"Can I have a hint?" They walked toward the boardwalk, passing 32 Below, the ice cream shop. Tourists gathered around the picnic tables seated alongside the ordering window, eating their ice cream and sipping shakes. She didn't recognize any faces, so the families laughing together had to be from out of town. She wanted what those families had or appeared to have, the gentle easy laughter of people who got along.

They passed the town auditorium where plays and concerts were held, and a sea breeze picked up as they neared the ocean, cooling her heated skin. Grant pulled her a little closer, warming her further. Yes, she could definitely get used to this.

"Now, what fun would that be if I gave you a hint as to our destination? Don't you trust me, Kassidy Russo?" His Southern accent splashed over her like the foam of a crashing wave.

People wandered up and down the boardwalk. Some still in their bathing suits. Others with bright-pink skin that poked out of their flowered shirts and beige shorts. Even in New Jersey, the sun reflected off the sand and water strong enough to burn the toughest skin. Growing up at the beach taught her to never underestimate the strength of the sun or the ocean.

"Is there a reason I shouldn't?" Her words came out with a harsh bite that she hadn't meant. She had wanted to tease back, to bring an ease to their conversation, but she had blundered, if the confused look across his face was any indication.

"I'm sorry," she said. "I didn't mean... I was trying to

joke." They crossed Ocean Avenue and headed north on the boardwalk toward the edge of town.

"Nothing to be sorry about. You were speaking your mind. I like that about you."

"Really? Because most people don't." Maren's words echoed in her head. She should try to not be so much herself.

Grant stopped and turned to her. "You and your directness are refreshing. I've spent a lot of time around people always pretending to be something they aren't. They always have something to prove or to hide. People from my neck of the woods smile to your face but turn their backs with their honest remarks. You are exactly who you are. There is no guessing. Don't change. Not for anyone."

"Who were these people you spent time with?" They began their walk again. A woman passed them. Her mouth hung open as she stared at Grant. He didn't seem to notice. She had to admit he was a very good-looking man who could probably get any woman he wanted and probably had many women gawk at him. But there was something about him that rang familiar to multiple people.

She wanted to know more about him. What did he do before he appeared in her town, living next door to her? Why didn't he have a woman in his life? She could ask that question, couldn't she? And if he asked her about her past, she would share some of it. She had already told him too much about the chasm between her and her sisters.

"Believe me, the people I used to know were not

important. I'm glad to be done with them. Here we go." He led her down the steps to the beach. The lifeguards had gone home for the day, so most of the people had left too. Only a few stragglers hung on to the very last bit of sun, but they were farther south on the beach, closer to the bathroom and changing rooms.

This part of the beach was quiet and secluded. The dunes jutted out more, blocking some of the view, and the sand hadn't been replenished because of some dispute with the neighboring town. The jetty invaded most of the sand here, making it undesirable for sun worshippers because of the small amount of sand to sit on.

But Grant must not have noticed or cared. Or maybe chose this spot because of its privacy. A table set for two waited for them.

Mr. D stood with a smile spread wide over his ruddy face. Instead of his bakery apron covered in sugar and flour, he wore a crisp white shirt and a pair of navy-blue trousers.

"*Ciao*, Kassidy," Mr. D said and held out a chair for her. "Welcome."

"I don't understand." She glanced between Grant and Mr. D.

"Mr. DeFazio helped me out. I wanted a quiet dinner, but somewhere special."

"Ah, sit, sit." Mr. D held out the chair for her. "Dinner is simple tonight. I made my special Italian bread. You have fresh provolone and an imported sopressata. There is a salad with fresh tomatoes from my garden. And for dessert, cannoli. *Mangia*."

"Mr. D, are you serving us tonight?" She really didn't understand how Grant had pulled this off or that he even knew Mr. D. "How do you two know each other?"

"I stumbled upon his bakery one morning when I went for an early walk. I've been back almost every morning since. When I asked you out to dinner, I figured who better to recommend a place in town except the local baker? Mr. D offered to help me with the food. I couldn't refuse. His bread is fantastic."

"Smart boy," Mr. D said with a wink.

"This is amazing. And so nice. I'm overwhelmed." She had expected a quiet dinner at the vegetarian deli or hot dogs on the boardwalk. She hadn't expected such a thoughtfully planned evening from a man she hardly knew. He put his heart into this night, and the gesture stole hers.

"I hope that's a good thing," Grant said. "I'll take it from here, Mr. D. Thank you for everything."

"You are both most welcome." Mr. D. shook Grant's hand and kissed her on both cheeks before climbing the stairs to the boardwalk and disappearing into the dusky night.

Tears snuck up on her, almost choking her. She hadn't cried in a long time. Not even when her dad died because she didn't have time for crying. But this night, on the beach, with the moon a guest in the sky, shook her. She blinked away the emotion, wondering if she should run before she broke into a hundred pieces. Grant couldn't be real.

He motioned for her to sit, then took the seat opposite her. The chair sank some into the sand from her weight, but she suffered no worry of falling over. A wind danced off the waves and chilled her more. She relished the cool breeze, calming the flush on her face like a soothing balm.

Grant turned on the solar-powered lantern in the center of the table. "I hope you don't mind the food choice. I let Mr. D pick it all. I just wanted something easy to transport and eat once we got here. Are you comfortable? Is this okay?"

"This is more than okay. No one has ever been so thoughtful on a date before." She must sound like a woman who didn't ask to be treated well.

Grant's eyebrows raced up his forehead. "Then you haven't been out with the right men. If you don't mind me saying, ma'am. You should be treated with respect and be told how special you are."

She folded and unfolded the linen napkin. "You are very unexpected." Right from the first day on the sidewalk to walking into her kitchen and offering to help.

The conversation during dinner flowed along with the bottle of red wine Mr. D. had tucked under the table for them. Grant told her about growing up in Alabama where he was surrounded by the mountains and lakes.

"I've never swam in a lake before. Not with the ocean in my backyard." Her insides hummed with the alcohol, good food, and great company. She hadn't been this relaxed in ages and didn't even mind the wind blowing her hair over her face only seconds after she moved it away.

"I'll have to change for you," he said. "I'll take you to my hometown and you can see how the other half lives."

The breath stuck in her throat. She swallowed hard against the possible meaning in those words. He could simply be saying something nice with no meaning at all, but her broken and lonely heart grabbed on to the idea and held tight.

"That would be nice." As nice as seeing where Grant grew up might be, she needed this conversation on safer ground. "Is it just you and Levi, or do you have other siblings?"

He pushed his food around on the plate, keeping his gaze on his task. "My brother Emmet died a little over two years ago."

"Oh, I'm so sorry. I didn't know. I wouldn't have asked." She wanted to hide under the table. So much for safer conversation.

"It's okay. You wouldn't know. It was an accident." He offered her a thin smile that didn't reach his eyes.

"I really am sorry." For all her bickering with her sisters, she couldn't imagine losing one of them for good.

He put a hand up to stop her. "No more apologies, Kassidy. Tell me something about you. Were you ever married?"

She didn't want to upset him further and answered his question. "Engaged. But it didn't work out. How about you? Were you ever married?"

His hand hesitated over the bottle. He dropped his gaze to the table again before meeting hers. "I was." He didn't elaborate, and she waited to see if he would say anything more.

"Am I being too personal by asking how it ended?" This was what she wanted to know. Who was the foolish woman that allowed Grant to get away? Because he had been nothing but a respectable man in her company who was willing to help without waiting to be asked. She was sure he had his flaws because everyone did, but leaving socks on the floor or the toilet seat up would never bother her enough if he could be counted on for nights like this one.

He sat back in the chair and dropped his hands to his lap. The lantern offered enough light for her to notice the darkness that passed over his face. Whoever this woman was, she must have broken his heart.

"You don't have to answer that. I shouldn't have asked that either." She tried to wave away her words, hoping to go back to the ease of the conversation before her multiple blunders, but like the sun, it was gone.

"She passed away two years ago. Two months after my brother."

"Oh, Grant. That's terrible. You've been through so much." She finished off the wine in her glass. The bread and cheese turned to lead in her stomach. He must not be over his wife. She was the foolish one thinking a woman had dumped him and left him available. She should have known a woman with her senses would hold on to a man like Grant.

"Thank you. It's getting late. I should get you back." He pushed out of the chair.

She willed her face to remain neutral and not show the disappointment in her heart. She hadn't meant to ruin the evening. But it was better that she knew what she was up against. A wife who passed before her time, Kassidy couldn't compete with that. Getting involved with a man who still loved his deceased wife would never work out. Kassidy wanted stability. A house filled with people who loved her. She wanted someone to come home to at night. Grant was not that man. And she couldn't wish it to be true. He was a stranger just passing through like so many people in Serenity.

"Let me help you clean up." She gathered the dishes and glasses and placed them in the basket Mr. D had left. Grant folded the table and chairs. His truck had been left at the top of the steps right out on the street. He really had thought everything through.

Everything except the part where he wasn't over his wife.

Chapter Thirteen

She couldn't wait another minute. She had used up all her time. Kassidy had come to the beach every morning this past week to look for sea glass and hoping for a glimpse of Grant. She hadn't seen him since their date.

He had driven her home and walked her to the door, ever the gentleman. But she had realized that was just how he was. His actions had nothing to do with feelings for her. He would walk anyone to the door.

She had pretended to search for her keys in her purse, while he stood on the stoop beside her with his hands in his pockets. She had hoped he would say more about their night together or ask her for another date. But he hadn't. He had simply placed a soft kiss on her cheek and watched as she went inside and closed the door.

Now, she scanned the boardwalk and the beach from her spot by the water. The sun popped over the horizon, warming her neck and already promising to bring a day of heat and humidity. Her curly hair expanded on her head with every second.

She had quite the find of sea glass today. Stones in light blues and whites. She didn't care that those colors were the most common. Every piece was beautiful, and she knew the perfect place to put them in her kitchen. After finding all the sea glass in her father's attic, she wondered if she would end up like him. Hoarding buckets of sea glass and alone.

But she was drawn to the beauty and the possibilities they held just like she had said to Grant the other day before the failed date. Even Peyton and Maren were sucked into the wonder of the sea glass. They had made mosaics and frames every day, placing them all around the house, leaning against walls to dry, ready for sale.

There was no sign of Grant on the boardwalk, and she couldn't hang around another minute. She had to get home and tend to the ritual of washing off the sand and salt from her legs before going to The Blue Dot. She climbed the steps up to the boardwalk and started her walk home. When Grant had walked her home from the beach the day he had asked her out on the date, it was as if her heart had unlocked for the first time since being with Bear. She wasn't in love or anything as crazy as that, but no other man had piqued her interest this way.

Grant was easy to talk to. And Sweet Lord, easy on the eyes. He genuinely seemed to care about her and The Dot. But he could just care about everything the way he was polite and respectful to everyone. He was probably someone who rescued dogs in his free time and volunteered at the children's ward in a hospital.

Tomorrow was Friday. He had promised to come to The Dot and work. She would shoot him a text later just to check in. Or she could ask him his opinion on a new idea for the menu. She also planned on running her menu change ideas by Maren today when she came by. Maren had a surprise for her.

Kassidy washed her feet off with the hose in the backyard. She let herself in through the back and into the kitchen. Peyton sat at the table with her head bent over her phone. Sea glass covered the table grouped by color, mostly shades of blue and green. Washed-out white wood frames were stacked on the chair, waiting to be decorated.

"Good morning," Kassidy said and dropped her sea glass into the mason jar on the shelf by the window over the sink.

"Hey."

"Whatcha looking at?" She grabbed a banana off the counter. This would have to opt as breakfast. She didn't have time for anything else.

"Insta. Just seeing what my friends back home are doing." Peyton placed her phone upside down on the table.

"Missing all the fun stuff, huh?" More than once she had been grateful social media didn't exist when she was a teen. She didn't need documentation of all the stupid things she had done as a kid. She didn't know how teens today handled the pressure, and she applauded Maren for raising a teen with all the added stress.

"They're all doing the same stupid stuff they always do. I'm over it, and I'm over high school. I can't wait to go to college where the kids will be more mature."

"I get that. High school can be a drag." It certainly had been for her. "Do you like being here? In Serenity. With all of us?" She held her breath. Peyton would deliver an honest answer, even if it wasn't the answer she wanted to hear.

"I do, actually." Peyton's face lit up. "I didn't think I would. All of us cramped into this tiny house and me sharing a room with Mom." She rolled her eyes like a pro. "But honestly, being near the beach and working at the tavern have been a lot of fun. Finding the sea glass at Grandpa's has been the best. I feel like it connects me to him more, like he sent me all of it. Come see the latest ones." Peyton grabbed her hand and tugged her down the hall to the bedroom at the end.

"I didn't know where to put them." Leaning against the wall were the mosaics made of sea glass. Each one was a different shape or style, using sea glass of beachy colors. Some looked like waves or trees. Some were more abstract, but still beautiful.

"Wow. These are remarkable. You have a real gift. I like the one that spirals." She picked up the one with the coil of sea glass that had started out with white stones and gradually turned blue as the curl broadened. She could picture the ocean's waves in this one.

"Yeah, that's my favorite too." Peyton snapped a

photo of her holding the mosaic. "I'm going to put that on my story. You have a big smile on your face while you're looking at it."

"I could make a spot in the shed for you to store your pieces if you want. Then you and your mom won't trip over them." Any excuse to make them more comfortable and want to stay longer.

"That would be great. She's not loving the space they're taking. She doesn't want to trip over them in the middle of the night."

"That sounds like her." She should give Maren some credit for sharing the room. She probably could use her own space as much as Peyton.

"Aunt Kassidy, I don't think Mom wants to stay for the summer. She wants to go home and see what Dad is doing. She hates him so much she can't trust him to handle anything." Peyton dropped her gaze and her cheeks bloomed red. "Don't tell her I said that."

Watching her parents disintegrate right before her eyes had to be twisting Peyton up inside. Without any siblings to talk with, did she have a friend she could lean on? Peyton couldn't possibly understand what Maren was going through and better that she didn't, but that didn't mean Peyton wasn't going through something of her own. "It must be hard for you watching your parents divorce."

"I get it that they don't love each other anymore. But why do they have to yell and scream so much? Can't they just talk? They used to talk." Peyton turned her gaze away.

"Because sometimes anger gets the best of us. Give her time. Divorces are hard." Especially when betrayal is involved. Maybe things would be different if Maren and Dave had just fallen out of love, but he fell in love with someone else, someone younger, and he had swapped Maren out for this new version. That sting was hard to get over.

"When you broke up with that guy when I was little, did it feel like a divorce? Mom said you guys were engaged." Peyton headed back to the kitchen and she followed.

"I guess it did. We lived together. We shared a life. I thought we would stay together forever. When he dumped me, I didn't see it coming." Much like Maren hadn't seen Dave coming with his big announcement.

She and Bear had been so wrapped up in their own things, work and her with night school, she never suspected he had wandered right into the arms of a woman with a real career and an impressive ivy league education.

"Wow. That sucks." Peyton slid onto the kitchen chair.

"It does. Well, it did. I moved on. And your mom will too. So, that's why I say give your mom a break. I'm meeting her in about twenty minutes. I'll try and talk to her about staying for the summer. Would you be interested in hanging around even if she goes back?" She hadn't thought of that idea until she had said it. But she liked the sound of Peyton staying with her.

"Thanks, Aunt Kassidy. That would be great. I

would love to spend all summer here. I really want to sell the things I've made. I also don't want to go back to our house with the reminders of our life before." Peyton picked up her phone and tapped at the screen. She waited to see if Peyton would lift her head again, but she remained entranced by whatever had her attention. A teenager's signal that the conversation was over.

She ran down the hall to the bathroom and splashed some water on her face. She changed her shorts and grabbed her tote. Peyton had moved to the backyard with her crafts. She gave a quick wave as she ran past. Maren hadn't been in the house. She must already be at The Dot. Kassidy took the car. It would be faster.

"You did what?" Kassidy's voice echoed against the silence in The Blue Dot. She shook her head to quiet the angry ocean's roar in her ears. Maren must have said something else because her sister could not have possibly deceived her this way.

Even though she knew they were alone amongst the empty tables, she still stole a glance toward the kitchen, hoping Grant would come out and shed some light on what Kassidy did not understand.

"It's just for research purposes. Don't you want to know as much information as possible? It won't hurt to talk to a real estate agent. It doesn't mean we're selling." Maren shuffled papers and stuck them in a pink folder. The folder matched the color of her nail polish. Maren wore navy-blue ankle pants with a white shirt that had tiny pink dots all over it. As always, Maren was impeccable and overly prepared.

What Maren had done meant selling to her. She hadn't expected this kind of betrayal of all things. She had thought—no, hoped—Maren had design ideas she wanted to share. Or ways to bring in money that she hadn't come up with. She wanted Maren to say that she wanted to run The Dot with her and she would never move away again.

Maren's big surprise was Charlotte Munroe, Serenity by the Sea's best commercial real estate agent. Charlotte was a powerhouse and due to arrive in five minutes. Kassidy wiped her sweaty palms on her wrinkled shorts.

"You should've talked to me first." Because then she would have tried to talk Maren out of this. She needed more time to find her miracle.

"You would've put up a fight like you're doing right now. I just want to see what the building and the land are worth. We're two blocks from the beach. That has to be valuable. Maybe valuable enough to sell the place, pay off Dad's debts, and walk away with a little cash."

"Is this because of your divorce? Do you need money? Because when we sell this place, all we're going to be able to do is pay off the debt. There won't be any extra cash." Her breath came in short spurts. She pinched the bridge of her nose.

Everything about The Blue Dot was stacked against her. The outdated image, the sparse staff, and the crushing debt. Was it time to throw up her hands in surrender? It would make more sense to start over, fresh. But her heart clung to the idea of keeping this place. Her heart was making her a fool once again.

"If Charlotte tells us a number we can't pass up, we have to sell sooner than later. You're the only one who wants this place. Bailey and I have lives elsewhere."

As if she didn't already know this. How many times did Maren have to remind her? "Did you talk to Bailey about this?"

"Last night."

Those two words stabbed her in the back like a grilling fork. She grabbed a chair and dropped down. They were plotting against her. They didn't want to give her the time to find the money to buy them out. They just wanted out from under the mess their father had created. They would never stay to help her dig out his house. They just hadn't been brave enough to tell her to her face. Instead, Maren brought in Charlotte.

"Maren, do you ever miss living near each other?" She had to know if her sister ever thought about her the way she did. Did Maren want her sisters around? Did she crave a family the way Kassidy did? Probably not. Maren had Peyton.

Maren cringed. "Sure. Yes, of course. When you lived in Chicago, I often wanted to call you and see if you wanted to go for coffee or shopping. But I understood why you lived there. I didn't try to convince you to move back."

"Why not?" If she had felt like they had wanted her, maybe she would have stayed. Maren had never called when they lived near each other. Kassidy was often the last person on Maren's list if someone else could fill a need. Bailey was always on an adventure, looking for the next exciting thing. Kassidy hadn't ever really belonged.

"Well, why would I? It's your life. And I have my life as does Bailey. Sometimes our paths can't cross. That's all. I know I said I'd think about staying in town longer, and I will, but I just can't live here. There's nothing for me here."

"I'm here." Her voice rang hollow even to her.

"No offense, but that's not enough." Maren scooped her hair away from her face.

"Peyton doesn't want to go home and listen to you and Dave fight." She pushed out of the chair and went around the bar. A whiskey tumbler held a few pieces of sea glass. She had forgotten about putting the pieces there. She ran her fingers over the stones, hoping for the familiar comfort from their soft edges, but this time they were nothing but rocks.

"Peyton doesn't know what she wants. She's fifteen. She changes her mind every day. By tonight, she could have decided she hates sea glass and crafts and have her bags packed."

"Hello." Charlotte Munroe glided into the seating area with her long black linen skirt that had a slit up the front, revealing her tan and toned leg. Her interruption stopped the words on Kassidy's lips.

Charlotte leaned in and placed a kiss near her cheek. The air around them filled with a sweet and flowery scent that clung to the air. Her sleeveless tank was white with large pink flowers placed strategically like handprints. Her makeup was professionally applied. Kassidy glanced at her wrinkled shorts and swatted her wild hair away from her face.

Charlotte seemed to suck all the oxygen out of the room. Charlotte pulled Maren in for a hug. The two women cooed over each other like long lost friends. *Totally not professional*, she wanted to say but bit her cheek.

"I have to go." She hurried past the two women before the banana she ate earlier made a reappearance.

"But we have an appointment," Maren said.

"No, you have an appointment. I'm not interested in selling. That's my final word." She pushed out into the fresh air and took large gulps. The salt air cleared her mind and settled her stomach.

She didn't want to drive the car in her frazzled state. The streets were narrow because no house had a driveway. Everyone parked in the street, taking up space. She'd walk home, but she didn't want to be there either. Maren could return, and they would only end up fighting. She needed someplace else to go. Someplace Maren wouldn't think of.

She walked a few more blocks along the boardwalk before turning inland. The Topside Community came into view. She had no right to show up at Grant's place. They hadn't spoken all week. He had even ignored a couple of her texts. He must have realized that he couldn't date or that his feelings for her, whatever they might be, weren't strong enough compared to what he felt for his wife. As much as that thought hurt, she would be okay with being friends. She needed a friend right now.

She approached the tent, stopping before the porch. Music drifted out to greet her on the sidewalk. She recognized that love song with the slow melody. It had been popular several years ago. The artist escaped her for a minute, but she racked her brain until the answer appeared like the sun poking over the horizon.

That was a Grant Hawkins song. She liked his music, had even followed his career a little, but he didn't play anymore. Grant Hawkins had walked away from the music world and never returned because of a bus accident he had caused.

She didn't want Grant to catch her listening to his music like some weird stalker. She had better knock before he happened outside. Hopefully, he'd hear her over the loud music.

She raised her fist to knock but hesitated. That song wasn't coming from a radio or a tablet or a Bluetooth speaker. The dots connected like a lightning bolt to a metal rod.

The man who had taken her to dinner, sitting right inside the screen door on the leather sofa, strumming a guitar, *was* Grant Hawkins, the famous musician.

Why had he lied? To keep his identity hidden, why else? But he had to know people would recognize him. Though she hadn't until now. She had sat across from him during dinner, laughing with him and asking about his wife, and she did not know who she was sitting with. "Pretty pathetic, Kass," she said under her breath.

But now she understood his reaction when she asked about being married. Grant Hawkins' wife was on that bus with him, and she didn't make it. He must feel responsible.

Add to that he also lost his brother around the same time. No wonder he wanted to hide from the world. Anyone would understand his need to be left alone until he could heal. Or maybe the fans didn't understand. Maybe they wanted him to come back for them.

She wouldn't dare ask him to give himself over like that. The man deserved his privacy. If he didn't want to be found out, then she would go on pretending she didn't know. His real name didn't matter to her. And even if she had developed a huge crush on him in no time at all, he wasn't going to stay in town. He wasn't in any shape to have a relationship, if he couldn't come clean with who he was.

She would have to do the only thing she could.

Walk away.

Chapter Fourteen

Something moved on the front porch. Grant put the guitar down to check. Maybe Kate was back with another cake. He could use the sugar distraction about now.

He opened the front door to the empty porch. The sun was still in the backyard at this time of morning, casting long shadows on the sidewalk. A petite woman with curly hair hurried away from his place. Not Kate.

"Damn it." He fisted his hands at his side. Kassidy must have heard him playing. He had all the windows and the storm door open. He never imagined she'd show up here. Not after how their date ended. He had shut down after her question about being married. The night had been going so well up until he mentioned Emmet, and when she has asked about how his marriage ended, for a brief second he didn't want to be a widower still in mourning. He just wanted to be a man on a date with a beautiful woman who made him feel things he hadn't felt —ever.

"Kassidy, wait." He would face the fact he had lied about his identity like a man. If she fired him, so be it. He had been avoiding her all week, but her absence drove him crazy. He had wondered what she was doing and who she was doing it with. He wanted to know how things at The Blue Dot were working out. He wanted her smiling at him.

He stepped onto the sidewalk in his bare feet. The cement was still cool and a little damp from his neighbor Joe watering his patch of land this morning. That had taken about all of five minutes.

She stopped but didn't turn. He held his breath for what seemed like an eternity. Finally, she looked at him. Her face wore a stone mask.

"What are you doing out here?" Levi appeared on the porch in his basketball shorts and nothing else. His hair was still wet from the shower.

"Get inside."

"Are we in trouble?" Levi stayed on the porch. "Ah. She found you out, didn't she? Good morning, Miss Kassidy. Lovely day, isn't it?" Levi waved.

Kassidy offered a small wave in return. His insides burned. "Stop acting like the fool you are and get inside. I'll handle this."

Levi sputtered out a laugh, but at least he went back in the house. Grant took the first step toward Kassidy. She didn't tell him to go away or stop. He took that as a good sign and closed the space between them.

"You were just on the porch." It wasn't a question, and he wouldn't insult her with one.

"You aren't wearing any shoes." She still didn't smile, but her sass, as if it mattered that he had on shoes or not, made his insides warm. Maybe she wasn't as mad as he thought.

"No, ma'am. I wanted to catch you before you flew away down the street."

"Let's get something straight, mister. You can turn off that Southern charm. It won't do you any good. You lied to me." She took a deep breath. "I can understand why. Your life is your business, and you haven't done anything wrong, but I still don't like it."

"If you know who I am, then you must know why I don't advertise my existence." And why he didn't want to talk about his wife on their date.

"The news said you wanted out of the music business."

"That's true. Could I make you a cup of coffee? I don't want to have this conversation on the sidewalk. Peering eyes and all." He wanted to take her inside and make her understand what drove him to be a recluse. He didn't want her to look at him as if he couldn't be trusted.

"You don't have to explain yourself to me. I'll keep your secret if that's what you're worried about." She brushed her hair away from her face.

"It's nothing personal, Kassidy. Other than my name and the omission of my music career, everything else about me is true. I just don't want to be asked all the questions that come with knowing who I am. I hope you can understand."

"I thought... never mind what I thought. It's stupid. I'll let you get back to whatever it was you were doing." She started to turn away. He couldn't let her go.

"Why did you come by? Did you need something? Is everything okay at The Blue Dot?" Or did she miss him as much as he had missed her?

She worked her bottom lip under her teeth, making it red and swollen. He bit back a groan and tore his gaze away.

"I shouldn't have bothered you with my problems," she said.

"You're not bothering me." He closed the space between them because he couldn't stand not being closer. "I want to hear what's on your mind."

She let out a hefty exhale. "Nothing is okay. My sister brought a real estate agent by this morning. I got so upset I took off and walked here. I didn't know where else to go."

There must be a hundred other places she could go, but she came to him. He squeezed her shoulder, wanting to pull her into a hug, but didn't. She looked up at him with wide eyes, moist with her frustration. He pushed reason and discretion aside and wrapped his arms around her. She came willingly into his embrace.

Her arms tightened around his waist as she pressed her cheek against his chest. Her breath warmed the skin under his shirt. She smelled like sunshine and fresh air.

He could stay like that all day if she wanted. To hell with the prying eyes.

"Thank you. I kind of needed the hug. It's been a while since a man held me."

"I'm sorry to hear that. Any man would be lucky to be your shoulder to lean on."

She eased out of the embrace enough to look up at him. Her eyebrows furrowed. "Is that a line from one of your songs?"

She could pull the laughter right from his gut. "No, ma'am, but it could be if you'd like." And it would be too. It would work in the piece he'd been toying with earlier this morning before she caught him. He had been struggling to get words down and switched to playing his old songs, hoping they would set something loose. They hadn't, but she had.

With some regret, he steadied her on her feet. He had spent enough time on the sidewalk in clear view of the other tents. "How about that coffee?"

"I should probably go over to my dad's place and clear through the clutter. Maren should've brought the real estate agent there instead, then I would have understood."

"I guess you haven't found a way to buy them out yet."

"I'm still looking. I could probably get enough money for my house to pay off my mortgage and make a down payment to them, but then where would I live?"

"Come inside. We can talk. You'd be doing my bare

feet a favor and saving them from the sand and rocks poking at them."

Her hand flew up to her mouth, and she covered a laugh. "I'm so sorry. I didn't realize how sandy the cement was. Okay, coffee would be great."

He placed his hand on the small of her back as he guided her to the porch. She didn't flinch or move away. She even allowed him to hold the door for her. She could hold the door herself, didn't need him to do it, but his momma raised him to be a gentleman first and that meant holding doors for women and standing when one walked into the room. And never assuming she needed him, but hoping she might want him.

"How are you liking the tent?" She turned in a small circle, taking in the place. "I love it in here. I wish I could spend the summer here myself."

Levi returned from the bedroom area fully dressed now. "Howdy. I'm taking a long drive, but I'll be back tonight. Don't do anything I wouldn't do, y'all."

He smacked Levi upside his head.

"Ouch. Whatcha do that for?"

Kassidy burst out a laugh like musical notes. "Bye, Levi," she said.

"Don't mind him." The screen door slapped shut on Levi's exit. Grant busied himself making coffee. He had no idea where Levi was headed. As long as it didn't involve him having to write any more songs, he didn't care.

"I always wanted a brother." She slid into the chair at the small kitchen table. She fit in that space. He could see her living here. He stopped with his hand over the coffee. Could he see her living in the tent or something else? Something was changing in him. Every time she smiled at him, it was like gasoline on his heart.

"You can have mine. Levi can be a real pain in the butt sometimes." He no longer regretted having Levi convince him to stay in Serenity by the Sea. Even if he didn't come up with any songs worthy of an album, he had met a smart and beautiful woman and she had taken his mind off his worries for a second.

"I'll swap you Levi for Maren."

"A sister might be nice. Are you certain she wants to sell?"

"She brought the real estate agent in to give us an estimate of the value of the building and the land. Sounds like selling to me. I had plans for that land." She pulled a piece of sea glass out of her pocket and worked it between her fingers.

"That doesn't mean she's convinced to sell. She could be weighing her options. How do you take your coffee?" He pulled milk from the fridge. He didn't remember seeing her drink that healthy stuff at The Dot when they worked together. She did offer it to the customers, which was smart.

"It doesn't mean she wants to keep it either. Black is fine."

"If you could walk away with a huge amount of money from The Dot, would you do it? You know. Crazy money." He brought over the mugs and joined her at the table built for two. The space was small and his long legs bumped hers. She blushed and focused on her coffee.

This was better than their date at the beach. He had wanted to impress her with the setup and the help from Mr. D. He might have done it too, until he clammed up. This was natural and easy, as if they had coffee together every morning with their legs bumping into each other.

"I don't want to lose this tavern. It's all I have left of my dad and it's my last chance to make something of myself." She glanced at him over the mug.

The tent heated up either from the coffee, the morning sun, or simply his interest in the pretty lady opposite him. "I can understand wanting something of your dad's, but if the debt is too large, you'd only be hurting yourself."

"I know I'm taking a big risk with The Dot. But I know in my heart, I can make her better. I wasn't aware of all the debt my dad had accumulated. That wasn't part of my plan. That one threw me for a loop. Maybe it's crazy to try and hang on so tightly to something."

He understood that too. He'd been hanging on to the past with both hands for a long time. It was wearing him out now. He missed making music and the way he felt when he did, as if he were flying that moment a lyric or a melody came together. And he liked the ease in his chest when he spent time with Kassidy.

"I'm not the person to give advice about walking away. I walked away from my career and nearly killed Levi's career too. That's why we're here. He wants me to write three songs I owe the record label. He thought the ocean would inspire me."

"Does it?" She sipped her coffee. "Ooh. Hot." She stuck her tongue out. He stifled a laugh.

"Sort of." He didn't want to scare her by saying she was as much of an inspiration as the ocean was. More, actually.

She was doing things to him, waking him up for the first time, but his grief for Noel tangled his insides.

He would leave town after the songs were done. Kassidy would dig her feet in the sand and stay put because she belonged here.

"Do you want to get some air?" He pushed away from the table.

"Sure." She followed him onto the porch. She took a seat on the rocker, but he stood a safe distance from her.

"Can I ask why you gave up your music career? The real reason."

He wasn't ready to tell that whole story out loud just yet. He and Noel had fought the whole day. She wanted a divorce because she was in love with someone else. She had picked five minutes before rehearsal to tell him. His playing had been off the entire night because he couldn't get thoughts of her with another man out of his head. Levi had plowed into him about his bad playing as soon as the last song was over.

Foolishly, he had believed driving straight through to the next stop on the tour would be the way to calm down. Anger had taken up residence in his soul. He had wanted to be free from both of them, away from the pain in his chest because he had missed Emmet's call only two months before. And right after Emmet's death, he had wanted to cancel the tour, but Levi wouldn't do it. So, if he could just get to the next town and play that last venue, he could be free.

"Sometimes life gets in the way of our plans." He wasn't sure that was a complete answer, but it was a part of the truth. He had planned on an entirely different life, touring and making music with his wife and his band. One bad decision changed all that.

"You can say that again. I had planned on owning The Dot outright. I assumed my father would leave the place to me. By leaving it to all three of us, everything I had hoped for fell on its head. I wasn't planning on buying them out or the amount of debt my dad left behind." She pushed the rocker with her toe. The chains creaked with each back and forth.

"I can see you love that place, but sometimes it's easier to cut your losses and move on." But he hadn't moved on, and he had cut out everything, even the thing he loved. He thought he owed giving up music to those who hadn't made it. He believed his muse died that night too. He stood there and told Kassidy to cut her losses, but he had, and it hadn't fixed a damn thing.

"I can't give up The Dot. We're selling my dad's house because it's not practical to keep, but I can't end up with nothing but a bunch of junk he stored away for years." She turned away from him, gripping the mug against her chest.

"I don't understand."

"My dad kept things. Kept everything he ever came across and then some." She let out a deep gusty breath. "The place is a disaster. It will take weeks to go through, and after I do, there won't be anything worth keeping. And the worst part is, I don't want to do it alone, but I may have to. Bailey might stay, but Maren is determined to go home."

He sat beside her and eased the mug out of her hands so he could hold them. Her skin was cold against his. "You think Maren doesn't want to be a part of what you're doing. Why doesn't she want to help pack up your dad's house? That seems like a simple request."

"I wish it were just a simple ask. For Maren, sifting through all that clutter drags up too many sad memories of the past. She doesn't like being in Serenity, and that's all she cares about, staying away. My feelings don't factor in. She completely disregards me."

"Disregards. Big word."

"I like big words. They don't fit in your songs?" She sassed him with her smile and the arch of her brow. She shifted closer to him, keeping her hands in his.

"Big words don't fit in my mouth. I'm just a simple Southern boy. Listen, Kassidy, you're going to have to face Maren again and make her understand that you need more time, and even though she brought in the agent, you're not ready yet. You can't keep running away from her. But I don't mind you running straight to me." Even though he should take his own advice and stop running from his past, the idea that she came looking for him flipped his stomach on its head.

She stood up and paced the porch like a bird flapping from branch to branch. He missed the weight of her next to him but wouldn't reach for her, trying to cage her against him. He sat back and took her in, instead.

"I'm not running away from her. Once she has her mind made up, she doesn't want to change it. She always thinks she's the smartest person in the room. She can be impossible sometimes. And unless I show up with a check for her portion by the end of the week, she'll just keep doing whatever she wants, because that's what Maren does. All the time. I shouldn't say this out loud, but it's exactly why Dave is divorcing her."

"Kassidy, you're running. Even now you're practically tearing up the porch with your pacing. Take a deep breath."

She halted and glared at him. "Take a deep breath? You want me to take a deep breath as if that will fix my life? Do you have any idea that I have been chasing my dreams and instead of reaching them, they just get farther and farther away? I didn't have a lot growing up. I believed that success would be a corporate career that made me money. When I couldn't make that happen, I came home, ashamed. I'm a bartender in my father's bar. I'm too old to start over. I've already lost everything once. It was taken from me. You had a career that other people dream about. You called all the shots. If I had had that, I wouldn't have thrown it away."

The air went out of his lungs. He hadn't thrown his career away. It had been snatched from him. If he could go back, he would do it all differently and still be living his dream. She didn't understand.

"I should go," she said.

He nodded because the words were out of reach. She hurried off the porch and he wanted her back, wanted her to understand him, help him forgive himself.

He fought to find his voice with each step she took away from him. "I stopped playing music because I couldn't give my fans what they needed anymore."

She turned to face him. "I hate to tell you this, but you didn't stop playing music for them. That's a cop-out. You stopped playing music for you."

She had said too much and wished the sidewalk would swallow her up. She had allowed her bad mood to get the best of her, and her mouth had opened and spilled ugly words right at his bare feet. He had nice feet, and she wasn't a foot person. She preferred legs and back-sides. And good arms. And boy, did Grant have good arms.

She shook her head. She had just insulted the man and now she was ogling him like a horny teenager while he stood there on his porch with hurt in his eyes. What was the matter with her? And she didn't even care all that much that he had lied. At first, she was spitting mad, especially because of their date. He had had plenty of chances to tell her who he was then. But this morning, when he had called her name, and worry darkened his chiseled face, her heart gave up. She understood—to a point.

"I'm sorry. I shouldn't have said that you stopped playing music to save yourself." She was a hypocrite. She had lied to her sisters to save herself.

"No, you shouldn't have." He turned his back on her which stung as much as a slap.

"But it's true." She should quit saying what was on her mind. Hadn't Maren told her to be less herself?

"You don't know me, Kassidy. You don't know why I stopped playing." He faced her. His eyes darkened, and his jaw twitched.

"You didn't just stop, Grant. You're hiding. I used to follow your career. I'm going to sound like a crazy groupie or something, but I did. I liked some of your music. And you were always so great in interviews. You did all that charity work for kids. You weren't like those other artists who tweeted about the tough day they had from their private planes. My heart broke for you when that bus accident happened." She hadn't expected to be affected by an accident that had nothing to do with her, but he had seemed like a genuinely nice guy, and anyone with half a heart would be devastated over the loss of loved ones. She would never have been able to forgive herself if she had caused an accident that took Maren or Bailey or Peyton.

"Stop. Don't make me sound like some do-gooder who caught a bad break. I was driving that bus." His voice rattled with anger. He wiped his hands over his face. "I don't want to talk about it."

"Maybe you should." She shouldn't poke at him, but he was missing out on the joy he brought the people who listened to his music. He had a gift he should be honoring.

"No. Not to you. Not to anyone. I made my choices. I'm not interested in being out in public anymore. I don't write music anymore. I don't sing. I just wish everyone would finally get on board with me."

"I heard you singing when I walked up. You sounded amazing. I thought it was the record, but it was you." He had the kind of deep, rugged voice that could shake her soul.

"That's not the same thing. I won't get back onstage." He regarded her with narrow eyes. "Did Levi put you up to this?"

"What? No. Except for today, I haven't spoken to Levi since the day he brought the groceries to The Dot. How could you think I'd go behind your back?" She would never help Levi force Grant onstage, but he didn't seem to know that. And how could he? It wasn't as if they'd spoken about his past life before this moment. Somehow Levi had betrayed him or duped him in the past. For all their problems, neither of her sisters had done that to her. No, she was the culprit in hiding the truth. But it was for far different reasons than what Grant was doing. She wanted her sisters with her, and without the lie, they would leave her. Grant lied to run away.

His hands clenched and unclenched at his sides. "I'm sorry. Of course, you wouldn't side with Levi." The apology was a little too little. And she didn't know why.

Maybe because Grant's attitude held a mirror up to hers and she didn't like what she saw.

"I didn't come here to argue with you too. Thanks for the coffee. I'll see you tomorrow for the breakfast shift?"

He stared at her. "I'll be there tomorrow. But you'd better find a replacement for me for Saturday and every day after."

Tears burned the back of her throat. She hadn't meant for this whole conversation to spiral out of control. She wanted to go back to the moment where he gathered her in his arms. His embrace made her worries dwindle. For a second, things seemed like they might work out. Now she was losing more than her cook. She liked him, but he wasn't ready to move forward. She couldn't get involved with that. She had enough of her own problems.

Problems that needed tending to. She left without another word. She wanted to look back to see if he was watching her, but she forced her head to stay high and her shoulders straight.

The slapping of the screen door echoed behind her. Nothing but silence filled the air. Not one note of music floated in the breeze.

Chapter Fifteen

Kassidy poured a glass of wine and sank back in the chaise lounge. The moonless sky stretched and yawned above her. Thick, wet humidity covered the night air like molasses. Building a fire in the heat was a bad idea, but she didn't care. The dance of the flames lulled her into a calm she hadn't experienced all day. She needed any trick she could give herself to ease away the stress.

The fight with Maren had scorched her insides and left her spent. She had avoided Maren's texts and calls all day because she didn't know what to say. Maren's attempt at research still hurt.

Peyton had shown up to host for the dinner shift with a handwritten note from Maren, but she had only tossed it in the garbage. She couldn't continue to avoid her sister. Especially not in the small house they were sharing. Grant had been right about that. She just wasn't ready to come to terms with the idea they would have to sell.

For a Thursday night, the dinner crowd had been pathetic. She had to send Peyton and two waitresses home. The beach was crowded during the day, but the customers weren't coming to the old, worn-out Dot. On her way home, the line for 32 Below went down the street and around the corner. A long line gathered for miniature golf, but those people weren't opting for her place to eat either. Maren might be right and that drove her mad.

She had so many great ideas to change the place around. Ideas that would never be seen because no matter what Maren said about redecorating or expanding, deep down she wanted to sell.

"Look what I have." Bailey held up a tray with all the makings for s'mores.

"Bailey, I can't have a gooey dessert every night. I'll look like a beach ball soon." But the idea of eating an entire chocolate bar appealed to her stress level. Chocolate could cure just about any problem.

"You're being silly. Tonight, I have dark chocolate. That's healthy for you. The graham crackers are low fat, and one marshmallow never hurt anything. I figured you could use some comfort food. Maren told me what happened today." Bailey set the tray down on the small glass table by the fire pit.

"I don't want to talk about it." She sounded as petulant as Grant had earlier today.

"You're going to have to some time." Bailey handed her a stick with a big, fat marshmallow on the end. And now Bailey sounded like Grant. She stifled a groan. She needed to get Grant out of the front of her mind. They would never make it as a couple. They both had too many obstacles getting in their way.

"I want to keep The Dot. I won't change my mind." She took the stick and the marshmallow anyway. She'd have to take a longer walk in the morning. She could call her mother and ask her to lend her the money. She didn't want to do that; in fact, it killed her to even admit she was failing to the woman who wasn't interested in her life. But she was out of options.

"Something will work out," Bailey said.

"We can get a lot of money for the building." Maren plopped down beside Bailey and swiped a bar of chocolate. "Why didn't you return any of my calls?" Maren's gaze held hers like a magnet. She fought the urge to look away but lost the battle.

She swung her feet over the side of the chair and walked to the edge of the patio. "Why did you bring Charlotte Munroe to the tavern?" Having this conversation with her back to Maren eased some of the discomfort from her chest.

"We need to know what we're dealing with. All possible solutions. Not just the option to keep the place. If an outside buyer can spend more than you can afford to buy us out, we have to consider it. The Dot has too much debt not to think about alternatives," Maren said around bites of candy.

"I don't care about another buyer. She's my business." She should have been. The foolish tears returned. She swallowed them back. Success didn't have to be defined by money or a long climb up the corporate ladder. She could change her definition of success to having repeat customers or being liked by the people of this town. Her shoulders sagged. All of that sounded good in theory, but deep down in her gut she believed if she couldn't keep The Dot, then all her hard work behind that bar and in that kitchen had been for nothing.

"Kass, I know how much the place means to you. But be rational. Do you really want to take on all of Dad's problems? Look at the house we're dealing with. And what if you have another Hurricane Sandy? Would you even be able to survive that much loss a second time?" Maren placed a cool hand on her shoulder. She shrugged her off and returned to the fire pit, shoving her marshmallow in the flames.

Hurricane Sandy had swept over the Jersey Shore and demolished her. Blew most shore towns to pieces, knocking over buildings and homes as if they were pieces of a board game. Everything had been sucked up by the ocean, including cars and roller coasters. The shore had been devastated, and some places had never recovered. The Blue Dot had been lucky. The dunes and the beachfront had taken the brunt of the disaster.

"Hurricane Sandy isn't going to come around again in our lifetime." She had been the rare occurrence of three storms coming together and landing in South Jersey. Maren was worrying about nothing. Or coming up with excuses to prove her point.

"Now you're a meteorologist." Maren threw her hand in the air.

"What did Charlotte say?" Bailey pressed her marshmallow between two graham crackers.

"Now you're on her side?" She couldn't stop herself from arguing. She was helpless to fix her situation. She had always relied on herself to solve her own problems. Even when she had come home after she and Bear had broken up, she had refused her father's offer of a job right away. But she had needed the money, and he had needed the help, so it had been a win for both of them in the end.

"I'm not on sides. I have my own opinions on this whole subject. Not that either of you ever ask me. You still treat me like the little sister who is really an outsider. We happen to have the same dad, but most days you forget we're sisters."

"How can we possibly forget? No one forgets a sibling. And even if I tried to forget I had two younger sisters who always tried to pull me in the direction they wanted to go, you remind us every chance you get that you've been left out. Except we didn't leave you out. If you're mad at someone, be mad at Dad. He was the one who had the affair." Maren stamped her foot. Her marshmallow fell in the fire.

A hush washed over them.

"You've gone too far, Maren," she said. Their father had never tried to hide the fact he had a child with another woman, and he didn't want either her or Maren to treat Bailey as if she wasn't part of the family, but they had excluded her because they were young too. She wasn't proud of that behavior. But Bailey didn't give up.

She was determined, with her wide eyes and set jaw, to make her older sisters love her.

Kassidy had fought with the guilt for eventually loving Bailey because her mother had been the reason Kassidy's mom left.

"I love you both, but I'm leaving. I want to be as far away from Serenity by the Sea as possible. Kass, I'm sorry I can't help you clean up Dad's house. And you don't need to buy me out. I'm giving you my portion of The Blue Dot. You'll make it great." Bailey's bottom lip trembled, but she squared her shoulders and stormed off, her wavy hair bouncing as she went.

"Don't go, Bailey. Please. We can talk it over." She lunged for Bailey, but she had made it to the door, slamming it behind her.

"I'm sorry," Maren said.

"You need to apologize to her. Not me. I'm used to you shooting off your mouth." She grabbed the stick and stuck another marshmallow on it. Tonight was a double s'mores night for sure.

"Let me tell you what Charlotte said." Maren sat beside her on the edge of the lounge.

"Fine." The arguing had worn her out. She would let Maren have her say, and then hopefully, she would go inside and leave her alone.

"We could get a lot of money for it. She knows a developer that would love to come in and build a small set of townhomes. The lot could hold about ten homes. State-of-the-art places that could be rented out all summer with ease. And the money that could come in from the summer rentals could pay the mortgages all year." Maren's face lit up as she spoke.

"What are you saying?"

"What if we sell? We could get enough money to pay off the debt and have some left over. Never mind what Bailey said about not wanting her share, we'd still give it to her, right?"

"Sure. Of course."

"I got to thinking. What if we bought one of those townhomes? The three of us. Together. Charlotte said she could get us a deal on a unit. Then we rent it out and make more money. It would be easier to deal with, less work than The Dot. And we could be landlords from anywhere. We don't have to live here to do it."

"What am I supposed to do for a job?" She couldn't start over again. Sure, she believed everyone was entitled to a few do-overs in their lives, but not her. She was supposed to get this right. She'd started over twice already. If she couldn't own The Dot, what the heck would she do? She wasn't qualified to do anything except mix drinks and wait tables. She took a huge bite out of the charred marshmallow and burned her tongue. Twice in one day. She had burned her tongue on Grant's bitter coffee earlier.

"I don't know. I'm faced with the same problem. I need a career now that Dave and I are over."

"Work at The Dot with me." If they both owned it, she wouldn't have to buy Maren out.

"The Blue Dot is never going to make enough money to get us out from under her. Everyone is going to want sleek and modern, Kass. Look at the restaurants on the boardwalk that are raking in the money."

Her heart broke. Maren was right. People wanted new and shiny. Technology and gadgets were what sold and enticed. She wasn't new and shiny anymore and neither was The Blue Dot. She couldn't afford to make it that way. No one wanted to come to a place that was old and tired. She was just too stubborn to admit defeat.

"Let me have a couple more weeks. I have an idea that is sure to bring in a crowd." What she was thinking wouldn't be fair, especially because she said she would not do this, but if Levi was the one pushing Grant to move forward and write again, then Levi might agree to convince Grant to play. It would be for his own good. He needed to move on, and so did she.

"Even if you could bring in more customers for the whole summer, what about the future?" Maren noted—always the practical one.

"What about nostalgia and sentimentality? Doesn't that count for anything?" Didn't connection and community weigh in?

"Those things don't pay the bills. I'm too old to start over. I have a teenager to worry about. College is around the corner."

"Dave will help with college." Dave might be a cheater, but he loved Peyton. "Come on, Maren. This is our chance to strike out. Haven't you always wanted something that was just yours?"

"Not The Dot. I never wanted The Dot. She took Dad away from us too much. Sometimes it felt like he loved that place and the customers more than us. I spent my teen years smelling like cooking grease. It hardly made the boys come running." Maren smirked.

"Then that's it. You're stuck on selling. Is that what you told Charlotte?" She pushed off the chaise and stood closer to the fire.

"I told her I needed to talk to you and Bailey." Maren stood beside her.

"Thank you for that much. You know, we could turn The Dot into something else. Something better." She had her teeth sunk in and couldn't let go. Just like Grant. They were more alike than she had realized.

"How are we going to do that? We don't have the money for major renovations."

"Did you look at my design ideas?"

"You are so stubborn, Kassidy. But not yet. I'm sorry. The day I said I would, I bumped into Charlotte at the beach. She put the bug in my head to sell. I could use that money. It would make me less dependent on Dave." Maren stared down at her hands and rubbed the spot where her wedding ring used to be.

"So would having your own business."

"But the business you're talking about could fail. Probably will fail." Maren kept her gaze on her hands.

"The money from the sale will run out. Then what will you do? You're the one who always talks about having a plan. You're the organizer. You won't feel any better when your bank account empties out if you don't have a way to take action. Yes, it's a risk, but The Dot has stood in that spot a long time. She's worth the risk." She could sense Maren's resolve faltering the way her head could tell when a summer storm rolled in. All she had to do was give Maren a tiny shove, and she would come around. She just couldn't allow Maren to know what she was doing. Maren was smart enough to pick up when reverse psychology was being used on her.

"I wish I had your confidence."

"Maybe it's just stubbornness like you said." She leaned into Maren with a playful push. "Because honestly, I'm scared out of my mind. Taking over The Dot and turning her into something special reminds me of all the sea glass I've collected."

"The trash from the ocean?" Maren narrowed her eyes.

"That's just it. Sea glass was once trash, but now it's beautiful, and it took a lot of hard work to get there. Sea glass is transformation. The Blue Dot needs transformation, and so do I." Her life had grown stagnant which was why she had nothing to show for herself except The Dot. If The Dot could shine again, then maybe she could too. And she could do it without a man beside her. She didn't need one like she thought she did last time when she followed Bear to Chicago.

"You're starting to sound like Bailey with her crystals and moonglow and those oils she puts in diffusers. And Peyton with her frames and mosaics she can't wait to sell."

"Maybe they're onto something. I don't know. I do know I have to try because if I can't make this work, then

I will have nothing too. At least you have Peyton. I don't even have a family of my own."

"You have me and Bailey and Peyton. We'll always be your family even if Bailey is mad at us." Maren squeezed her hand.

"We will always be family." But being family didn't make them close. It made them related. She was tired of being alone. Tired of facing every day by herself. Spending time with Grant reminded her of what she didn't have. Someone to love and to love her. Someone to come home to at the end of the day, someone she could wrap her arms around and breathe in his comforting scent. She didn't need a man to complete her. She wanted a man to share her life with. And she wanted her sisters too.

The kitchen window creaked open on rusty hinges. Bailey stuck her face near the screen. "Hey Kassidy, you have a visitor."

Chapter Sixteen

Kassidy came in through the kitchen, but Bailey was gone. The door to the middle bedroom was closed. She must be in there, still angry at her. No one was in the living room. She had no idea who could be visiting her at ten o'clock at night, but she hoped it was Grant. She hated how they had left things earlier. He had been right about her running away from facing Maren, and she would tell him so. She still wasn't ready to say anything to her sister. She would stick to the lie for now.

With no one in the house, she went out the front door and stopped short. Levi stood on the walk with his hands in his back pockets and facing the street. He turned at the creak of the screen door.

"Hi." His face lit up with a high-voltage smile. The same smile as Grant's with a slight curl to the upper lip. But on Levi something was missing. She couldn't put her finger on what it was, or maybe what was missing was Grant.

"What brings you by?" She forced her gaze to stay on Levi instead of looking down the street for a glimpse of Grant outside the tent. Had Grant sent him? Was he watching from the shadows? God, she hoped not. If Grant had something to say to her, she sure hoped he would be man enough to say it himself.

"I wanted to talk to you about something."

"Does Grant know you're here?" That wasn't asking about him exactly. And she couldn't figure out what Levi could possibly want to talk to her about anyway. They had barely spoken because their paths had hardly crossed this whole time. Still, her curiosity was piqued.

Levi stared at his shiny dress shoes. He was the opposite of Grant in so many ways. She no longer preferred the suit and tie look with polished lace-up shoes. She wanted the grittiness of worn-in work boots.

He lightly tapped at a weed coming up through the sidewalk crack with the toe of his shoe as if he were testing to see if the sidewalk would crumble right under him.

He looked up and held her gaze. "Grant and I spoke tonight. I'm going to come straight to the point, if that's okay."

"I appreciate that." Though the accelerated speed of her heart said differently.

"I want to buy The Blue Dot. Grant told me you're selling it."

She had never said she was selling. She thought

Grant understood how she felt about keeping her father's business. What it meant to her to continue to own it. Was he so mad at her for telling him he was a cop-out that he sent Levi here to cut her knees out from under her? He hadn't seemed like that kind of man, the opposite in fact.

"Um... well, we might sell it. We haven't completely decided yet." She would not entertain any offer from this man. He had no right to come here and try to take her dream away while she was vulnerable. Grant was using her pain against her to get back at her for hurting his feelings.

"I did a little quick research on the building and the land. I'm prepared to pay top dollar for it. I think it would make a great place for singers and songwriters to come to work out their new material. I'd like to bring a little rock and roll to the Jersey Shore." Anticipation crossed his face. He practically bounced on his toes as if he were a puppy waiting for a pat on the head. Well, she wasn't about to applaud his grand idea.

"Grant likes this idea?" She couldn't get her head around what was happening. A top-dollar offer would have to be considered. Her sisters would need to be told, and Maren would jump at it. But why Levi? And why now? Because she had spoken her mind too truthfully to Grant, and he must hate her for it.

"He does. In fact, the idea was his. He thinks a pub for musicians to work out their material would be a good direction to take my business. I agree. I've been waiting for the right opportunity to come along. You're it. Here's the offer." He pulled a folded piece of white paper from his dress-shirt pocket. "I'm prepared to move on it right away, if you agree."

She sat down on the top porch step and stared at the number. Buying The Blue Dot was Grant's idea. She had completely misunderstood him. What else was new? She had been misunderstanding men most of her life. She hadn't understood Bear and his ambitions. She had believed he actually loved her for her. She hadn't understood what drove her father to hoard things. She thought Grant actually cared for her, but it had been some kind of an act. To what end? Had he been planning to buy The Dot out from under her since the day Charlie quit?

The paper creased in her sweaty hand. Levi could solve all the debt problems in one quick motion. She pulled her knees in close to her chest. A mosquito bit her leg. That would become a big red welt and itch tomorrow.

With Levi's offer, they wouldn't have to wait for some developer to come along. She could send Maren on her way home. Her sisters could have what they wanted, and she would be left alone with no business and no family.

"Kassidy, what do you say?" Levi's voice dragged her away from her worries and right back to the humid night filled with bugs and disappointment.

"I'd have to talk to my sisters about this. Can I have a week? We have a lot going on right now." She needed time to digest what this actually meant. Without The Dot, she had nothing. What would she do? Who would she be? Would it even make sense to remain in Serenity by the Sea? One piece of paper with some pen scratchings on it had the power to destroy her life like a shipwreck.

"Sure. But you'll let me know if another buyer comes along. I want the chance to outbid them." Levi seemed so sure of himself, as if he was used to getting his way. Grant wasn't pushy. He was gentle and subtle, not wanting to be noticed. So, how could he send his brother here to derail her?

"There are no other buyers at the moment." And there wouldn't be if she had anything to say about it. Maybe she shouldn't have told him about no other buyers. Maybe Maren would want to negotiate an even better offer from Levi. But Kassidy didn't care about negotiations. She didn't want to let The Blue Dot slip through her fingers like the sand. She wanted to renew her. Make her beautiful in a new way. Like sea glass.

"Take my number. I'd like to keep the dealings between us. Grant needs to stay focused on writing songs. I don't want him distracted by this, okay?" He handed her a business card. Levi Hawkins, Business Manager was printed in silver block letters against a shiny black background. Sleek. Shiny. New. Everything The Blue Dot and she were not.

She had no intentions of talking to Grant about this offer or anything else for that matter. He had deceived her, and she had played the fool. He had probably even faked the date to butter her up for Levi's appearance here tonight. He might not even be writing any songs. For all she knew, they had been scouting the place, waiting to pounce.

"Yeah, sure. Whatever you say." She stood and pocketed the card.

"I'll be in touch. Good night, Kassidy." He turned before she answered and slipped into the darkness as if he'd never been there.

For her, he never had.

She went back inside. The house was quiet. The backyard was empty except for the burning embers of the fire pit. Maren had cleaned up their s'mores and probably gone to bed. She hesitated outside Maren's door with her hand poised to knock. Levi's offer could wait until morning. She left without saying a word and went into her room and closed the door.

Her room was about the same size as the front room but had the better closet. She supposed it might have been considered the main bedroom back when the house was built because of the closet and the proximity to the only bathroom in the house.

She flopped on the bed and stared at her phone. She had a call to make. She didn't want to do this, but she was out of options. She couldn't let Levi take her tavern and upturn her entire life. She couldn't allow Maren to sell. Maren would leave and go back to the life she built on the other side of the state. Maren had lots of friends and volunteered for different groups. She was settled. Kassidy could understand wanting to return to what felt comfortable. But she would have to totally start over. She didn't want that. Not alone and not again.

Her heart ached at what Grant did to her. She had finally allowed someone to nudge open the armor around her heart, only to have it broken into pieces. And they hadn't even kissed yet. She would not wonder what his lips might feel like.

Instead, she searched her contacts for the one person she tried to avoid and hit call. The phone rang without end on the other side. It was late. The call would go to voicemail at this hour.

"Hello? Kassidy? Is that you?" The voice, familiar and strange at the same time, came across the line in a breathless exhalation.

"Hi, Mom." One thing she would say for her mother, she understood how to use a cell phone. Still, she braced herself for her mother's reaction to this unusual communication.

"Do you know what time it is? You scared me half to death calling at this hour. I thought it was the hospital saying someone was dead. Is it Maren? Or Peyton? Are they okay?"

Not—*was she okay*. Her mother always assumed the worst when it came to Maren or Peyton. Her mother's fear of losing either one of them was palpable. And it only managed to turn her stomach sour, not because she didn't love her sister and her niece. But because her mother loved Maren more and in turn that included Peyton. She often wondered if she had had a child, would her mother love that child as much. Families were not perfect, especially not hers.

"No one is in the hospital." And even if they were, her mother would be the very last phone call she'd place.

The woman panicked first and asked questions later. "I have something I wanted to ask you."

"Oh. Well, it must be important if you're calling this late." Rustling went on in the background as if her mother was moving around. Probably pouring a glass of wine to help her get through a conversation with her youngest child.

"It is." She closed her eyes and took a deep breath. Once she said it, there would be no going back. "I was wondering if I could borrow some money." The words tasted like dirt in her mouth.

"For what?"

"I want to buy The Blue Dot from Maren and Bailey." *Here it comes.*

"Joe left that piece of junk bar to all three of you?" Her mother hacked out a laugh. "Of course he did because he never paid attention to what was going on right under his nose. You've worked there for what, fifteen years, most of your adult life, and he leaves the bar to Maren who is, let's say, above it and to that flighty one who can barely tie her own shoes."

She didn't want to dissect her mother's comment, but she had worked at The Dot for ten years since she'd been back. And the *above it* statement translated to Maren was too good for the tavern. Maren was too good for most things. "Bailey is not a flake."

"Whatever. Why do you want this place so badly? Wouldn't it be better for you to work at something other than pouring drinks? You spent all that time going to college. Why don't you use that degree?"

"Mom, I don't want to have this conversation again. Can you lend me the money or not?" Her mother had found fault with all her decisions. She had argued going to Chicago with Bear was a bad idea. She had been right, but that wasn't the point. Her mother had turned her nose up at Kassidy's choice of college degree and her decision to go to school part-time so she could continue to work. When Kassidy had a job in an office, her mother thought that was a bad idea, and when she went back to bartending, her mother had scoffed at that too.

"I'm sorry. I just think you were destined for more. Just like Bear thought about you. I always liked him."

Her mother had never said so much as one word about liking Bear. "Mom, Bear did not think I was going to do great things. And he's been out of my life for ten years. Can you please move on from that?"

"Are you seeing someone new?"

Her mother did not understand her life choices and no matter how hard she tried to explain them, her mother remained unconvinced that she could be happy in a bar without a man. For a New York second, she entertained the idea that Grant might offer her some company. That had been a huge mistake that led her to asking her mother for money. Because if she hadn't fallen for Grant, she wouldn't be so affected by his betrayal. Affairs of the heart were nothing but trouble.

"I don't have time for a relationship right now. What do you say? Will you lend it to me? I promise to pay it back with interest if you want."

She made a tsk sound. "Where would I get the kind

of money you need to buy out your sister and that other one? That would be tens of thousands. I can barely make the rent."

"You have plenty of money." Maren had told her how much their mother had squirreled away. Maren was her mother's executor if anything should happen to her. Maren had been to the bank, the lawyer, and the safe deposit box with their mother. Mom was loaded thanks to smart investing and a rich third husband who passed away while they were still married, leaving her mother three-quarters of his estate.

"Kassidy, I'm in my golden years. I don't have the earning potential anymore. I have to live off my savings, which isn't much. And if I end up needing a home health care aide or God forbid a nursing home, I want my money to be used for that. You'll have to figure something else out. I'm sorry."

Her mother always complained she didn't have enough money. She had been doing that for as long as Kassidy could remember. She shouldn't be surprised by her mother's rejection, but it still cut deep. She kept waiting for the moment her mother threw open her arms and said she would do anything for Kassidy, no matter the cost. That day never came. To her mother, she was practically nonexistent.

"We're clearing out Dad's house. Is there a chance anything of yours is still there?"

"I doubt it, but if you come across anything, throw it out. I don't want any memories from my time with your father. Okay, honey, I have to go now. Say hello to Maren and Peyton for me. Bye." Her mother hung up without waiting for an answer.

Kassidy sank back into the pillows and made one more call. Maren would kill her when she found out, but she had to put a stop to this runaway train.

This time the call went to voicemail. She left a message. "Hello, Charlotte. This is Kassidy Russo. I wanted to let you know we no longer need your services to sell The Blue Dot. Thank you for coming by today. Good night."

Chapter Seventeen

Kassidy had nothing to lose because she had lost it all. She had no way to buy The Blue Dot from her sisters. Her career was over. She had lost Grant because he wanted to take her dream away from her so his brother could create a bar for singers and songwriters. Levi hadn't even offered her a job. She may even lose her home because without a job she couldn't pay her bills.

She was feeling sorry for herself. Well, she was entitled to a little self-pity.

The Friday dinner rush at The Dot was underway. Fridays were their best nights with the biggest crowds when they had a crowd. She had a full staff tonight so she worked the bar, the place she enjoyed being the most. Way more than the kitchen. She mixed drinks and laughed with customers. Kate and Howie from down the street were at the bar, drinking martinis and making friends with the tourists.

When Kassidy was behind the bar, everything made sense to her. She had a purpose. She brought joy to people for a few hours—especially Kate since she was on drink number three. Kassidy listened to their stories, laughed at their jokes, and gave them a shoulder to lean on when things went sour.

The Dot even had a local band playing tonight, the Body Stuffers. They played alternative music, and they were loud. She wanted to bring back live music for a long time now, but her dad always argued with her. He thought families wanted to be able to talk during dinner. She wanted a younger crowd to come in after dinner who would want drinks and spend more money. Money they had desperately needed.

She would enjoy whatever time she had left here. Once she told her sisters about Levi's offer, the place would change hands. All her employees might be out of work, and nothing would be the same. She might have been mad Levi hadn't offered her a job to stay on, but she would never stay here if she couldn't own it.

Levi had texted her three times today, asking if she had an answer ready. She had avoided him, unable to face her reality. She didn't know how much longer she could hold him off.

"Hey, Kass, there's someone here to see you." Bailey stuck her head out of the kitchen doors and yelled to be heard. Bailey had calmed down after their fight the other night and decided to stay in town until the end of the summer. She could handle her clients over the computer or phone. She had sublet her apartment in

Hoboken to a friend. But Bailey hadn't made any promises after that.

"Now? And who is it? I'm kind of busy." She shook the metal drink mixer and poured the Cosmo into a glass.

"I'll watch the bar." Bailey gripped her by the shoulders and directed her to the doors. "Go. You'll be glad you did."

She couldn't imagine who this visitor was and why she would be glad. At least it wasn't Levi because she doubted Bailey would be so calm and helpful if she found out about the offer and that Kassidy had kept it secret all week.

The kitchen bustled with the usual activity but was decibels quieter than the dining area. Kiri and Steve manned the griddle and the oven. They were the best cooks around. Steve had been Charlie's replacement and was working out well. Teri washed the dishes and stacked the plates for the next orders. The waitstaff hustled in and out. Her insides hummed because of the efficiency around her.

"Kassidy." The voice came from the office area.

Her heart stuck in her throat. She must be seeing things. "Grant, what are you doing here?"

He looked great in a fitted t-shirt and faded jeans. He had on the scuffed work boots that only made him sexier. He wore his cap backward. A week ago, she would've run into his arms.

"Can we talk a second?" At least he had the decency to look contrite.

"I have a restaurant full of people. Can this wait until

later?" It didn't matter how handsome he was with his Southern charm. He had still sabotaged all she had worked for. Now he stood in her kitchen, asking for her time. She almost couldn't believe it. The band ended their song, but the ringing in her ears continued.

"It's important. I don't have a lot of time."

"Yeah, well, neither do I." She turned on her heel and went back to the bar. If he had something to say, he could damn well say it while she worked.

He followed and took her elbow. "I don't want anyone to overhear us." He leaned in near her ear. His warm breath sent shivers over her skin.

She motioned for him to follow her to the end of the bar, closer to the stage where the seats were empty and they could have some privacy. She had to lean in to be heard too, and the smell of his soap or cologne invaded her attempt to stay distant. "Just say what you have to say."

His shoulders sagged. "I came to apologize for the fight we had."

"That's it?" She had hoped he might mention his deception, but that must be asking too much.

"That's not enough?" His eyebrows shot to the edge of his cap.

"How dare you come here as if nothing has happened between us except some stupid fight. I don't care about that. What I do care about is how you told your brother about my money problems and suggested he buy the bar from me." She lowered her voice so Bailey, still at the bar handing out drinks, didn't accidentally hear her. Though she was pretty sure Bailey snuck sideways glances in their direction. The questions would come as soon as Grant walked away.

Grant's face twisted in confusion. "My brother Levi?"

"Do you have another brother in town?" She slapped a hand over her mouth at her indiscretion. "I'm sorry. I shouldn't have said that."

He arched a brow. "Well, no, you shouldn't have. What are you talking about? I haven't spoken to Levi about you."

"Don't treat me like I'm stupid." The least he could do was be honest with her. Denying the truth only hurt worse.

A band member brought his guitar to life with a loud riff. One of the other guys in the band tapped the microphone for a sound check. Music would begin again, making it impossible to have this conversation inside the tavern. She would be forced to go into her office or outside with Grant, and she didn't trust herself not to cave if she wasn't surrounded by people.

"Kassidy, I never suggested anything to Levi about this bar. I would never reveal something you told me in confidence."

"Ladies and gentlemen, we want to thank you all again for coming out tonight to hear us play. We've got one more set lined up for you, but first, there's something I have to do because I can't believe my good luck tonight. One of my heroes is in the audience. Put your hands together for the one and only Grant Hawkins."

The drummer rattled off a few beats, and the guitarist tapped out a celebration on his strings. A hush fell over the room, but like fireworks, after a long pause, the customers burst into applause. Her stomach dropped as the color drained from Grant's face. He swayed on his feet as if punched in the jaw.

If he fell over, she would blame herself. Not a week ago she had considered doing this very thing to him. The pain on his face was tangible. He wanted to be left alone, and no one—not her or even Levi—would honor that.

"Grant, man, would you come up here and play with us?" The singer motioned for Grant to join them. Grant didn't move.

How could a fan of Grant's not know he hadn't stepped onstage in two years? She wanted to march right up next to that singer, she didn't know his name, and yank the microphone away from him. Grant wasn't going to sing for this crowd or any other. And he shouldn't. Not until he was ready. The hell with what everyone else wanted.

The audience started chanting Grant's name. Bailey's voice rose about the rest. She spun around and motioned for Bailey to shut up. Bailey's lips clamped shut.

"Grant, one song. We'll play whatever you want. We know all your stuff," the singer said.

The guitarist made his instrument sound as if it agreed.

"Alrighty. I'm a little rusty. I warn y'all." Grant laughed, but she didn't miss the hollowness in its echo.

She gripped his shoulder and pulled him closer. "You don't have to do this," she said in his ear so no one would be able to read her lips.

"Don't I? If not for me, then for all these people here chanting my name." Grant walked away before she could answer. He didn't have to prove anything. Not anymore.

The singer whispered in Grant's ear. Grant nodded, then signaled to the rest of the band. In the light pointing at the stage, his skin had taken on the hue of smoky white sea glass. He looked as if he might pass out.

The music began. She recognized it. An upbeat number with a rock edge to it. Something about driving fast cars, drinking beer, and hanging out with the girl he loved. Typical rock song, but on the record, Grant's deep gravelly voice brought a rough romantic edge to it.

Grant missed his cue, the part where the singing should begin. The band's singer shot him a weird look. He motioned for the band to keep playing.

Sweat beaded on Grant's face while he gripped the microphone with both hands. He closed his eyes, opened his mouth, but shut it again. The guitar stuttered to a stop. The band stared at him. Tension filled the room, pushing against the walls and taking up all the air.

"Sorry, boys. Not feeling it tonight." He shook his head and hurried from the stage amidst calls from the band and the audience to return.

Her heart broke as he bolted through the doors and out of The Blue Dot. Someone probably got his exit on video. His humiliation would be all over social media by morning. Grant Hawkins was washed up. She still didn't understand what made him take such a risk. Or maybe she did.

"Oh, Kassidy, honey, go after him," Kate said, standing beside her and gripping her elbow. "That poor man. He must be so embarrassed."

She blinked a few times to make Kate come into focus. "You know him?"

"Of course. We said hello a couple of weeks ago. His brother has been to our house a few times for dinner. Nice young men. Now, go. He needs you."

She stared at the door, unable to move. All she wanted was for her life to press forward, doing the thing she loved most in the world right in the place she stood, and she had no power to keep her dream alive. Grant wanted to do what he loved, but he was stuck because he had lost it all.

Maybe they were both wrong. Or very, very right.

Chapter Eighteen

Grant struggled to breathe as he hurried to his truck parked in the back of The Blue Dot. He had to get out of there before someone followed him. But the air was as thick as lard, making it damn near impossible to cross the parking lot without his heart coming straight through his chest. He reached the truck and flattened his hands on the hood, then sucked in a few deep breaths.

What the hell was he thinking going onto that stage? He had wanted to prove he was fine to everyone, especially Kassidy. When he couldn't start the song, the pitying look in her eyes about knocked him over. The words were on his lips, he knew every one of them the way he had memorized the feel of soft grass against his skin, but nothing came out. Nothing. He kicked the tire and cursed under his breath.

He could pretend all he wanted that he chose not to

get onstage. That not writing songs was up to him, but it wasn't true. He was as stuck as a bear in a trap. His past had its claws in him good. And all he wanted was to get over it, to start over with that beautiful woman inside that run-down bar, but who was he kidding? She would never want a man like him.

"Grant, are you okay?" Kassidy's voice echoed behind him.

He groaned. The last thing he wanted was to see her right now. Keeping his back to her, he said, "Kassidy, go inside."

The gravel rustled with her footsteps. She stopped close enough for him to catch her sweet scent. "I just want to make sure you're okay. What happened in there—"

"Enough." He jerked away from her before she could put a hand on him and break him into unfixable pieces. He didn't want her pity. "I don't want to talk about this with you. Go back inside now."

She tilted up her chin. "You don't get to tell me what to do."

"Not now. Please don't give me your sass now. I need to get the hell out of here." He fished his keys out of his pocket.

"Where are you going?"

"As far away from Serenity by the Sea as possible. Someone in there has my worst moment on their phone and they're posting it right now." He tried not to imagine it. His emails would start blowing up. Every blogger and disc jockey across the United States would be hassling him again for an interview. And if he wasn't careful, Levi would agree to them.

"Even if they are, you can't run from it."

"I can, and I will. I've been doing just fine for the past two years until I came here and met you. You made me think things and feel things I was better off not going near. I forgot for a second about what I've done to the people I love, and I stood on that stage believing I could do it. But I can't. And I can't stay here with you because I'm liable to hurt you too."

"You'll hurt me more by going."

"Oh, come on, Kassidy. Not ten minutes ago you accused me of going behind your back to Levi. I would never do that to you. I know what that tavern means to you. It's in your eyes and the way you exhale every time you talk about it. You sure as hell don't look at me that way." He was jealous of a bar, and he couldn't be any more pathetic.

"How did he find out?" She crossed her arms over her chest.

She still could believe he'd do that to her. He had misread every one of her signals. He had been so lonely for so long he didn't even know when a woman wanted him.

"How the hell do I know? Ask him. Because I'm leaving." He yanked open the truck door.

"So, that's it. You're just going to go and forget about us?"

"There is no us, darlin'. There's only me and my truck and the gravel I'm going to kick up."

"Great line. Why don't you put that in the song you're not writing?" She turned on her heel and marched across the lot, madder than a wet hen and passing Kenny from the music store heading in his direction.

"Kassidy, wait." He took a few steps but stopped. She didn't know him at all, but that was his fault, wasn't it? He had hidden his true self and then clammed up when she had asked about his wife and Emmet. Why wouldn't she believe what Levi had said? If he wanted to get Kassidy back, he was going to have to find a way to convince her he would never hurt her. Prove his worth to her.

Kenny jogged the rest of the way to him. His white hair bounced on his shoulders. "Wow," he said, watching Kassidy storm inside The Dot. "You've got problems inside and out."

"Tell me about it." And no idea how to fix them.

"Listen, what happened in there could've happened to anyone. Plenty of artists freeze onstage." Kenny clapped him on the arm.

"I wasn't always that way. I loved the stage and hearing the crowd sing along. When I looked out at the people in The Dot, my throat closed up. I couldn't suck in any air." He had searched for Kassidy, hoping to see her and sing looking at her, but her crestfallen face had scared him more. He thought he was ready to try again, but he wasn't.

He would scratch together those last few songs for Levi because he owed Levi. And maybe he did owe his fans a little, but he would not perform onstage. Whether he liked it or not, his career as a performer was over. And so were his chances with Kassidy.

Chapter Nineteen

K assidy grabbed the last tote from the back of her car and hefted it over to the folding table on the boardwalk. The annual beach festival came to life on the boardwalk. Serenity by the Sea businesses and many from adjacent towns set up their wares. Tables were covered in multicolored cloths that displayed everything from handmade crafts like scarves and hats to jarred honey to silk kites. Tourists and locals strolled from table to table, touching items that made their faces light up.

The Blue Dot had a table too. Normally, she would set up a station where she could mix drinks made special for the day or one great item from the menu like Charlie's pulled pork sandwiches. But since Charlie was gone and Peyton wanted the space to sell her sea glass creations, Kassidy opted for a standard six-foot table. She wasn't going to be able to keep The Dot anyway. Promoting it seemed like a moot point.

Peyton and Maren manned the table. Peyton smiled wide for everyone who came by. It was hard to resist such a bright and cheerful young lady. She was doing a great job selling, convincing everyone who came to the table that they just had to have a mosaic or a frame to commemorate their vacation. She wooed them with stories of finding the sea glass in her grandpa's attic. It didn't hurt that the frames and mosaics were beautiful. Kassidy planned on buying one for herself.

"Here is the last of the frames," Kassidy said, opening the tote.

"Thanks, Aunt Kass. I can't believe how well this is going. The boardwalk is packed and everyone wants what we made. I wish I had made more." Peyton displayed the frames on the table.

"I hope the weather holds." Maren squinted up at the gray clouds in the west, threatening to ruin the festival if they moved in too quickly.

Thunderstorms were unreliable. They appeared out of nowhere, uninvited, and never stuck around for long. Kind of like deadbeat dads.

"We'll see," she said.

"What's bothering you? You've been awful quiet today," Maren said.

"Nothing. I'm just tired." Because she hadn't slept much after her fight with Grant last night. She had tried to text him during the night to apologize for her harsh words, thinking he would be up, or hoping he would be up, but he never responded.

She had also hoped he would calm down enough to

talk, because she wanted to make sure he was okay. He was embarrassed and frustrated with himself. She wanted to tell him not to be, but she doubted he would listen to her. Not after what she had said to him. If only she could take it all back.

She searched the crowd every few minutes, expecting him to appear, but that was foolish thinking. He was hiding. He would never want to be in such a public place. She checked her phone one more time, but still nothing from him.

Instead, she noticed Levi a few tables down, talking and laughing with Maria Lopez of Intentions Clothing. Levi. He would probably wander over and start asking questions if she didn't get to him first. She still hadn't mentioned his offer to her sisters. She had been waiting for a miracle that had never shown.

"What are you waiting for?" Maren said, dragging her away from thoughts of money and deception.

"What?"

"I asked if you wanted to get us some ice cream and you nodded. Then you didn't budge. Are you sure you're all right?" Maren put a hand to her forehead, but she swatted her away.

"I'll go. Sorry about that." She had her excuse to move away from the table and intercept Levi, now at the only local farm table filled with plums, peaches, and jams.

She placed a hand on Levi's arm. He turned and his smile spread wide as if he'd found a long-lost friend. "Well, howdy, Kassidy Russo. I was hoping to see you here today. Have you given any more thought to my offer?"

"Hi, Cheryl," she said, acknowledging the owner of the Happy Trails Farm who spent a lot of her free time in Serenity by the Sea. Cheryl waved.

She turned back to Levi. "Have you seen Grant?" She wasn't going to talk about his offer now. She wanted to make sure Grant was okay.

"Not since last night. Why?" He handed Cheryl a twenty. "Keep the change."

"Wow, thanks." Cheryl shoved the money in her apron.

"Let's talk over here." She directed Levi away from the table. "When last night?"

"Not sure. Maybe around ten or so." Levi peered inside the bag at his purchase.

"You haven't seen him since last night?" Then Grant could not be at the tent. He went somewhere else. He left town like he said he would.

"Nope. He doesn't check in with me. I wish he would sometimes, but my big brother likes to take off for parts unknown. Sometimes it's days before he shows back up. Did you see the size of these tomatoes?" Levi held the tomato up like a prize.

"So, he did leave," she said more to herself than him, not caring one iota about tomatoes or vegetables. Grant had made good on his word. He couldn't stick around, not even for her.

"He packed a bag. Said something about getting out of this town for a few days to finish writing the songs he owes me. As long as he comes back with the music, I don't care where he writes it. I thought the ocean might inspire him, but I misjudged that one."

"You aren't worried about him?" The pain and hurt on Grant's face when he looked at her last night had made her chest ache. And all Levi seemed to care about was his damn tomato.

"Honestly, the publicity will do him some good. I told him not to worry about what happened on the stage. Social media is going crazy with the video of him falling apart. He's going to sell a ton of albums."

"Is that all you care about, selling albums? Your brother is still in a lot of pain." She couldn't believe her ears. She could only imagine what it cost Grant to go up on that stage and not be able to go through with performing. He had wanted to prove to himself he could still do it.

"It's been two years. My brother needs to get back to work. There are people counting on him."

"Who can he count on?" She had believed Grant had taken advantage of her situation, but she realized she had that wrong. "He doesn't know anything about your offer on The Blue Dot, does he? You made that up."

"Don't take it personally. I figured you'd be likely to sell if you thought Grant wanted it. I can tell what's happening between you two. You're the first woman in a very long time who has made him open his eyes to the world around him. I'm grateful, darlin', really."

"You need to stop calling me darlin' before I deck you."

Levi threw up his hands. The plastic bag swayed. "Easy now. No need to get hostile."

"How did you know about my money problems? You're a tourist. Locals don't share our business with outsiders."

Levi arched a brow. "You might not have that completely right. My adorable neighbor Kate, who can bake a mean coffee cake, told me about your debt problems. She didn't want to gossip, but she did."

She wanted to smack her head. Of course it was Kate. She should have known. Kate was lovely and funny and did make a good coffee cake, but she also had a mouth the size of the Atlantic Ocean. Kate talked to anyone who would listen.

"My offer still stands. Take me up on it, Kassidy." He tapped his two fingers to his forehead in some kind of a salute and walked into the crowd of people.

Grant had not been behind the offer. She never should have suspected him. She needed to apologize for that too—if she could find him. And if it wasn't too late. Because of her past experience with Bear, she wrongly suspected that all men would use a situation to their advantage and disregard her feelings or desires. Grant was not Bear.

Please call me. She sent the text.

The dark-gray clouds continued to move east and brought air thick enough to walk into. Maybe the thunderstorm would break the humidity—her hair could use the help—but not before the end of the day. Peyton was having so much fun. It would be a shame if she had to end her day early. It also seemed even Maren was enjoying herself talking to the customers. She was so good at drawing people out. Maren had a gift for design and for sharing.

"I saw you talking to Levi," Maren said as she returned to the table. Peyton had wandered down the boardwalk, looking at the other vendors' items. Kassidy took the camp chair beside Maren.

"I asked him if he had heard from Grant." She averted her gaze. Maren would suspect there was more to the conversation with Levi. She would tell her sisters about the offer. Soon.

"And?"

"He said Grant left town last night. I feel terrible about what happened to him. I just had no idea what the band was going to do. I never imagined that stunt would bother him so much he would leave." Levi had said Grant had gone to finish writing songs, but was that the truth? Was he halfway back to Alabama by now or some other place where he could hide deeper than he had been hiding?

Maren put a hand on her shoulder. "Kass, maybe this isn't the right man. He has a lot to still work out."

"I thought we had a connection. I thought for once something was going to go my way." But she had accused him of hurting her. She might be the one who wasn't ready for a commitment.

"Excuse me, ladies." A tall man with salt-and-pepper hair, smile lines around his warm eyes, and an athletic body dressed in a t-shirt and cargo shorts beamed down at them.

"Yes. Hi, I'm Maren. I mean hello. It's nice to... how can we... help you?" Maren pushed out of the chair with too much force, knocking it over.

Kassidy righted it and stifled a chuckle. The stranger, however, offered a small laugh absent of malice. Maren blushed.

"I was admiring your art from across the boardwalk. I'm new in town. I thought The Blue Dot was a tavern. Is it a craft store too?"

Maren smoothed down her hair. "You're right. The Blue Dot is a tavern. My family and I own it." Maren pointed at her. "This is my sister Kassidy."

"Hi." Kassidy waved.

The man stuck out his hand to Maren. "Hello, Maren, I'm Mav. And hello, Kassidy," he said with a quick glance in her direction, but he returned his gaze to settle on Maren.

She should leave Maren alone, but this was too good not to witness, so she plopped back into the chair for a front-row seat.

"I don't understand all the sea glass artwork if you own the tavern. Not that I'm complaining. It's very nice," Mav said, turning a frame around in his hand.

"We found a ton, and I mean a ton, of sea glass in our father's attic. My daughter wanted to make the crafts. This seemed like the perfect place to bring them. You might like this one." Maren handed him the frame with the pieces that must have been from old bottles. Each piece was green or blue with numbers etched in them. Peyton had turned it into an impressive frame made from distressed wood.

"Your daughter is very talented. I'd like to buy all five of these frames." Mav gathered the frames and handed them to Maren.

"Oh, that's not necessary." Maren waved her hand.

"Let him buy them," she said through the side of her mouth. If the weather didn't hold, a storm would dump on their heads and Peyton wouldn't be able to sell all the pieces she had made. And not that she would point it out now, but if Maren took the man's money, she would have a reason to ask for his number.

Maren shushed her.

"I have five nieces who would love these. I'll be their favorite uncle. You wouldn't deny a guy a chance to be the favorite, would you?" He smiled again, igniting those adorable smile lines.

Maren blushed again. Oh, her sister may have developed the fastest crush ever.

"I suppose I couldn't allow that." Maren wrapped each frame in ocean-blue tissue paper. Mav handed her the cash. Their hands touched during the exchange. Maren batted her eyelashes.

"I have one more question," Mav said.

"Yes, she's free for dinner." Kassidy crossed her arms and gave Maren what she hoped was a *don't you dare tell him no* face.

"Kassidy," Maren said with horror. "Please excuse my bossy sister."

"She's also a mind reader."

She wouldn't allow Maren to miss a chance to enjoy herself. She deserved to be treated the right way by a man and not the way Dave had been treating her. This little exchange may go nowhere, but it would do wonders for Maren's self-esteem.

Kassidy grabbed a piece of paper and jotted down Maren's cell number. "You can reach her here. She's only in town for a couple more weeks. Don't wait."

Mav folded the paper and stuck it in the pocket of his shorts. "I'll be in touch. Thank you for the frames." He held up the package and nodded goodbye.

"I can't believe you did that," Maren said.

"Oh, come on. He was flirting with you, and you liked it. You should go out and enjoy yourself."

"I'm not ready to date." But Maren's gaze followed the handsome Mav until he was no longer visible.

"Sure you are. That guy was cute. Go enjoy dinner. And if you get to have some great sex afterward, go for it. Life's too short." She certainly knew that. All the plans in the world could be snagged away in a second. All it took was for a fiancé to come home and say he didn't love you anymore or for the kindest man she'd ever met to flee from her life without a look back.

"You're so vulgar." Maren scrunched up her nose.

"Just truthful. You do still want to have sex, don't you?" She certainly did, and she wanted to know what it would be like with Grant. Now, she may never find out.

"I'll think about it." The blush crept back up Maren's neck.

"Good. You should." She checked her phone. Still nothing from Grant. She should just give up. He wasn't going to call or text her. They were over before they even started.

Thunder rolled in the distance. The gray clouds hung low, almost touching the ocean's surface. A wind picked up, pushing the ends of the tablecloth into the air and sending someone's cards tumbling end over end down the boardwalk. A few of the vendors started packing up with half their gaze aimed at the sky. Even the crowd had thinned.

"I guess we should think about closing up," she said.

"That's disappointing. We still have that whole tote to sell." Maren pointed at the tote she had brought over earlier.

"There's another festival around Labor Day. You could come back."

"I suppose." Maren shrugged.

Kassidy caught a glimpse of Charlotte Munroe heading their way with determination in her step. She had to be coming for her about the message she had left. She needed to intercept her before Charlotte made it to the table. Maren would chop her head off if she found out she told Charlotte they didn't need her.

"Why don't you take the tote back to the car? I'll start packing up the rest of this stuff before the rain comes." She handed the tote to Maren before she could argue.

"Are you sure? It was just a little thunder. Maybe we should wait it out." Maren looked up at the sky.

"Let's get started in case the storm starts sooner than

later. Then when Peyton gets back, we can decide to stay or go. You still have the mosaics to sell." She stole a quick glance over her shoulder at Charlotte who had stopped at a neighboring table.

"Well, all right. Here. Take a few frames just in case." Maren handed her three frames.

"Perfect. Now go." If she could, she would have pushed her. Thankfully, Maren hadn't noticed Charlotte nearby and headed toward the car.

Charlotte marched toward her. "Kassidy Russo, what do you mean by leaving me that kind of a message? I already had two buyers lined up to tour the tavern."

Charlotte was sophisticated in her pressed white sleeveless blouse and wide-legged black linen trousers. She wore her hair pulled back in a low knot. Her makeup hadn't slipped off her face from all the heat. Kassidy was impressed. She was pretty sure her own hair had grown wider exponentially as the day wore on. Her clothes were wrinkled, and she was a smelly, sweaty mess.

"I'm sorry for the inconvenience. But we've made other arrangements. We didn't sign a contract with you. We aren't obligated to you or your buyers. But believe me, we would love to use you for the sale of our father's house. I think we'll be ready to put it on the market by the end of the summer."

"Fall is not a great time to sell. People want to be in before the school year starts. Buyers want our little seaside community because of the schools too. Can we list it now?" Charlotte's purse dangled at her elbow while she spoke with her manicured hands.

"We're still cleaning it out." And had a long way to go. And if her sisters found out she had lied about their father's last wishes, the cleanup would take longer because she'd be doing it by herself.

"Oh, how bad could it be? He lived alone."

Little did she know how bad. "Trust me. The house isn't ready to be seen."

"Well, I can't say I'm not disappointed about the tavern. I wish Maren had said something. She had seemed so sure of this arrangement." Charlotte retrieved her cell phone from the front pocket of her purse. Her thumbs moved effortlessly across the screen. Something so important it can't be missed. Kassidy's phone remained silent, with no contact from Grant.

"Things changed suddenly. She wanted me to apologize to you too." No matter how many times she told herself to throw in the towel, she couldn't do it. Maybe she was too stubborn for her own good, but The Dot was in her blood.

"I'll call her this week and talk more about the house," Charlotte said.

"No, she's busy with her daughter and some personal stuff. I'll call you and set up a time for you to come by. But like I said, it won't be for a few more weeks." She might have to come up with a way to keep Maren from calling Charlotte. She hadn't thought about that until this moment. Her lies dug her in deep trouble.

Charlotte narrowed her perfectly plucked eyebrows. "Okay. But I'll just put in my calendar to call you if I don't hear from you. I'm sure you're agreeable to that?" Her fingers skated over the screen again.

"Of course, but you'll hear from me."

Charlotte glanced at the darkening sky. "You should get out of here before the storm comes in."

"I was thinking the same thing. Thanks for stopping by." *And please go before Maren returns.* Charlotte sauntered off in the opposite direction of the parking lot. She let her shoulders drop. At least she had dodged that catastrophe for now.

Peyton returned to the table with a skip in her step. "Aunt Kass, look at all this great stuff." She held up a weaved handbag, a wide-brimmed sun hat, and pink flip-flops.

"You spent all your profit." She couldn't help but laugh. Peyton's face lit up like the afternoon sun, which they weren't seeing any of today.

"I just couldn't pass this stuff up. I love all the little shops here. We don't have anything like that by us. All the cute shops closed. No one wants to come to our part of town. Not that I blame them. If I could, I'd love to live by the beach. You're so lucky."

"You can come and visit me anytime." She hadn't been the best aunt. She should have been spending every summer with Peyton, getting to know her better. But Maren was always so wrapped up in her own life with little time for her. She hadn't wanted to impose and used the excuse that the summer was her busiest time. If she could go back, she would make better decisions. Going forward she would have to.

"Thanks. I'd like to visit more often. Where's Mom?"

"She went back to the car. We should clean up. We're one of the last ones. I think the pending storm has scared most of the people away." The wind blew sand against the boardwalk as if thousands of pebbles hit the wood.

"That's too bad. I was hoping to have sold out."

"You almost did. A man stopped by earlier and bought five frames. You're very talented." He may have bought all those frames to impress Maren, but Peyton didn't need to know that.

"That's great. Thanks for saying that. I didn't even know I was creative."

Kassidy's heart swelled. Maren and even Dave had raised a bright, beautiful young lady. She had hoped for a family of her own for years, but time was slipping away from her. She had been standing in the same place for so long she forgot to look around and notice the changes. She wasn't getting any younger. She needed to acquire some new skills now. And at the end of the summer, she would be alone.

Her phone vibrated in her pocket. Her stomach clenched as she pulled it out.

I'm sorry. Been writing. Be back soon. Can we talk then? Grant's words pulsed behind her eyes. He wasn't ignoring her after all. She would talk to him whenever he returned. Her thumbs hovered over her phone, aching to respond.

"Kassidy. Kassidy. How could you?" Maren hurried

toward her. The deep crease between her brows and the clenched fists said it all.

She put the phone back in her pocket.

"Do what?" She needed time to figure out how to handle this. Whatever crisis this was.

Maren swatted the hair out of her face with an exasperated sigh. "Don't play stupid with me. I just saw Levi Hawkins in the parking lot. He strolled right up to me with all that bravado and Southern charm and the smile of a snake. At first, I couldn't imagine what that man could want, but then I thought maybe he had a message from Grant. I was feeling so badly for you. But that wasn't why he walked over to me. No, apparently, he made a sizable offer on The Blue Dot to you a week ago that you have conveniently decided to not mention."

Words jumbled in her brain to form a response, but none made sense. She had had an obligation to tell her sisters about the offer and hadn't. There was no denying what she was accused of, but how could she make Maren understand? "I was hoping to find a way to buy you and Bailey out. Then we wouldn't need his offer."

"You can't buy us out." Maren shook her fists. "When are you going to figure that out? You're so thickheaded. It isn't fair to keep that albatross wrapped around all of our necks."

"I just need a little more time."

"To do what? Rob a bank? Sell drugs? Maybe you're foolish enough to call Mom and ask her for the money."

"I did." Heat climbed up her neck and burned her cheeks.

Maren's mouth fell open.

"Why can't you understand that I don't have anything besides that business? I don't have a family like you. I don't have a life of chasing my every adventure like Bailey. What am I supposed to do without The Dot?" Her voice shook on each word like a rusted fire escape with the weight of a hundred evacuees. She berated herself for allowing any emotion to show. She needed to stay calm and sure of herself on this. She didn't want to fall to pieces over The Dot. But it was more than The Dot. It was everything.

"I don't know. Start over. Like the rest of us. Life happens, Kass. You don't always get to like it. Dad died. He left the bar to all of us. We have to sell it." Maren raked her hands through her hair.

"Why can't you stay here?" Why was she holding on to this idea like a drowning person? It would be so much easier to give in, but her pride or her heart wouldn't let go.

"And do what? Run the bar with you? That's crazy." Maren spit out a laugh.

"Why? Because you don't want to start over? Because you don't want to give up the life you have to try something new here? Stop being a hypocrite, Maren. You wouldn't even have given that good-looking guy your number if I hadn't pushed you. Your marriage is over. When will you see that? You need to move on just as much as I do."

"A guy hit on you?" Peyton said.

She said yes and Maren said no at the exact same time.

"Wow. Good for you, Mom. You're hot. You should go out on a date."

"See?" Her niece was one smart cookie. Maren could learn a thing or two from her daughter.

"Both of you, stop it. I'm calling Bailey and telling her about Levi's offer. Then we're going to accept it. All three of us." Maren wrestled the rest of the frames and mosaics into her arms and marched away.

She turned to Peyton. "Can you help your mom clean up the rest? I think she and I could use some space." She needed to catch her breath. A long walk on the boardwalk and a stop to search for sea glass would help her calm down enough to have an adult conversation unlike the one that just happened.

"Sure, Aunt Kass. I get it. She can be a lot sometimes." Peyton tucked her hair behind her ear.

"That's an understatement." She pulled Peyton into a hug. Her hair smelled of ripe strawberries. "Thanks for the hug. I know it's uncool to hug at your age. You're great. I love you."

"Back at you." Peyton made some sign with her fingers that she assumed was teenager for all good.

She put as much space as she could between her and the table without looking back. She ran down the steps leading to the sand, pulled off her sneakers, and headed for where the white foam floated over the sand. Except for a few dedicated surfers who wouldn't miss a chance to catch a wave before a storm, the beach was empty. The ocean was dark and angry with whitecaps cutting its surface. Thunder clapped an outraged tune again. She didn't have a lot of time so she wouldn't look long for sea glass. Running her hands over the wet sand and discovering a small treasure would put her world right. Oh, that was wishful thinking.

Yet, her hunt for sea glass turned up nothing. Sometimes that happened—and she hated it each time. Sea glass was becoming harder and harder to find because ocean dumping happened less and less. Some of the best beaches for sea glass these days were in other parts of the world. Maybe she should take up where her father left off and go hunting in other countries.

She was avoiding all her problems, the way her father had avoided his. Maybe she didn't collect every object she came into contact with, but she didn't want to face the reality she would lose The Dot. She hadn't been completely honest with her sisters about missing them. She had wanted them to discover what they were missing on their own. She had been afraid to take a chance and let them see her heart. Because her heart had been broken so many times before.

The first fat raindrop fell on her shoulder. She'd never make it back to the house without getting soaked once the rain really started and Maren had taken the car. She would find some shelter, then tell her sisters it was all over. She would sell The Dot to Levi.

She glanced at her phone and the text Grant had sent.

And hit delete.

Chapter Twenty

Kassidy hurried down Main Street, ducking between the fat raindrops splattering the sidewalk and seeping over the sides of her shoes. Trees bent in half against the force of the howling wind gusts. She had stayed too long at the beach and really wouldn't make it home. With the way things had been going, lightning was likely to strike the center of her head.

She jumped inside Mr. D's bakery and out of the storm. Her clothes dripped on the clean floor. The fluorescent lights were a harsh contrast to the dark skies.

"Mr. D, are you here?" She craned her neck to see through the portholes of the doors leading to the kitchen area.

Except for the tables and the sparse pastry case because this time of the day most of the goodies were sold, the store was empty.

A cup of tea and a sfogliatella would hit the spot

while she dried off and the storm passed. This kind of weather never lasted long.

Mr. D, in his white t-shirt and tan pants covered in a multitude of baking ingredients, came through the door with a vibrant smile that lit up his blue eyes. Mr. D was always happy to see everyone, and she needed that right about now.

"*Ciao, Bella.* What brings you to my bakery in this weather, ah?" His Italian accent decorated every word much like his homemade buttercream frosting on decadent cupcakes.

"I stayed at the beach too long. The rain has started. I don't think I'll make it all the way home without needing a boat." She didn't want to go home anyway. She would have to face her sisters and the lie—well, the lie by omission. She should also come clean about her father's make-believe last wishes. She had deceived them into staying in Serenity by the Sea longer than they had wanted. But it sure had been nice for a while. A real family.

"Can I get you anything?" The pastry case door scraped against the track as Mr. D pushed it open.

"I'll have the sfogliatella and a hot tea, please. Can I stay for a while? Till the rain passes?"

"*Si. Si.* Make yourself welcome." Mr. D put the pastry on a plate with a fork and a knife. A few minutes later he brought her a white chipped teacup filled to the brim with hot water and a tea bag staining the water brown.

"Thank you." She wrapped her hands around the

cup. The warmth seeped into her fingers, pushing some of the chill away.

"You look like... how do you say...? Like you have the weight of the world on your shoulders." Mr. D cleaned the inside of the cases, moving the remaining pastries out of the way as he wiped with a rag.

"It feels like it these days." She cut into the sfogliatella. The thick beige custard spilled out onto the plate like sweet lava. She dipped a finger into the cream and licked it off. A moan escaped her lips. Honestly, she could die right now having lived a complete life. Mr. D's pastries were heaven on earth.

"Good, yeah?" His smile pushed up his ruddy cheeks.

"Excellent."

"So, these problems. Tell me about them. How can I help you? It's not your friend Grant, is it?" Mr. D moved around behind the counter, straightening up. He was finishing his end of day routine. She recognized it from her own routine at The Dot. A routine that was over.

"Things didn't work out for us. He left town." She wasn't trying to blame Grant for what had happened between them, or what hadn't. She was as much at fault. They just weren't right for each other.

"I'm sorry to hear that. He was a good man. I can tell." Mr. D tapped his chest and gave a definitive nod.

She couldn't help but smile. Mr. D prided himself on knowing the character of a person from the first time he met them. She sat back in the chair and cuddled the cup. She could sit here all night even after the rain passed.

"Grant is a good man. We're just too different. We want different things."

"Sometimes opposite attract, no?" Mr. D packed up the remaining pastries in a white bag. "Here. You take these home to your sisters." He put the bag on the table and went back to wipe the counter down.

"You don't have to do that, Mr. D. Bring these home to your wife." Opposites didn't always attract. She and Bear were more opposite than the same, and they didn't work out. She and Grant seemed to fit. He was easy to talk to. He made her laugh.

"I know I don't have to give you the food. I want to. My wife, ah..." He waved a frustrated hand in the air. "She no want more pastries every day. Tells me they make her fat. Ah, fat. Nonsense. My sons have gone home. You take them. Sharing food in my country is how we show we care."

How did her family show they cared about each other? The only thing she could think of was by staying away from each other. But that wasn't entirely true. She and her sisters had bonded many nights these past few weeks over something as simple as s'mores. She had begun to look forward to Bailey bringing the tray out to the fire pit. She and her sisters, and even Peyton, had grown closer over all the sea glass they had found. They had laughed and reminisced about the old days. They had started to understand each other. And she went ahead and lied to them.

"Mr. D, if you couldn't have this bakery anymore, how would you feel?"

He scratched his chin and narrowed his eyes. "Well, I'd be sad because this is the place I started when I came here. But as long as I had my family by my side, nothing else would matter. We could start another store maybe. Or I could take some classes. I'm not too old, no?"

"No, you are not too old to learn something new." She smiled and shook her head at his sense of humor. "But would you feel like you lost a part of yourself if the bakery closed? It's been who you are for so many years."

"Ah, no, it's not who I am. It's what I do, *Bella*. I am a simple man who likes to bake. I can bake in my own kitchen when my wife isn't chasing me around with a washcloth, cleaning up the crumbs I drop." His belly shook as he laughed. "Life changes. This I know because I was a child living on a goat farm in Calabria, then I was a young man in a strange country. I had never seen snow before I came here to America. That was some change. If I lost my business, I would be mad for a while, then sad, but as long as I had my health and my family, I'd move on. Why do you ask?"

She had been blinded by her plans and her definitions and her expectations. Here was a man who had traveled across an ocean to a foreign country where he couldn't speak the language and he had made something of himself. And the only thing he cared about was being with his family. She could certainly give up The Dot to save hers.

"Mr. D, you are one smart man." She brought her cup and plate to the counter.

"Me? No." He waved his hand through the air again.

"You. Yes. I have to get home."

"You don't want to wait until the storm passes?"

"I need to find my sisters. Thank you for the visit. You cleared things up for me."

"*Prego.*" He offered a definitive nod.

She hurried out into the rain and wished for the car, but then stopped. She didn't need the car. She was lucky to be able to be outside in the rain with the wind blowing in off the ocean hard enough to push her clothes against her skin in the town she loved most. She tilted her face up to catch the raindrops on her skin. Thunder shook her, and lightning cracked open the sky over the sand. The storm had something to say just like she did.

She would go home and tell her sisters how sorry she was and come clean about the house. It still hurt to lose The Dot, but she would gain more by being honest about needing her family.

But one more stop before she headed home.

Grant parked outside the tent. The rain fell in sheets over the windshield, blocking his view. From the passenger window, the drops left room to see the lights on inside. Levi was still there, like he said he would be. His little brother had come to enjoy Serenity by the Sea. Maybe a little too much, in Grant's opinion if what Kassidy had said was true. She had no reason to lie to him, but neither did Levi. Levi would have to explain why he went behind Grant's back and made an offer on The Blue Dot.

He grabbed his phone and ran for the front door. Time to get this over with. He had the songs for Levi. Well, he had two of them. Levi couldn't have the third one, at least not yet.

"Levi, I'm back." He shook off the rain and kicked off his boots so as not to track water all around the small space.

Levi came through the doorway at the back. He wore a t-shirt and basketball shorts. He had been trading his designer clothes for a more casual look every day. Yup, Levi liked Serenity. "About time. I was getting worried."

"Save it." He pulled up the songs on his phone and sent them to Levi. "You have the songs."

Levi lunged for his phone and tapped at the screen. In seconds, Grant's voice and instrument playing filled the tent. He had recorded each part of the songs himself. He had been up all night doing it. His body ached from lack of sleep and the drive back to Serenity by the Sea from New York City, but he wanted this arrangement behind him. After what happened to him onstage the other day, he wasn't so sure he ever wanted to play music again for anyone except himself.

He had thought he could not write or perform because he had lost Noel. He used that accident as an excuse to avoid what was really going on with him. Somewhere along the way, he lost sight of who he really was and what he wanted his music career to look like. He had allowed Noel and Levi to dictate what he did. He wasn't going to argue that he enjoyed the accolades from the fans, but the two of them had pushed too hard to outdo the album and the tour before. The entire band had worked nonstop for three years. He had wanted to take a break, but when he had suggested it, Noel and Levi fought him hard. He would always feel guilty for the harm he had caused. He should have been man enough to say no and understand that Noel didn't love him anymore. Well, he was going to take control of his career and his life now when Levi asked for the third song.

"Grant, these suck." Levi's words knocked him off-balance.

"You don't like them?" He wasn't expecting that response. They weren't his best work, but they didn't *suck*.

"Your heart's not in them. You cut corners. They're cliché. I can't turn these in. The label will go nuts, and the fans will hate them. Where's the third song?"

"You're not getting it. I'm done, Levi. Hand those songs in. I don't care if the label doesn't like them. I owed them songs. They have them now." He was done taking care of Levi too. There had been a time for him to watch out for his little brother. After the accident and after Emmet died, he felt obligated to make things right for Levi in any way he could, but no more.

"You owed them three songs."

"They're only getting two." The third song he wanted for himself. He had some ideas for it, maybe a way to build an album from it, but he would see. One thing he knew, he had put his heart in that song.

"They'll sue you and me. You can't let that happen."

"Here's the thing. I'm not saving you anymore. You

needed me to do that for you when we were kids. Now, as my manager, you find a way to make the label take these last two songs and end the contract. I can't save your career any longer. I'm done. I have dreams I want to go after. I'm going to run my career my way from now on."

"Did you fall on your head? You had the dream to be the singer, playing on stages around the world. I made that happen for you."

"I appreciate that. I do. But these past two years I have been wandering around looking for myself, thinking I lost who I was the night of that accident. Problem was, I had never left. I've been standing right here the whole time. These past few weeks in Serenity by the Sea have shown me that. And it has shown me what's important and how I want to live my life. On my terms."

"You aren't trying to tell me you're in love with the bartender, are you? She's just one woman in a small town."

"I care a lot for Kassidy." And he wanted the time to be with her, if she would have him. "Did you tell her I wanted her to sell her bar to you?"

"I needed a way to convince her." Levi shrugged.

"So, you lied. I would never have asked her to give up the thing that mattered most to her. That's something that you do. When you love someone, you support what they do even when you don't agree."

"If you're talking about how I managed your career, it was my job to make decisions you didn't know how to."

"Wrong, little brother. Your job was to support my decisions. What you did to Kassidy was crap. You're going to go next door and apologize and tell her this was your stupid idea. Then you're going to rescind your offer."

"I want that bar. We can really make something of it. Especially if you're going to write bad songs. You're going to need a new career."

"You can't have the tavern. If she has to sell, it's not going to be to you. As for a new career, maybe you're right. Maybe I won't be a famous singer on the radio anymore. Maybe I'll stay a cook in a small town. But whatever I do, I'm going to decide for myself."

"They have to sell that place to somebody. Wouldn't you rather it be me? I'm not going to screw her over."

A frantic knock came at the door.

"Grant, are you home?" a female voice said. Not Kassidy. Grant swung open the door. The rain bent sideways and wet the screen. He let Maren and Bailey in.

"What are you two doing out in this storm?" he said.

Maren wiped the water from her face. "Have you seen Kassidy?"

"Not for a couple of days. Why?" The hair on the back of his neck stood up. It didn't take a genius to figure out if they didn't know where Kassidy was in this storm, there was a problem.

"She's missing," Bailey said. "She's not answering her phone. In fact, she turned it off because we can't track her. We don't know where she is."

"We're afraid she went looking for sea glass and got swept up by the ocean," Maren said. "She's so stubborn, always doing what she wants. She knew the storm was coming and how dangerous it would be to be near the ocean. The rip current could have grabbed her and pulled her out to sea in minutes."

"Did you check the beach?" Levi said.

"We came here first just in case she was here," Bailey said. "We'd better go down and look."

"How about your father's house?" Levi asked.

"We checked. She wasn't there. We swung by here, hoping she went home, but she isn't there." Maren tugged at the hem of her jacket.

"What about The Blue Dot? Did either of you go there?" That would be the first place he would look. "Maybe she just wanted to get in out of the rain."

"We went by there too, but she wasn't there. I think she's avoiding us," Bailey said.

"Why would she do that?" He must have missed some sisterly drama while he was away. Maybe that was why Kassidy hadn't answered his last text. He had checked several times, was tempted to send another one, but he didn't want to press until he had dealt with Levi. Now, he wished he had made her talk to him.

"We had a fight," Maren said. "Because of you." She stabbed Levi's chest with a skinny finger.

"What did I do? I just made a legitimate offer on your property." Levi backed up, his hands in the air.

"She wants to keep that place. I should've seen how much it meant to her. I'm the older sister. I'm supposed to protect her. But I didn't. All I did was force her into selling the only thing she has in her life. Grant, please help us find her. I can't lose her in the storm before I get a chance to apologize."

"It's going to be okay." Bailey pulled Maren into a hug. "She's smart. She knows to respect the ocean."

"What if she climbed up on the jetty and slipped?" Maren wiped a tear away from her face.

"I'll go. I'll find her. You two stay put." He wasn't ready to lose Kassidy either. He had things he wanted to discuss with her. Things he hadn't been clear about until he had driven away from Serenity.

"What about the songs?" Levi said.

"I told you. You get those two and nothing more. Now I have something far more important to take care of." He pushed past them and out into the rain.

He would find her if it was the last thing he did.

Chapter Twenty-One

Wind howled around the sides of The Blue Dot like wolves coming in for the kill. The roof leaked from the intense rain, making puddles in the kitchen. Kassidy grabbed buckets to catch the water. She would need to bring a roofer in to patch it for the rest of the summer. She would ask Levi if they could have the summer before having to close their doors for good.

Her cedar siding slapped against the building as the wind bullied it. She was certain pieces of the shakes would be all over the parking lot by the time the storm was over. Except she couldn't assess the damage without the risk of getting blown away. Whatever was happening to the building would have to wait.

The trees at the edge of the parking lot shook in the wind's angry grasp. She moved away from the window just in case something came flying. Storms at the shore might not always last long, but they hit hard, wreaking plenty of havoc in their paths.

The overhead lights flickered, then went out. It was early evening, but the sky had turned battleship gray, offering little outside light to filter into The Dot. She found a flashlight and a seat. She might as well get comfortable. She'd be sticking around until it was safe to go home. Maybe she'd sleep here tonight. It wouldn't be the first time, but it would likely be the last.

She would have a list of lasts with the tavern. The last breakfast she served, the last drink she mixed, the last band that would play here. Her heart ached for the loss, but maybe, like sea glass, something beautiful would show up in the future. She hoped it wouldn't take a hundred years, that's all.

She could call her sisters from the tavern's phone, since her cell's battery was dead, but the stillness inside passed over her like a warm blanket. She had come to say goodbye. Her favorite time at The Dot was when no one else was there. If she stayed quiet, it was as if The Dot could whisper her stories to Kassidy. So many stories between these walls. Her father teaching her how to make a drink before she attended bartender's school. The regulars who sat at the bar night after night nursing their beers. The years when bands played regularly, and as many years watching the crowd thin. The fights she had had with her father to make changes to the business. All the times her sisters walked out the door promising never to return. The day Grant saved her.

"The stories are coming to an end, my old friend."

The Dot had been a companion to her, reliable, steadfast, warm, and safe. It shouldn't hurt so much to lose a building. But it did. She had to remember what Mr. D said. She might be sad, but as long as she had her family, nothing else mattered. The Dot could be given away.

She would be starting over soon. This was her chance to remember all the good times here. The storm raged on, as did the fear inside her. Standing on the edge of the unknown made her stomach queasy and her heart thrum with excitement at the same time. She was mixed up like a great drink.

Someone knocked on the door. She debated on even answering. She couldn't imagine who would be out in this weather, but it could be Maren or Bailey, searching for her. With some regret, she pushed out of the chair and unlocked the front door.

"Kassidy, are you okay? Everyone is looking for you." Rain dripped off the brim of Grant's cap. The light from the flashlight showed the concern on his handsome features.

"What are you doing here? Come inside." She motioned for him to pass her, then locked the door against the wind. "I lost power, but I have dessert from Mr. D's if you're hungry."

"You're offering me food? What are you doing here?"

He smelled like rain and leather. The shoulders of a t-shirt and his strong arms were wet. All she wanted to do was fall into them.

"I could ask you the same thing." Her insides hummed as she took him in. He had come for her. She had ignored his last text, had accused him of something he hadn't done, and he was right here, making sure she was okay.

"Your sisters are worried about you. They've been looking everywhere. They thought you might've drowned." He tossed his cap on the table and combed his fingers through his hair.

"Really? Do they really think I'd be dumb enough to go into the ocean when the riptides were nuts?" She marched away from him, unable to believe how naive her sisters thought she was. She was the one who had lived most of her life at the shore. She understood the ocean and what it could do. And if they had been so concerned, why hadn't they come? She almost burst out laughing but bit her tongue. Families would argue. Families would love fiercely, but they would be the very same people who would drive her batty—and she loved every piece of it.

"They love you. They were thinking the worst. For a second, I was too. Why didn't you call?"

She would make sure she told her sisters she loved them every day from here on out. "My battery is dead, and honestly, I was enjoying the quiet. Hang on a second. You were worried? Then why did it take you days to answer my texts?"

"I really am sorry about that. I was trying to finish the songs for Levi. I can be a grouch when I'm working. But you never responded to my last text. I wanted to talk to you. Was that your way of saying you didn't want to talk to me?"

She had deleted his text. She regretted that now. "I

wasn't sure what was left to talk about. You had made yourself clear when you ignored me."

"I wasn't trying to ignore you. I needed to get my head on straight." He laced his fingers through hers.

"Well, did you?" She didn't pull away. Instead, she looked at their hands tangled together. Separate, they were two people on very different paths, but together, they fit the way sea glass could become jewelry.

"Let me text Maren first and tell her you're okay. Then could we talk?" He pulled out his phone and tapped the screen. She missed his touch immediately.

While he sent texts to Maren, she went into the kitchen and grabbed some old candles from the back of the pantry, arranging them on a table in the dining area. Their flames flickered in the draft, but they provided a romantic glow. She was getting ahead of herself. He wanted to talk to her. That could be about being friends, and not anything more. She might have wanted to throw herself into his arms and kiss the heck out of him, but there was still that little issue of his late wife.

"The candles are a nice touch," he said and pulled out a chair for her to sit. "Maren says to stay here until it's safe to come home, and she's sorry."

She sat with a plop. "She isn't the only one. I guess she and I have a lot to talk about too." There would be no more hiding. She would put her heart on the line from now on. She had missed out on so much trying to play it safe.

He sat beside her and took her hand again. "Levi told me about him making the offer to you. You have to know I had nothing to do with that. I would never hurt you that way."

"I know that now. He told me Kate mentioned my money problems. I'm sorry I suspected you."

"Levi can be very persuasive. It's what makes him so good at his job. He thought if you believed the offer was my idea, you'd be more likely to go for it. He didn't know how much keeping The Dot meant to you."

"I want to take his offer. It's more than fair, and it's time. That's why I'm here in the storm. I just wanted a few minutes to myself before I went home to tell my sisters we have our answer."

"I told him to forget it." He gave her a sideways glance.

"What?" She sat up. "We need him. There aren't any other buyers, and I really don't want to use that Charlotte Munroe. She's so uppity."

"You don't need his offer. I have a better one." His smile eased across his face.

"I'm not taking money from you." She would not be indebted to this man or be his charity case. She had to keep some of her dignity, especially if there was any chance of them continuing their relationship.

"Just hear me out." He held up a hand.

"Grant..."

"Please, Kassidy. You might like my idea."

"Okay. Go ahead." It wasn't as if they had anywhere else to be at the moment. Though instead of all this talk, she could think of something she'd rather do in a candlelit room with the sexiest man she had ever met.

"I spoke with a friend of mine from the music business while I was in New York. He is willing to lend you the money to buy your sisters out."

"Grant, I can't take money from your friend even if it is a loan. Thank you, but no."

"If I had it myself, I'd give it to you, but I don't. Think about it, Kass. He's a good guy and likes to invest in small local businesses."

"Who is this friend of yours?"

"Carl May."

"The Carl May? The biggest country singer of our time?"

"The one and only. I met him years ago at the Ryman Auditorium. He became like a mentor to me. He's happy to help. Seriously."

"Why would he do this? It's not the smartest financial risk."

He cupped her face. The heat from his hands sent waves of desire over her. "Why? Because I asked him to. And because, Kassidy Russo, when I drove out of town the other night after that humiliating experience on your stage, the only thing I kept thinking about was coming back to you."

"But you left." Her words tangled around her tongue. She couldn't concentrate with him so close and smelling good enough to lick.

"I didn't leave because of you and me. I was mad as hell at myself for looking like a fool in front of you."

"It is not possible for you to look foolish to me." She

wanted to see every part of him, the good and the not so good.

"You say that now, but you haven't seen me at my worst. I had to finish those songs. And I had to be sure that I could give you what you deserve." He placed a kiss on her lips, but he didn't linger. She wanted to twist her fingers in his hair and pull him back.

"And what is it you think I deserve?" Because she knew what she wanted.

"You deserve it all, but particularly a man who isn't afraid of his past. A man who can stand beside you and support you and help you make your dreams come true. I want to be that man." He slid his hands to her shoulders. All the heat in her body flowed south.

"I thought you were gone forever because of me. I'm sorry for the things I said in the parking lot the other night."

He sat back in the chair and wiped a hand over his face. "I froze when I went up there. The faces of the people watching me and the band waiting for me to break into song made me want to throw up. I've never felt like that onstage. Then I looked over at you and thought, she must see a coward. I had to fix that."

"I didn't see a coward. I saw a man hurting. I wanted to help you."

"I'm not good with asking for help. I hope you'll be patient with me on that one."

"So, where are we going with this? I want to be with you." No more hiding her heart. "I want to spend time with you, get to know all the things you like and hate. Are you sure you're ready to put the past in the past?"

"Sweetheart, I was a fool for far too long. I was stuck and didn't know I had the way out. But I do now. I knew the minute I drove over the town line. My past doesn't define me. I made a mistake, and I've paid for it. But you woke up something inside me that had been dormant for a long time. You made me see and hear and feel again. I want to walk among the living, and I want to do it with you by my side, if you'll have me."

She wrapped her arms around his neck. "Oh, Grant, I want that too. You showed me what a real man is supposed to be. I thought I wasn't good enough before, but in all my worst moments, you didn't judge me. You just helped me, stood beside me. I want more of that too."

"I want to stay in Serenity by the Sea with you. I want to work here at The Blue Dot, if you'll let me."

"I will think about your friend's loan. What about your music? You can't give that up. And what did Levi say about the songs you gave him?" She pulled him out of the chair and wrapped her arms around his neck, wanting him close to her.

"Levi hated the songs. I thought he might. I threw them together. I want out from under the label. Those songs will take care of my obligations and set me free to do what I want. I want to write music from my heart. I want to remember why I loved music in the first place. You helped me see that I needed to do that with all your fighting for this place. Your heart is in here. In every inch." He dug his phone out of his pocket. "I want to play something for you."

He tapped the screen and music floated into the air around the flicker of the candle flames. His deep sultry voice sang words about finding love for the first time and remembering what was important. He sang about becoming new after a long time of being something else. He sang about transformation and the woman who had helped him do it.

Tears she didn't have the power to stop ran down her face. "How could Levi hate that? That was the most beautiful song I've ever heard."

"That's because it's about you and how you make me feel. But I didn't give that song to Levi. The record label can't have my heart and soul anymore. That belongs to only you, if you'll have it."

"Will you sing that song to me every night?"

"I will sing that song for you for the rest of our lives." He took her mouth with his. Their kiss was long and hot and deep, familiar and yet brand new. She wanted more. So much more from this man. She wanted his hands on her body and his love and commitment. She wanted to laugh with him and share with him. She wanted to make his dreams come true the way he did for her.

He eased out of the embrace. She let him go with regret. "Now, what should we do until the storm passes?"

Chapter Twenty-Two

Sweat ran down Kassidy's neck. The heat amplified the rancid and musty smell in her father's house. She tried to breathe through her mouth as often as she could.

Serenity by the Sea battled yet another heat wave and everything and everyone in its path was losing. Anyone sitting on the sand would cook. Today was a day to be inside in air-conditioning or in the water. She wished for both, stifling in the living room as she was.

"Why can't we just throw all this stuff out?" Maren said, holding up a bundle of brown paper bags tied with twine. "It's worthless."

"And it's hot and smelly in here." Bailey twisted her hair into a knot and secured it on the top of her head with a pencil.

Only Peyton happily had climbed into the attic to retrieve the last of the sea glass. She brought down buckets and boxes and lined them up on the lawn. They still had pounds and pounds of it.

"Let's just stick to the piles. Garbage, donation, and keep." She had organized space in the living room for the sorting. The garbage pile was the biggest by far. Her heart ached a little for her dad and his condition. He had hung on to all this junk because it somehow gave him peace, and here they were doing exactly what he didn't want to have done. But they couldn't sell the house unless it was empty and clean. The sooner the task was over, the sooner the house would be out from under them.

"We aren't keeping any of the stuff from the down-stairs rooms." Maren waved an arm over the boxes.

"Some items might be valuable or sentimental. I don't want to miss anything by being hasty," she said. So far, they had combed through two black garbage bags and found two hundred dollars.

"You know, if Dad hadn't put it in his will that he wanted all three of us to sift through his garbage together, I would have hired someone to come and light this place on fire." Maren hauled the brown bags outside.

"She doesn't mean it like that," Bailey said after Maren left.

"I know she won't set the house on fire." It was time to tell the truth. "I have a confession to make."

"Oh no, no more confessions," Bailey said. "I can't take the drama. We've had more than our share this summer."

She put down the old plastic reusable food containers

and let out a long breath. "I wasn't completely truthful about something."

"Besides omitting Levi's offer and telling Charlotte Munroe we didn't need her to sell The Blue Dot?" Maren returned, pulling the hair tie from her hair and resecuring it in a tight knot on the top of her head.

She had told her sisters after she returned from her night with Grant at The Dot about his proposition and firing Charlotte. Bailey had understood. Maren came around a day later. She couldn't have been too mad. She was still in town.

"Yeah. It's about this house and Dad's last wishes. He never said he wanted us to clean up the house together. I made Mr. West say that he did."

"Why did you do that?" Bailey leaned against a stack of boxes but must have misjudged her space and fell over.

"Are you okay?" Maren said.

Bailey stood, laughing. "I really am a klutz. Go ahead, Kass, tell us why you made that up? We would've stayed to help with this once we saw it."

"No, we wouldn't have," Maren said.

Maren's honest answer shocked Kassidy. She had been right about Maren's reaction, after all. "I didn't think you would either. I'm sorry. I just couldn't face this all by myself."

"I disagree," Bailey said. "I would have stayed."

Maren got up off her knees and dragged a box to the garbage pile. "Come on, Bailey. We would've run and left all this for Kassidy to deal with. I'm ashamed to say it, but it's true. When I got here, I was so wrapped up in the loss of my marriage and still reeling from losing Dad. The last thing I wanted was to be stuck in Serenity a second longer than I had to be. I would've used any excuse to go. I only stayed for Dad. I'm sorry, Kass. I should've stayed for you."

"I just want us to be a family again. I look around at the people I know in this town and even though I shouldn't, I feel alone all the time. Holidays are the worst. I thought maybe if you stayed, you'd remember how great this place is and we could maybe try again to be a family."

"You want us to live here?" Bailey said.

"I do. In my tiny house that we pack to the rafters with all four of us. I know Peyton loves it here. She would do great in the high school. Maren, I haven't seen you smile this much in ages since you've been here."

"I signed my divorce papers." She blushed.

"You did? When?" Kassidy said.

"Last night. I overnighted them to Dave this morning."

"And the hot guy she met on the boardwalk keeps texting her." Bailey bumped hips with Maren.

"Stop that now. I'm still not sure about dating. The idea scares me."

"Which is exactly why you should do it," Bailey said. "Kassidy and Grant can double with you."

The sound of her name paired with Grant's sizzled her insides. They were an actual couple. She still had to pinch herself to believe it. He was planning on renting a house on the north side of town at the end of the summer when the Topside Community closed up.

"I'm only going on a date with Mav if I decide to stay in town," Maren said.

"And?" Kassidy said.

"Come on, Maren, do it. My suitcase can't handle another sticker from all my travels. I'm staying put too. I want to work with Kassidy at The Dot. We make a good team."

"So, you've decided to take Grant's famous friend up on his offer?" Maren said.

"I am. It's just a loan. Grant helped make my dreams come true. And so are the two of you." The idea of borrowing that much money from Carl May still didn't sit quite right. She should be able to do this by herself, but she was out of options and it was just a loan. She, Grant, and Carl had mapped out a payment plan. Carl had arranged for her to make payments to his corporation and not directly to him. And if she could turn The Dot around the way she hoped, maybe she could pay him off sooner.

She could reinvent The Blue Dot by using sea glass as the model and the theme. Blues and greens. White-washed walls. Peyton's mosaics hanging everywhere. They could open the back wall and make outdoor seating. Wicker chairs and soft cushions. A garden. They could even rename her. Give her a fresh start. The kind of start she deserved. With the people who loved her the most.

"I'm not sure about staying," Maren said. "I need to go home for a while and see if any of my old life still fits."

"What about Mr. Hotty?" Bailey said.

"If he's still interested after I've decided on a few things, then we'll see. Peyton and I are going back the day after tomorrow. But how about if we come down right after Labor Day?"

Her heart sank. She had wanted both of her sisters to stay so they could be a real family. "That would be great. You're only an hour or so away. We can see each other all the time." She hoped that would be true.

Maren brushed the dirt off her pants. "I hate to leave you two in this hot mess, but I have to get back to the house. I want to get some laundry done before we pack. And school supplies are on sale. I thought I'd stop by the stationery store and pick some up for Peyton. I saw some note cards with pretty pictures of sea glass on them." Maren hugged her. "Thank you for lying about the house. Staying here these past weeks reminded me how important the two of you are to me." Maren squeezed Bailey's arm and left.

"Well, that's that," Bailey said. "She'll probably be gone by morning, not wanting to wait around, if I know Maren."

"You're right. Now that she has the idea in her head and the issues with The Dot settled, she'll be gone." Kassidy only hoped it wasn't going to be for too long.

"Don't look so down, Kass. She'll be back. And you have me." Bailey poked a finger in her cheek, tipping her head from side to side like an amusement park ride.

"I do. And I'm so glad." She wrapped Bailey in a tight hug.

"We'll get this place cleaned up. I promise. But I have to go too. I promised Kiri I'd take her shift tonight."

"That's nice. I don't think I'll be in tonight. I want to do as much work here as I can." She was ready to let this house go. It would be a weight off her chest.

Bailey grabbed her tote. "I'll see you tonight."

"Hey, Bailey."

"Yeah?" Bailey turned.

"Do you feel like making s'mores when you get home?"

"Count on it." Bailey skipped out the door.

The click of the lock echoed in the silence. The house overwhelmed her. There was still so much to go through. Maren was probably right. They should just throw everything in the trash.

Needing to stretch her legs, she climbed into the attic to work up there. It was hotter than the first floor, but the one window gave a small glimpse of the ocean. And the attic had room to move around now that all the sea glass was gone. Most of the boxes had been moved too.

They had found a few old photo albums of Dad and Aunt Joanna when they were kids. Kassidy was pretty sure she'd stumbled upon Aunt Joanna's prom picture from high school. She had brought the albums back to her house for safekeeping and so she could tease her aunt next time she came to town.

The only thing left in the attic was Dad's record collection. It seemed a shame to throw those out. Maybe Kenny had a use for them in his store. She'd have to check.

She ran her fingers along the album jackets. Dust danced in the air. She pulled one out. An album by a country artist she had never heard of.

"Kassidy, are you up here?" Grant's voice echoed into the attic.

"I am. Come on up."

He stuck his head through the opening in the floor. His face glowed like the sun. "Hey, beautiful."

"What are you doing here? Not that I'm complaining. I didn't think I'd see you until later tonight."

He gathered her in his arms and kissed her neck. "I missed you and wanted to see if you needed any help. Mmm... you smell good."

"I smell like sweat. But thank you anyway." She tilted her chin to make room for his sweet kisses on her neck.

"What have you got here?" Grant took the album from her.

"It's nothing much. My dad had some old records. I was thinking Kenny might want to buy them or have them. Whatever." The albums were probably worthless. Kenny would laugh at her when she showed up with these old things.

Grant studied the album jacket. He pulled the record out and inspected that too. "Do you know who this artist is?"

"Nope. But I'm guessing you do."

"Damn straight I do. He's only the most famous original country music singer of the past century. Do you have other albums of his?"

They looked through the box and discovered nine

others. "Grant, I don't understand. Why is this guy important? Is he someone who inspired you to play music? I've never heard of *the most famous original country music singer of the past century.*" She made air quotes with her fingers.

"You have the entire collection of Bob Hecht albums. Do you know how rare that is? Hecht had had a fight with his record label and they stopped production of The Devil in Blue Jeans. That alone is worth a ton. And you have two original presses."

"That's good?" She knew nothing about any of this.

"That's very good. Sweetheart, you have solved all your money problems if you want to part with these."

"Please tell me you're not joking." In all the garbage, her father had actually collected something valuable. She couldn't believe it and had almost thrown it out.

"I wouldn't joke about that. This is museum stuff. You'll have your pick of buyers. Carl May would take these as payment in full. But they're worth a hell of a lot more than what you borrowed." He wrapped his arms around her waist and picked her up.

She threw her arms around his neck and laughed. "Thank you."

"For what?" He placed her back on her feet.

"For being you. For loving me. For making my dreams come true."

"Loving you is easy. But this time, I think your dad had a hand in helping."

She said a silent thanks to her father. Hopefully, he was watching and could see how happy she was.

"I think we should tell my sisters. Maren will die when she finds out. And she'll want to scour every single piece of junk lying around the house after this."

"We should, but one thing first."

"What's that?"

He pulled a small black box from the front pocket of his jeans and flipped the top open, revealing a round cut diamond surrounded by smaller sapphires.

"Marry me, Kassidy. Make me the happiest man alive."

"The ring is beautiful."

"I picked the blue stones because of the sea glass you like to collect. They reminded me of the ocean. I know it's fast. And we still have a lot of getting to know each other. We don't have to set a date or anything yet, but I want the world to know you're mine."

"Are you really sure about this?" The worries about making a mistake took flight, but she grabbed them and put them away. She had waited her whole life for Grant.

"Never more sure of anything. So, will you?"

She wrapped her arms around his neck and pressed her lips to his. He held her close and kissed her back.

"That's a yes, then?" He rested his forehead against hers.

"That's a yes."

Epilogue

One year later

Kassidy stood arm in arm with Bailey and Maren. The hot summer sun beat down on them and the Jersey Shore air was thick as molasses. But she didn't care about the sweat running down her back. She had too much to be happy about these days. Just a year ago her life had fallen apart, but now, things were different.

"Smile," Peyton said as she pointed her cell phone at them and took a picture.

"I hope I wasn't squinting. Let me see." Bailey took the phone.

"I still have a few more things to do before this afternoon." Maren checked her notebook. "I swear my lists need lists."

"It's all going to be fine," she said. "Everything is in place."

"Does that everything include Grant?" Maren raised an eyebrow.

"He's inside doing a sound check now. Don't worry." She was too excited to worry. What a switch from last year.

Kenny, from Beach Rhythm, had orchestrated a sale of her father's albums for more money than she could ever have dreamed. There had been plenty to pay off The Dot's debt and give her a makeover which Maren had engineered. First from her home in Hunterdon County, but after about six months, she purchased a home in Serenity by the Sea. Peyton came out on weekends until the school year had ended. She would be there for the summer before returning to her dad's for her senior year. Maren had blossomed under the work to renovate The Dot.

Instead of the old tired dark place, she had become open with large windows on every wall and the back wall was complete sliding glass doors that opened to a large veranda for sitting. They had put a new stage in for local bands to play along with some more well-known names that brought a whole new group of customers. They had painted her in the colors of a modern beach house. Bailey had changed the menu to a lighter fare and even coached clients from the new office.

The Blue Dot had been transformed from something that was once useful but neglected to something brand new and beautiful. Like her.

As she watched her sisters and Peyton taking more pictures for their grand opening in a few hours, her heart swelled with pride. She had her family back. She had reinvented herself and her business. The new marquee announced Grant Hawkins would play tonight. The tickets had sold out in minutes. He was opening his first set with her song. The song he sang for her every night like he had promised.

She stole a glance at her hand. Her beautiful engagement ring was flanked by an equally beautiful wedding band. They had been married on the beach two weeks ago.

"Let's go home. I want to freshen up." Bailey put an arm around her shoulders.

"Let me look at the sign just a little longer."

"You can look at that sign every single day from now on," Maren said.

"It's the best part of the whole renovation," she said.

"I don't know about that," Maren said. "I could think of a few other things that required more time and effort."

"She's right," Peyton said. "It is the best part."

When The Blue Dot transformed, the sisters had agreed the name needed to change too. The Dot was about the past.

But the future. The future belonged to Sea Glass.

But wait, there's more! Take a sneak peek at book two in the Serenity Series.

Sea Glass Hidden in Plain Sight
    Chapter One

. . .

Planning this wedding was the absolute the worst idea Maren ever had. She should have said no from the start because deep down she wasn't a major event planner booked by some of New Jersey's wealthiest. She was small town and happier in her flip-flops than chasing entitled, spoiled women around in pounds of tule and hairspray. Only she forgot until tonight.

Organizing an extravagant wedding for a famous baseball player and a social media influencer should have been a walk in the park. That didn't look to be happening tonight.

Maren stood in a magnificent ballroom with expensive crystal chandeliers dangling from a twenty-foot ceiling and cutting prisms into all the diamonds on the ears, neck, and fingers of every woman in the room. Maren wanted to plan special events for each and every one of them, in fact, some of these women were her clients, but she should have declined the offer to be Paris's wedding planner.

If she had said a big fat no, the last four months with bridezilla extraordinaire would not have aged her faster than Maren's teenage daughter had.

If she had said no, she wouldn't have been able to glance across the crowded room tonight and see Shane Sutherland, brother of the groom, leaning against the wall by himself with a whiskey glass in his hand and looking better than he had in decades. Her body wanted to remember Shane. Her mind did not.

Maren pushed a long breath over her lips. She should have said no.

At least the dance !oor was full. The bride in her ten-thousand-dollar dress and the groom in his custom-made navy-blue suit swayed to a Sarah Vaughan tune.

Paris looked up at her new husband. Maren expected the typical expression of love and adoration sculpted into Paris's high-end makeup. Instead, Paris's mouth curled into a snarl. Her Botox "lled brow attempted to furrow.

Maren took a step forward. She needed to get a hold of Paris before she threw one of her tantrums in front of all the guests. Maren pushed through the crowd of warm bodies, but the center of the dance !oor moved farther and farther away with each step.

Paris pulled back her arm and in one quick, !uid move slapped her groom across the face.

READ MORE

Acknowledgments

~

It truly takes a village to bring a book to its readers. I could not do it alone. Believe me, I've tried.

I need to say a huge *thank you* to Joanne Gelderblom. One day she asked, "how can I help you?" and changed my life. Her bright light and brilliance shone on the areas of my business I didn't have well lit. I don't know how I existed without her. You're stuck with me now, Joanne!

I must also shout *thank you* to the incomparable Lisa Olech. She is a fantastic critique partner, author, and friend. Whenever I send up the bat signal, she comes running with her cape and a shovel to dig me out of many plot holes. No questions asked.

Jen Talty helped me brainstorm the series name and saved you all from a tongue twister. Thank you, Jen.

As always, I must thank my content editor, Robin Rottner. She makes sure you all see the best version of my stories.

Diana Carlisle made me the beautiful cover. I'm grateful for her talents.

But most importantly, I must thank you, my readers. Because of you, my characters and their world come to life. I'm honored that you choose to take this journey with me over and over.

Read On!

xo

Stacey

Also by Stacey Wilk

Serenity Series

Sea Glass Made with Second Chances

Sea Glass Hidden in Plain Sight

Sea Glass Out of Balance

Sea Glass Wrapped in Red

Heritage River Series

The Risk for House and Home

The Bridge Between Love and Lies

The Essence of Whiskey and Tea

Hometown Series

Taking Root

Raising Winter

Defining Chances

Beginning Over

Steeling Hearts

Whispering Christmas

Winter at the Shore Series

No More Darkness

Through the Darkness

Light Upon the Darkness

The Brotherhood Protectors World

Winter's Last Chance

The Last Betrayal

Her Last Word

The Last Days of Christmas

Seduced by Denial

Chill in the Air

Fighting for Tessa

Nash's Promise

Cruz's Watch

Harlan Unleashed

Big Sky Country Series

Time Won't Erase

Stay Awhile

Love Never Ends

Dare to Tell (coming 2025)

About the Author

From an early age, best-selling and award-winning author, Stacey Wilk, told tales as a way to escape. At six she wrote short stories in composition notebooks, at twelve she wrote a novel on a typewriter, in high school biology she wrote rock star romances in her binder instead of paying attention.

But it wasn't until many years later, inspired by her children and a looming birthday, that she finally took her story-telling seriously. And published her first novel in 2013. Since then, she's gone on to publish twenty-nine more so women everywhere can indulge in books that hook them heart and soul.

She isn't done telling stories. Not by a long shot. If you want to read her emotional and honest books about family, romance, and second chances, visit her at www.staceywilk.com

To see what she writes next, follow her Facebook

group for her amazing readers – Stacey's Novel Family
https://bit.ly/2FK8Lae

Or join her newsletter - https://bit.ly/2AojEFk